As the Distant Bells Toll

As the Distant Bells Toll

By

Aleksandar Žiljak

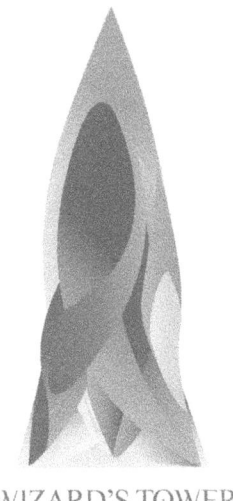

WIZARD'S TOWER

Wizard's Tower Press

Trowbridge, England

As the Distant Bells Toll

First edition, published in the UK November 2020
by Wizard's Tower Press

This edition, text and interior illustrations © by Aleksandar Žiljak, 2020

Hardcover ISBN: 978-1-913892-07-4

Translations by Aleksandar Žiljak
Engish Language Editing by Charlotte Bond

Interior illustrations by Aleksandar Žiljak
Cover illustration and design by Ben Baldwin
Design by Cheryl Morgan

http://wizardstowerpress.com/

Contents

A Unicorn and a Warrior Girl

You must know that countless years ago there lived a potent Prince. He was of great ability, valour, and worth. He conquered the Warring States and brought them all laws, money, measures, and writing. His name was Ch'in Shih Huang Ti, and all men know for a certain truth that he was the greatest Lord that had ever been. I tell you the truth when I say that Ch'in Shih Huang Ti decreed the Empire should be shielded by the Great Wall, thus stopping the northern hordes and bringing peace to his Realm. Five hundred thousand people built the wall, and many left their bones beneath it. Furthermore, Ch'in Shih Huang Ti ordered channels to be dug through his Empire and roads to be paved, so that merchants and armies could travel with ease. Know this, too! To ensure that nobody brought disorder into his Empire, he decreed that all the rebellious scholars were to be buried neck-deep in the earth and then beheaded. Others he had stoned to death. He also instructed that their books be burned. And let me tell you that the Emperor feared nothing and no one but Death herself. So, he had a great tomb built for himself and placed inside it treasures on a scale so wonderful and costly that it is hard to bring oneself to describe them. And he instructed a huge army to stand guard next to the tomb, so no thief dared to desecrate it.

I speak the truth and I shall not lie when I tell you that there's no one in the entirety of Cathay who did not hear at least one tale of the great emperor Ch'in Shih Huang Ti. I, too, heard them countless times. Hear this, too! The Great Khan himself in his city of Cambaluc told me a tale of the First Emperor, that nobody else in Cathay knows. Now, I am going to tell you of this tale.

Like crows above a forest, Choo-kheng thought when all the nobles, secretaries, and scribes scattered, black robes rustling, at the barely noticeable wave of the Emperor's hand.

Choo-kheng remained kneeling thirty paces from the Emperor, closely watched by black dragons coiled around the pillars to her left and right. Two huge dragons rose behind the Emperor, facing each other in a monstrous duel. The Emperor caressed his beard, studying the girl carefully. Then he nodded, satisfied, and waved for her to come closer. As a reward for her courage, she had the honour of kneeling just ten paces from the Emperor, but not before he beckoned her – this had been whispered into her ear before she was led into the Hall.

They had brought her to the Imperial City in a carriage escorted by horsemen under black banners.

When all the gates closed after Choo-kheng, leaving behind the soldiers guarding her, she found herself before an elderly lady-in-waiting, surrounded by servant girls. They ordered her to undress. Having been instructed to do everything she was told, she obeyed without question. The girls took her simple peasant clothes away and bathed her in complete silence, washing away dust and sweat after a ten-day journey. They dried her hair, combed it, and arranged it the way ladies of the court wore it. Still naked, Choo-kheng was thoroughly examined by another elderly woman, who did not pay attention to the girl's blushing cheeks as she skilfully probed her private parts with her fingers. Finally, they dressed her like a princess, pale green silk embracing her like a breeze whispering in the bamboo forest.

Afterwards, they took her into the Hall, before the Emperor surrounded by the noisy flock. And then the Emperor, after she was announced and kneeled thirty paces before him, sent his crows away and remained alone with Choo-kheng.

"You vanquished five of Our enemies bare-handed, Yeoh Choo-kheng," the Emperor said, finally breaking the tense silence. "That requires great courage and skill."

"Trifling bandits, Your Majesty," the girl replied, bowing so low she almost touched the floor with her forehead.

"Trifling or not, the bandits are enemies of the Empire. The enemies of the Empire are Our enemies. And you vanquished five of them." Hundreds of great butterflies rested on the stairs leading to the throne, their velvety black wings embellished with shimmering green triangles. Choo-kheng forgot the Emperor for a moment, awed by the fragile beauty of the butterflies she had never seen before. Here and there, a butterfly would flicker his wings, as if he were not at the feet of the most powerful man in the world. "You admire Our butterflies?" The Emperor did not miss her admiration. "They were brought to Us from distant southern lands under great hardships."

"They are beautiful, Your Majesty," Choo-kheng admitted. "So peaceful."

"They tell Us what is in the souls of those kneeling before Us. Their peace means that you are peaceful, Yeoh Choo-kheng. If there was an assassin or a traitor before Us, someone with dark thoughts..." The Emperor placed his hand on the hilt of his sword. "Once We had burning candles for that purpose. Little did they help Us. And now," the Emperor sat up in his throne, "show Us how you defeated the bandits."

Choo-kheng bowed again. "There were five of them, riding horses. I was leading a buffalo from the paddy field when they surrounded me. One—a leader, I think—jumped off his horse and drew a sabre. I'm ashamed to admit it, Your Majesty... I was scared..."

"Even the bravest warrior gets scared." The Emperor smiled. "It would be insincere not to admit that even Our own heart trembled occasionally before a hard battle. But if the true hero controls his fear, then there is no enemy he will not defeat."

"The bandit grabbed me, grinning. I pushed him away. At that, the remaining four dismounted." In her mind, Choo-kheng was back on the dusty road, swords and spears pointing at her. "I couldn't escape! Then the first one grabbed my blouse again and I hit him with my fist." She leapt briskly from the floor, completely forgetting before whom she was kneeling. Her fist hit the imaginary opponent like thunder. "He staggered, surprised, and then he cursed and struck at me with his sabre! I dodged, repelled the blade, grabbed his sword arm and twisted it. Something snapped inside. He screamed and dropped his sabre into the dust. The one behind me tried to pierce me with his spear! I evaded his attack, too, and kicked him into thicket with my foot. The third…" The girl became a wild wind and all the butterflies were sucked into a whirl of black and green: fragile wings flurried as the finest silk and lightning-fast kicks showed how she'd mown down the five enemies the way a sickle mows the sheaves. Before the Emperor's delighted eyes, the unequal fight unfolded until the last kick, a fight in which five armed bandits stood no chance against a tiny peasant girl. "And then, when it was all over, a dozen peasants came by the road, and when they heard the racket and saw what was happening, they jumped to my aid and tied the bandits up."

Winded, Choo-kheng fell back to her knees and bowed before the Emperor, as if she had danced a difficult dance or performed an acrobatic feat. Only then did it dawn upon her that she had acted very, very improperly. "You commanded me to show you, Your Majesty," she stuttered quickly.

"True! True, We did!" the Emperor laughed, caressing his beard. The butterflies, one by one, settled back on the stairs and peace reigned in the Hall once again. "You possess great skills, Yeoh Choo-kheng! You could defeat a hundred of my soldiers. You must have been trained by a great master."

"My grandfather," the girl said with modesty. "He has been teaching me since I was ten."

"You do him great honour." Choo-kheng glowed at the praise. Grandfather would certainly be glad when she told him that the Emperor himself had praised him. She had not understood the tear in his eye when they had said goodbye to each other. "And we know for certain that you are also a virtuous girl. Isn't it so?"

Choo-kheng blushed. Her eyes met the Emperor's. She had expected a spark of lust there: her grandfather had taught her about many things. He had replaced both her father and mother—taken away by contagion—and she was not naive.

10

The Emperor suddenly turned serious. "We need a girl untouched by the hand of man." At that moment, Choo-kheng would have preferred lust to that piercing stare measuring and weighing her, assessing whether she was the best choice. Lust was something she understood; something she had resisted successfully, but understood nevertheless. "If she is also a skilful warrior like you, it would do no harm, although you will not go alone. We wish to send you on an important mission, Yeoh Choo-kheng."

The day faded in a flash of colours. Evening descended upon the river. The hills on both banks resembled dragon teeth. Choo-kheng imagined them biting into the purple sunset, tearing a piece of sky away and swallowing the Sun. Several junks were silhouetted against the other bank. Soon, the rectangular sails on two-pronged masts would melt into the feathery curtain of bamboo separating the river from small fields, squeezed between the peaceful course of the river and the hills etched by eternity. By day, the overgrown hills reminded the girl of stones by a brook, covered in moist, soft moss: the beauty of the small reflected in the rapture of the great.

A soldier lit a lantern on the stern. Mild warmth spilled across the junk carrying Choo-kheng to her mission. More lanterns glowed down the river. Fishermen were preparing for night fishing. They stood on their long rafts of bamboo, pushing themselves away with poles, gliding silently across the quiet surface of the river. Their cormorants waited on prows, black wings spread, eager to dive for fish that would end up in large baskets laid on the rafts. Soon, they, too, became just a string of lights in the darkness swallowing the world.

Choo-kheng was guarded by twenty soldiers and their commander. The girl looked at them. Several soldiers gambled in a strange silence, a quietness inappropriate to the spirit of the game. Others were finishing their supper. One was carefully sharpening his sword. He would wash the blade in blood when the time came. The Emperor had chosen them personally from his guard, the best warriors to accompany the virgin.

"We have many enemies," the Emperor had frowned. "You saw all those courtiers. Nobles, counsellors, and scribes. We trust none of them. None!"

"But, Your Majesty—" Choo-kheng uttered.

The Emperor raised his hand and the girl hushed at once. "They think We summoned you to express Our admiration. True, We did. But that is not the whole truth. It is Our wish that you do something important for Us, Yeoh Choo-kheng. Something secret. You will receive an escort, a small one, so that it does not draw attention, but sufficient for someone with your skills. Together, you will sneak out of the City. We have already instructed the Commander where to go."

Choo-kheng felt unease growing deep inside her, something evil, threatening to paralyse and devour her. Fear. It fluttered in her innards like one of those butterflies before the Emperor's feet. But what had the Emperor said just a moment ago? The real hero controls his fear. And then there is no enemy...

"Have you ever seen a unicorn?"

The girl started. A unicorn? "No, Your Majesty, I'm afraid I haven't. I've seen deer. Wild boars. Bear and martens, foxes and squirrels. And many birds, which Grandfather taught me to tell apart. I even caught a glimpse of a tiger once, I think: it was in the forest and it was dark... But a unicorn? Never, Your Majesty. In my province, people say it's a fabulous beast, one that perished long, long ago—"

"It is not fabulous and it did not perish," the Emperor interrupted her. "It very much exists and We know where it lives. What else do they say about unicorns in your province?"

Choo-kheng recalled what she had been told by her grandfather and their neighbour, a woman so old no one was counting her years anymore, and what she had heard from other peasants: "They say that it's a magical creature. And that nobody can catch it. There's no trickery it won't see through, no trap it won't sense, no arrow it won't dodge."

"They also say," the Emperor added, "that it will believe only a girl untouched by the hand of man. Innocent and pure. And they say that the horn of the unicorn is used to detect poisoned drinks. Is it not so, Yeoh Choo-kheng?"

"True, Your Majesty," Choo-kheng confirmed. "They say that, too."

"Therefore, you will bring Us the horn of the unicorn, warrior girl. So that We can see if any of the snakes surrounding Us spits poison in Our wine."

The early morning mist veiled the valley like a fine curtain hiding ancient secrets from prying eyes. The hills, that were only yesterday devouring the Sun, were merely blurred floating shapes, distant worlds high above the peaceful river. The mist lingered in the grey light of the dense bamboo forest, bringing with it fresh dew. Choo-kheng shivered and drew her shawl higher around her shoulders as she walked quietly among the green stems. Bamboos leaned above the water, trembling baldachins woven of pointed leaves whispering at the slightest breeze, revealing to the chance traveller whatever the mist hid.

The soldiers already waited at their posts, bows in hand, deployed by their Commander.

They had left the junk upstream, rushing here on foot. It was still dark when they got off the road leading through paddy fields to a distant village, crossed an irrigation channel—one soldier, following orders and apologising, lifted Choo-kheng and carried her across to keep her feet dry—and cut to the river bank. The soldiers were well-trained, the girl noticed. The Emperor had chosen them well: they were moving almost without a sound. Only a long-tailed blue magpie called from a tree of heaven on the forest edge, uncertain who it was that stalked through the bamboos. Magpies miss nothing, her grandfather had said once.

A river forked here, outlining a forested island. On one side of the fork, a vertical rock rose to heaven: a giant sporting an overgrown stony chest with lush green hair atop a powerful head, watching the world beneath him with approval. Below the giant, a meadow spread from the bank to the steep hills which were emerging from the fog. This was where—as it had reached the Emperor's ears, and as he told the Commander—a unicorn would come early in the morning.

"Now, we have to wait," the Commander whispered. Choo-kheng nodded.

Time passed, carried by the river. It called in quiet voices of tits high in the bamboos, little birds of yellow bellies, white cheeks and black caps. It flashed with the Sun, tore the misty veils apart, spilled the colours across the world. Choo-kheng sank into the emerald cool of the bamboos. Her spirit flowed with the river, fluttered after the tits, spread her wings and flew high above hills and rocks, forests, and fields. Her shadow startled a herd of deer, caused a peasant rushing to the field look up at the blue sky, and trembled when she heard hooves trampling.

"It's here," the Commander said, dragging her back to reality. The girl looked at the meadow. On its edge, beyond the range of the farthest-shot arrow, she saw a white shape emerging out of the forest. "Move!"

"Wait," Choo-kheng whispered. "Let the animal come closer. Patience." With patience, she could approach timid stags and roes to within a step or two. The Commander understood. The unicorn had to be lured to the centre of the meadow, where there were no trees to shield him.

The animal paused, cautious. He pricked his ears, lifted his head, and smelled the air. Then he stepped into the grass and went slowly to the bank. Two black-and-white wagtails took the wing before the unicorn's hooves. One settled back in the tall grass, while the other flew in a circle and, calling, landed on the unicorn's back, wagging her long tail. The animal paid no attention to the bird. He came to the water and began quenching his thirst.

Choo-kheng could see him better now. Just like stories said, the unicorn was indeed like a horse. He was not too tall, rather resembling horses ridden by nomadic barbarians from the north. His tail was straw-coloured, and so was his bristling, erect mane. A twisted horn protruded from his forehead, as long as the girl's arm. But it was only when the unicorn came closer that she saw he had three hoofed toes on each foot: the middle one just like a horse's and a smaller one on each side, barely touching the ground. Choo-kheng wondered if that helped him walk on the soft soil of the river valley that was his home.

"Now, without a sound," the girl whispered into the Commander's ear. The soldiers were disciplined, with clear instructions of what to do and when, at the price of their lives. The unicorn was too far away. They had to wait patiently and quietly for the girl to lure him closer, within the range of arrows. The Commander nodded.

The unicorn reared the moment Choo-kheng stepped into the grass. The wagtail flew away from his back, protesting loudly, while he paused, nostrils flaring. His ears turned towards the girl. His muscles twitched under his skin, ready to launch him into wild gallop. The warrior girl froze like a statue. The unicorn studied her. Choo-kheng was unfamiliar to him: he had never seen her before, he did not know her scent. He could not know whether she was dangerous. He did not move. Neither did the girl. The river flowed peacefully, taking time away into oblivion.

For a long time, they stood facing each other, keeping their distance, afraid that the slightest move would break the spell in which they floated. She, fascinated by the unbridled beauty of the magical beast, free and elusive, and spellbound by the purity of the otherworldly creature living high above greed, power, and lust, untarnished by blood, misery, and fear; the unicorn, dazzled by the beautiful girl dressed in the finest silk, calmed by her innocence and unaware—as Choo-kheng realised with shame—that her untouched purity hid cruel treachery.

The unicorn made the first step towards Choo-kheng. Her heart stopped. She wanted to scream, to wave her arms, to drive him away. Hidden behind her innocence, twenty arrows waited in ambush. But the calm beauty of the white animal froze her as the unicorn approached, slowly, as if afraid he would scare her. And then he stopped, lifted his gaze, pricked his ears, shook his head. Did he feel the girl's shame? Or was it the call of a blue magpie that stopped him in his tracks? Whatever it was, the unicorn turned, cast another glance at Choo-kheng and ambled with dignity back into the forest he came from, out of range of the archers, elusive, mysterious.

14

Choo-kheng was sitting on the straw mat, lying in the grass. The morning was already well-advanced, warm and bright. The girl's eyes followed a dozen white egrets flying in a stately manner above the arm of the river, carried by slow wing-beats. Several more perched peacefully on the bare branches of a dry tree on the island. Choo-kheng looked across her shoulder at the bamboo forest and the hunters hidden there.

Last night, the Commander had been furious.

Worst of all, there was no one to wreak his rage on, no one to punish for the failure. Every soldier had done exactly as ordered, nobody had revealed his position. He could not blame the girl either. The confounded beast had run back into the forest without any cause or reason, before anybody could shoot an arrow.

"Perhaps there were too many soldiers," Choo-kheng had remarked cautiously, not mentioning the magpie. The Commander paused in the middle of sipping his wine and stroked his beard thoughtfully. Then he nodded and pointed at five of his men. "You'll lay in ambush tomorrow! The rest stay here. These are my best archers," he explained to the girl. "If they don't hit it, nobody will."

They reached the meadow before dawn, taking the same path as the day before. The soldiers deployed without a sound, stealthy, immersed into the green semi-darkness. But time flowed away with the river, the morning Sun tore the veils above the valley, and heavenly warmth waked life from misty stupor. Still the unicorn did not appear. Did he suspect something?

"Let me step out," Choo-kheng suggested.

"Hmm," the Commander pondered. Perhaps the beast was there and a glimpse of the girl would draw it out. If they stayed this way, who knew how long they would have to wait? Indeed, no one could predict what was on the unicorn's mind or how he would behave. "All right, go."

And so, Choo-kheng was alone in the grass, bait for the unicorn. Caressed by the Sun, lulled by the rustle of breeze in bamboos and the buzzing of insects around her, she was enchanted by the lives of all these creatures, big and small, that did not even suspect—busy with their innocent preoccupation with life—that soon blood would be spilled on this meadow.

Choo-kheng recalled the Emperor's words, whispered as he was leaning towards her. "If you succeed, girl, you will thus have proved loyalty to Us and

Our Empire. And We shall not be ungrateful." They were seducing her, promising her all she had ever dreamed of and more. Riches and honours she could not even imagine, what with being just an ignorant peasant girl who only knew how to lead a buffalo and thoroughly thrash, bare-handed, anybody who dared to jump her with dirty thoughts. Choo-kheng was well aware that the words were not empty promises: a great ruler must be ready to reward generously as much as punish severely.

Once, when she was a little girl, she had followed her grandfather down the road by the meadow. Her attention had been caught by a great spider's web, stretched between low branches. A large spider waited patiently in the middle of it, striped black and yellow. She stepped towards the web to take a better look. Several small brown grasshoppers leaped away before her feet and one, unwary, flew straight into the web. It struggled helplessly as the spider dived across the web in an instant, paralysing it with a single bite and wrapping it in dense cobweb. Where there had been a grasshopper a moment before, there was now just a silvery bundle in the web.

"Poor grasshopper," Choo-kheng muttered, sad and angry. She looked around. She spotted a stone to throw at the web, to tear apart that illusion of fragile beauty bringing only death.

"Stop!" her grandfather shouted. Choo-kheng looked at him, surprised. "There's no malice in what the spider did. It must eat in order to live and so somebody must be eaten. That's the way of the world and there's no malice in it. Only man does evil that he does not have to do, and then it is a crime. Remember that, Choo-kheng."

Choo-kheng shook her head angrily as she recalled her grandfather's words. Why did she remember them just then? Anyway, did she have any other choice? The Emperor himself had given her the order, and his orders were carried out without question. And then the girl looked at the edge of the forest, towards the darkness from which the unicorn had stepped into the meadow the day before. And she recalled the fascination they had both felt for each other.

A grasshopper, a spider, and a web. A sudden thought coursed through her. It was her grandfather talking to her: once more, he shouted for her to stop, and it was only then that she understood the tear in his eye when they parted. A grasshopper, a spider, and a web. She was the web.

Something rebelled in Choo-kheng, who was sad and angry, just as she had been when the spider had caught the grasshopper. She remembered the way she had reached for the stone. And now she was the web. And who would cast the stone in righteous wrath? Because, she realised, an unnecessary act of evil would be committed here.

Everybody knew about the Emperor's quest for immortality. One thousand virgins had been sent by his command on a long journey across the sea—to fetch him water from the fountain of life about which he had heard from some self-proclaimed sage—never to be seen again. And Choo-kheng knew well enough, taught by her grandfather, that there was no immortality and that death was inevitable, even desirable: merely an ending of one circle to begin a new one. The Emperor's quest was as futile as much as it was senseless. Only none of his crows dared to tell him that. And because nobody had the courage to warn the tyrant of his fallacy, a beautiful animal will be killed. A crime will be committed and Choo-kheng will be an accomplice, as guilty as the Emperor who commanded it and the soldier whose arrow will hit the innocent beast. And no matter how great the rewards and honours bestowed upon her, they would never wash away the blood of the unicorn, splashing her like mud.

But what was she to do? To rise that very instant from the mat and run away? Where to? As much as Choo-kheng knew that death was part of life, she did not feel like dying. Not yet and not in the ways the Emperor would have her die.

Suddenly, several wagtails rose from the tall grass and flew above the girl, calling loudly. *He's arrived*, Choo-kheng thought with a mixture of joy and desperation, and she turned. And froze.

A tiger had stalked to within ten paces of her. Choo-kheng's heart stopped as she looked on the animal, a strange beast she had never heard of, not even from her grandfather in all his wisdom, not even from their neighbour, the old woman whose years nobody counted anymore. *What kind of tiger is this?* Choo-kheng wondered. Because this tiger was not like the one she had seen. His coat, although striped with black stripes just like any other, was not yellowish in colour, but greyish, almost blue.

The green eyes stared at her. Was the tiger merely passing by? Or had he been stalking her since she went out into the meadow, waiting for the right moment? Maybe that was why the unicorn did not show up. But why did not somebody warn her? Where were the soldiers? Why didn't they shoot? It was unlikely they would have hit the tiger as he was at the edge of their range, but the arrows and a shout or two would certainly have driven him away. Or were they just like her, stunned by the blue beast?

The tiger took a step towards Choo-kheng. His whiskers twitched, the stripes above his eyes gathering in tense concentration on the prey before him. The warrior girl clenched her fists, ready to let the tiger charge, and then jump aside at the last moment to confuse him and gain the precious time needed to strike back. If she could beat up five armed bandits bare-handed, why couldn't

17

she vanquish a tiger? Even a blue one that had to be—since he was so unusual—a beast of great powers. Choo-kheng took a deep breath. Strange, she did not feel fear, not before this beast. And that gave her new strength: what she was not afraid of, she would defeat easily.

But Choo-kheng asked herself something else: what if the tiger was merely a stone thrown at the web by angry gods?

And who was she to oppose the will of powers mightier than her, mightier than the Emperor himself? Strangely, Choo-kheng felt great relief before the striped face of death. Fate had shown her the right path, sending a messenger to guide her along, and all she could do was obey. She looked at the beautiful bluish beast once again and then took a deep breath, closed her eyes, and relaxed her body, waiting for the end.

A heartbeat behind closed eyelids. The breathing of the beast. Another heartbeat. A powerful paw softly stepping on dewy grass. Beat. Tensing of mighty muscles. Beat. The cat ready to pounce. Beat, the last one before death.

And then, a sudden stamping of hooves and the surprised, raging scream of a hunter startled within reach of his prey. The girl opened her eyes and found herself before a whirlwind of neighing, snarling, and trampling as the unicorn—his head low, his mane bristling, his horn pointed—drove the tiger away from her. The cat lashed out with his paw, claws tearing the air, but the horn would not let him close. The tiger jumped aside, murder in his eyes, and circled, trying to catch the unicorn defenceless, but the horn kept pointing at him. The slightest mistake and the tiger would end up impaled. The unicorn and the tiger measured each other for an eternity. No matter how hungry he was, the tiger grew indecisive, facing the unicorn's spiralling horn. And then the unicorn charged angrily and the tiger barely avoided the sharp point ripping his belly apart. Then the cat decided he'd had enough: there must be an easier meal in the forest. He snarled once more, fangs bared, and finally, quite inappropriate for the lord of the forest, he escaped quickly from the unicorn that no predator can catch unawares.

Choo-kheng remained helpless in the grass. The unicorn whinnied victoriously and then, with the tiger lost in the forest, returned to the girl. She cast a glance at the bamboo. The soldiers must have seen all this but they were too far away, their arrows could not hit her saviour.

The unicorn approached the girl, touched her cheek with his nose, warm breath spilling over her face and down her neck. Choo-kheng lifted her hand slowly and touched the unicorn, caressing him and fondling his horn, that object of the Emperor's desire. There were no more obstacles between the girl and the animal, the enemy had been driven away. Only the two of them remained, alone in the meadow by the river; the unicorn, unaware of the betrayal woven around him; the girl, grateful that he had saved her and diverted the hand of fate, thus paving the path to his own doom.

The unicorn laid his head on the lap of the girl untouched by the hand of man. Choo-kheng caressed his white hair, leaned her cheek against his strong neck, felt the hot blood of the unbridled animal against her skin. That was what the soldiers had been waiting for, the moment that the Emperor had commanded them to discharge their arrows. But they would have done so in vain because they were too far away. The Commander knew well enough that there was no point. They would merely scare the beast and perhaps never have another chance. And so the soldiers remained hidden: another morning passed without them carrying out their mission. But the Commander was cunning. He realised that the trust between the girl and their prey could not be established just like that. And so, when the unicorn lifted his head, looked at the girl once more, and trotted back into the forest, the Commander just smiled with satisfaction, certain that soon it would be possible to lure the damned thing quite close.

Night swallowed the world, covered it under a black veil, wrapped it in silence. The soldiers slept. The lantern on the stern illuminated the sentry leaning on his spear. The soldier looked at Choo-kheng without interest and then returned to his night thoughts. It was as if she did not exist: the soldiers were strictly forbidden to even speak to her without need, let alone smile at her or make an improper remark. The threat of the headsman's axe had made them true eunuchs, at least on this mission.

The Commander had been very pleased at supper: he was expecting to carry out his mission tomorrow, or in two or three days at the latest. Choo-kheng knew he was right. The unicorn trusted her now. Tomorrow, the animal would approach her on his own. Tomorrow, she would tempt him. Tomorrow...

Tomorrow, or in two or three days at the latest, noble blood would stain Choo-kheng for eternity. And not even the finest silk and the most precious jewellery, nor the greatest of honours would wash that stench of treason from her soul. All that afternoon and evening she had been thinking of nothing else but those eyes, the eyes of the unicorn, and of what she would see in them as the first arrow hit. If only he had not saved her from the blue tiger! If only he had not stepped between her and the beast, it would be all over now: everything would be decided, and Choo-kheng would be free, released of all responsibility.

But fate would not have it that way. The hand that wanted to throw a stone at the web had paused and placed all the burden upon the girl's shoulders.

A string of lights along the river: fishermen with their faithful cormorants. Choo-kheng looked at the sentry and then down the river. One light, nearest to them, was apart from the others. It seemed close to the bank. Who knew why that fisherman lagged behind? Perhaps he had already filled his basket, but did not feel like going home. Or he had problems with his raft or bird. Choo-kheng did not care. She could swim to him.

By the time the Commander posted sentries and went to sleep, Choo-kheng had decided. She had realised she had no strength to face those eyes filled with pain - pain of the arrow tearing his flesh, pain of the friendship let down, pain of betrayal. She knew she must save the magical animal, even at the price of her own head. And she knew there was only one way to drive the unicorn away, before it was too late for them both.

At first, she had planned to use one of the sentries. But their loyalty to the Emperor was unfailing, and their fear before his wrath was infinite. Therefore, she had settled on this lonely fisherman, far enough away that he could not be seen by the others but close enough that Choo-kheng could swim to him, guided by his lantern like a desert traveller following the North Star.

The girl looked at the sentry as he passed her by, walking to the prow. If only he would fall asleep! But no, the Emperor's best soldiers would never fall asleep on duty. *It doesn't matter*, Choo-kheng decided and withdrew quietly to her cabin; it was small and cramped, but it hid her from stares. She undressed quickly, threw her finest robes onto the bed and opened the doors a little. The sentry was looking down the river, his back turned to her.

Choo-kheng sneaked out of her cabin, tiptoed across the deck, and slipped silently overboard before the sentry turned. She held her breath. She heard the sentry's quiet steps on the deck. For a moment, he stopped right above her and she was afraid that he would lean over and spot her alongside the junk. But the sentry kept walking. As far as he was concerned, Choo-kheng had retired to sleep.

Feeling relieved, the girl pushed herself off from the junk and swam in quiet strokes towards the bank, towards the lantern and her destiny.

There was only one way to save her saviour.

"You betrayed Us, Yeoh Choo-kheng."
        The Emperor was sitting on his throne. His hand rested on a sheathed sword lying in his lap.

He had commanded Choo-kheng be brought to him, chained, to a pavilion amidst the lake that graced the very centre of the Imperial City. They dragged her across the wooden bridge—the only one leading to the pavilion—and threw her down on her knees. She rose. They kicked her back to the floor, and then the Emperor shouted "Enough!" and ordered her manacles removed. The Captain of the Guard opened his mouth to object, for Choo-kheng was now a dangerous traitor, but his eyes met the Emperor's, and he released her himself before standing two paces behind her. The Emperor dismissed his guards with an impatient gesture of his hand, so the two of them remained alone, face to face.

Choo-kheng noticed that there were no butterflies before the Emperor's feet. Whether this was because it was late in the evening, when they flew no more, or because he knew precisely what was in her soul, she could not say. "We shall not ask with whom you betrayed Us. It does not matter: We had your entire escort decapitated today, thus punishing the one who touched you with his hands, as well as the rest for not preventing it from happening."

Choo-kheng suppressed a bitter laugh at the Emperor's cruel fallacy. Let him believe that he punished the guilty ones. Because who knew what revenge would he exact against the innocent people by the river if he learnt that she had given herself to an ordinary fisherman. In what inconceivable ways would he torture entire villages if she told him the whole story? How she had swum in complete silence to the young man's raft, rising from the water before his wide-opened eyes, naked like some river goddess, and extinguished the lantern flame so that no one could see them. And how she approached him without a word, kissing him and surrendering to his rough hands. And how she let his callous palms fondle her and fingers tease her. How she allowed, in blood, her teeth clenched, a man to make a woman out of a girl.

"What We wish to know is *why* you betrayed Us, Yeoh Choo-kheng."

The piercing cry of a white crane spilled across the lake. The crane was one of many that adorned the shores, their wings pinioned, to make the Emperor's heart glow with their lovely beauty. Another bird replied to the crane, and then they all fell silent: cranes and egrets and gaudy ducks, spotted deer in the park, ladies twittering merrily as they strolled, and frowning men-at-arms marching with determination. It was a time for dreams. The night lay a shroud of peace upon the Imperial City. Only lanterns in the pavilion remained burning, casting flickering light over the stage on which two actors, the warrior girl and the Emperor, were about to act a deadly play.

"Well, Yeoh Choo-kheng, why? Did We not promise a worthy reward for your success?"

"If I had failed the unicorn that saved me," Choo-kheng replied, "that would be worse. No reward would wash away the stain of *that* betrayal."

"Hmmm," the Emperor became thoughtful. Then he rose from his throne and stood before the warrior girl. "And you are not afraid of punishment?"

She did not reply immediately, merely looked the Emperor in the eye. She had stopped fearing him when she climbed back onto the junk and sneaked into her cabin, unseen. Neither was she afraid on the third morning, when the unicorn approached her and then stopped suddenly, sensing some change in her, then reared and galloped back into the forest, into safety, way beyond the reach of the arrows. The Commander realised quickly what had happened and had ordered Choo-kheng to be bound immediately. He spent the entire day fuming across the deck, trying to find out which soldier had taken her. If he had dared, he would have beheaded Choo-kheng himself. Finally, he had the guards on duty that night whipped. All he could do was return, qualms in his heart, to the Imperial City, job not done. And now, he and his twenty soldiers had been executed.

"Have You ever seen a unicorn, Your Majesty?" Choo-kheng asked finally.

"Unfortunately, no. We heard, however, that it is a beautiful beast."

"True. And I couldn't allow it to be killed."

"Even if We commanded it?"

"Even if You commanded it, Your Majesty," Choo-kheng replied, wondering why everybody feared this man. Fat, grey, his stare revealing his fear now and again. Where was his power? And did he truly have any? Or was everybody around him so helpless, chained by fear? Not even the sword in his hand scared her anymore. The five bandits seemed faster and stronger opponents. "You created Your enemies Yourself. Your quest for immortality is as futile as it is unnatural. Your life is not worth the life of a unicorn."

"Our life is the life of the State," the Emperor hissed. He grabbed the hilt of his sword, squeezing it so tight his fingers went white. "Our life is the life of the people! One state, one people, one ruler! You forgot that, warrior girl!"

"The people lived before You. They will live after You. *You* forgot that."

"How dare you?" the Emperor roared. He drew the sword from its scabbard and struck. The blade flashed like lightning, but it did not land a blow, frozen by some unexplainable force. The Emperor trembled when he understood. The blade stopped right in front of the warrior girl's face, squeezed firmly between her palms. The Emperor pulled his sword free. Choo-kheng jumped back, ready for another attack. "Is that so? You vanquished five bandits, We praised you a little, and now you feel strong enough to forget that We are not some village cutpurse!"

The Emperor brandished his sword once again, but she evaded his attack, and another, and another. She was thinking feverishly what to do. Sentries were on the bridge. Perhaps they had already heard the struggle that troubled the peace of night and were speeding to the aid of their Emperor. She knew she did not have much time. Even if she defeated the Emperor, what then? His merciless ministers would put her to the severest of tortures until she begged them to execute her. All she could do was escape.

"Where will you go?" the Emperor snarled, sensing her intention. "Do you think there will be a single place in Our Empire where you can hide from Us?"

"The world spreads beyond Your Empire, Your Majesty," Choo-kheng replied mockingly. This chubby old man was tiring her. How could she listen to him and feel the same awe for him that she had the first time they had brought her before his throne? A new gratitude to the unicorn rose up inside her. And to the tiger, the blue one, and the other one she had seen once. And to the deer and the birds, the spider and the grasshopper, gratitude to all those creatures that had opened her eyes, liberated her, shown her the way. Her destiny did not depend on any Emperor, she realised. It depended only on her two hands and whether she would step through the thicket of evil or walk down the path of good. That was her choice alone, the choice that had freed her of every fear.

The way her grandfather had taught her, she skilfully dodged another of the Emperor's attacks. The cold blade whizzed a finger's breadth from her ear, cutting a tuft of her hair off, flashing before her eyes. Lightning-fast, Choo-kheng grabbed the Emperor's sword hand and twisted it in a relentless squeeze. The Emperor screamed in pain and dropped his weapon. She grabbed it, and in a moment, the sword tip was under the Emperor's throat. Silence descended upon the pavilion; only the Emperor panted heavily, his eyes riveted to the shiny blade.

"I will not kill You, Your Majesty," Choo-kheng soothed him. "For You, realisation that You were defeated by a simple peasant girl will be worse than death."

And with those words, Choo-kheng ran to the rail like a doe, jumped over, and threw herself into the lake, taking with her the sword she had wrestled from the Emperor's hand.

"Guards!" the Emperor bellowed. "Guards! Over here!" Loyal soldiers on the shore heard his call and thundered across the wooden bridge. Torches were lit, somebody called for more soldiers to spread along the shore. Swords were drawn, bows tautened, arrows pointed into darkness. The Emperor commanded angrily that the impudent girl be caught alive and brought before him.

At that moment, a sudden dry wind howled above the Imperial City, swooping down from nowhere on them all. The lake's surface, peaceful a moment before, became choppy with high waves. The branches moaned, leaves rustled, bamboos bent, captive cranes and egrets and ducks cowered before the elements. Roof tiles fell and shattered, window blinds rattled, flags on the walls flapped wildly. It was as if some mighty dragon was coiled above the lake, extinguishing the torches and tearing the lanterns, throwing the City into complete darkness with his furious breath, drowning all the Emperor's commands and all the soldiers' cries with his angry howls.

Whipped by the wind, a sentry on the shore thought he saw someone swimming in the lake. He shouted, calling for reinforcements, but in vain: nobody heard him above the wind. His torch was extinguished by the wind so he could not see any more. He drew his bow taut, but the arrow he loosed was sent swerving by the wind. The bough above him screeched and cracked, and he dived nose-first into the grass lest be killed by it on the spot.

For half the night, the wind savaged the Imperial City and did a lot of damage. In all that confusion, nobody noticed Choo-kheng crossing the dam that cut the river and surrendering to the flow to take her far away from the City. It was only when she swam out, far downstream, that the wind calmed down. As if the dragon had blown out its wrath.

And somewhere far away, as the first pinks of sunrise painted the eastern sky, Choo-kheng sank into the protective embrace of the forest. She startled a herd of deer, almost stumbled upon a bear, and alarmed a blue magpie. A tiger gave her a wide berth. For a moment, she thought she heard hooves. She paused and listened, raising her sword: it could have been her pursuers.

Then she heard whinnying, so familiar, and ran without hesitation after the hooves that led her through the forest, away from the Emperor's wrath, beyond the reach of the swords and arrows of his soldiers, to a place safe from the whips of his jailers and the axes of his headsmen. Laughing free, Choo-kheng ran like wind on the trail of the unicorn.

You should know that the great Ch'in Shih Huang Ti died less than two years after the events I told you about. His dynasty was overthrown four years later. Know this, too, as a truth indeed! A fire devoured his castle for two months, so immense it was. But the Great Wall survived the First Emperor, and the mighty army still guards his tomb against robbers. You must also know that impudent Choo-kheng disappeared without a trace. Not even the Great Khan himself in his city of Cambaluc did know what happened to her afterwards. Neither did he know anything else about unicorns, except that they are seen in Cathay no more. So now I will speak no further of this adventure of the unicorn and the warrior girl, but I will tell you of another story.

ALEKSANDAR ŽILJAK

The Divine She-Wolf

Jana almost stumbled across the body lying in the snow, two arrows in its back. Breathless, running to her house, she did not stop to see who it was. She ran through smoke biting at her eyes. Around her, flames devoured thatched roofs. Something dishevelled and bloodied hit her, screaming. Jana pushed the woman away like a rag doll, only one thought in her mind as her heart was beating like crazy.

Mishko!

Somebody was yelling, calling people to put out the fires. A warrior was cursing, brandishing an old sword helplessly. Mooing in horror, a cow ran into the mud and trodden snow, trampling the beleaguered warrior, his curses dying under the heavy hooves. Jana left all that behind, ducking out of the way as a fire swallowed a barn.

Mishko!

Blood! Screams, curses, wailing, whinnying, pitiful mooing, and above all that, the merry crackling of rampant fires. Blood! Bodies; cut down, their heads split, shot with arrows, blood in the snow like roses scattered across a white table cloth. Blood! Tickling Jana's nostrils through heat and smoke; hot and salty, waking something in her that she thought was long behind her. Blood! She was not herself anymore; the village and the poor people ceased to exist, all her senses were taken over by the instincts of her tribe.

Mishko!

Jana knew instincts were all that was left to her now. Only instincts could help her: older than memory, older than the new pack she had joined. The pack that was really just a herd bleating and mooing helplessly, scattered by the horde of the merciless dog-heads. Instincts of a hunter. A cut-throat. A beast.

Her home was at the edge of the village, somewhat away from other houses. Jana dropped to her knees with relief when she saw it was not on fire. And then she saw hoof prints leading straight to her house. She cursed and forced herself to run that last hundred yards, following the trail of the horde, their still-fresh scents. Instincts.

She rushed into the yard; the wicker fence was down, the trough turned over. Yambrek was lying in the snow next to the well. *God, no!* Jana wailed and dropped next to him, taking him into her arms and raising him. He was breathing, thank God, and moaning. His forehead was bloodied. Jana looked for the wound in his blood-soaked tufts. She found a shallow cut, bleeding worse than it was.

"Jana," Yambrek opened his eyes with effort.

"Mishko? Where's Mishko?"

"They snatched him!" Yambrek sat up, blood flowing from his hair. Jana took her kerchief off and pressed it to the wound. "The dog-heads, curse them!" Yambrek reached across the snow for a bloodied hatchet. His callused hand squeezed the handle. Yambrek tried to rise but stumbled, still stunned by the blow, and Jana sat him back into the snow.

"They took him away. What are we to do, Jana? They took our Mishko away!"

Jana looked back at the arson and death that was the village. She knew there was no one to follow the dog-heads. *It will take people a whole day to put out the fires, gather the scattered cattle, and tend the wounded*, she realised. *And who knows how many were killed by the dog-heads.* No, there was no one in the village. And even if there was, there were no horses good for pursuit. The few horses that the village did possess were the peasant horses, good for a plough and cart, but not as swift as the horses the dog-heads were riding.

Jana took Yambrek's face in her hands. The anger in his eyes became flooded by pain and despair. Yambrek also knew the dog-heads were out of reach by now. And with them, their Mishko...

"Where did you hide my wolf-skin?" Jana asked grimly.

Chilly air cut at Tzeven's face as he grinned, satisfied, and spurred the horse beneath him. Hooves were scattering the snow, faster than any pursuit. Tzeven: as swift as *dzheiran*, a gazelle, speeding across the desert on her thin legs.

He had planned well. He had been scouting for three days, sneaking with his men around the village without the villagers realising he was there. Tzeven: as cunning as *manul*, a steppe cat, hiding behind a rock to jump on a sand grouse, never showing so much as a hair.

Bows, arrows, sabres; today, they drank blood. The attack had been sudden and ruthless as only the riders of the horde can be. Tzeven: as deadly as *bars*, a leopard, claws drawn, fangs as white as death.

He left behind blood and fire, wailing and screaming. The *khan* had said it right: Tzeven had heard him with his own ears and remembered every word. *Nothing better than the shrieks of your enemy's children and the weeping of their women.* Thus had spoken the *khan*, roaring with laughter, as he kicked a girl out of his *yurta*; some Cathay princess he'd possessed that night while flames devoured her father's palace. Nothing better... Only Horlo had been a bit careless, and a peasant had managed to cut him with his hatchet. Tzeven scowled.

29

Oh, Horlo, Horlo, always trouble with him. But he was strong and the wound was nothing, it would heal.

But the prey was here, tied up in Tzeven's strong arms. Biting at his fist; teeth never letting go, biting till hot blood flowed. Tzeven did not even wince.

The shaman had spoken right long ago: he did foretell Tzeven's destiny after all.

Tzeven recalled that night, years ago...

"Why kill all these people, Tzeven?" Blood had been running down the steel blade, he and his men slaughtering the entire tribe without mercy. The wind was covering the last screams with snow. Men were chasing scattered horses and camels, looting *yurtas*. There was only one *yurta* left, away from the others, with an old man in it.

"And why not?" Tzeven spat with contempt. "I hold a sabre in my hand, they don't."

"Do you know what you want, Tzeven?" the shaman—wrinkled by wind, sun, and snow—asked him as a blizzard was roaring above the steppe and wolves were howling in the mountains.

"Do you want to be a great warrior, the greatest of them all? As swift as *dzheiran*, as cunning as *manul*, as deadly as *bars*? Everything you survey to be yours? Is that what you want, Tzeven?"

The mysterious smile on the old man's thin lips, the sabre in Tzeven's hand. *Who is this old man to mock me like this?* Tzeven wondered. And how did he know his name? How did he know who had burst in, pushing the hides aside, letting the chill and snowflakes in? And the old man nodded; he knew the answer already.

"Yes, that is what you want, Tzeven."

Then he sighed and closed his eyes, as if Tzeven and his sabre were not there.

"That will be your destiny, Tzeven. If," the old man's eyes opened wide, finger darting up, "if you find the Feeble Sun first."

"The Feeble Sun?"

"Follow the Sun, Tzeven! Go where it sets! And look for a boy! Of blue eyes, as blue as the sky above the mountain. And of shiny hair, as shiny as gold. You will recognise him when you find him, Tzeven. You will know. He is the Feeble Sun. He is the key to your destiny." At those words, the old man burst into laughter. Tzeven scowled at his impudence and cut him down.

He was about to step out into the bloodied blizzard when a death-rattle and a knotty hand rising towards him stopped him.

"Only, beware of his mother, Tzeven... The she-wolf... Beware of her!"

Thus the shaman had spoken long ago. *Who knows if his mother was really a she-wolf,* Tzeven thought, *but the kid is indeed a wolf-cub.*

His scout, spying at the village seven days ago, had informed him that he had seen a little boy with eyes as blue as the sky above the mountain and with hair as shiny as gold. Those were his very words. And when Tzeven heard them, he recalled the old shaman immediately; he had forgotten all about him until then. After all, the shaman had been just one of many whose blood was spilled by Tzeven's sabre. His prophecy came before Tzeven's eyes. The great warrior, the greatest of them all! As swift as *dzheiran,* as cunning as *manul,* as deadly as *bars*!

A finger of destiny, nothing else, Tzeven knew right away. Because the scout spoke the same words as the shaman, words Tzeven himself had heard from the old man's wrinkled lips, but which the scout had not. Therefore, Tzeven— not wasting a moment—raised his best two *arbans.* He led them in the direction of the sunset, and when they neared the village, they prowled around it for three days before Tzeven found where the boy lived. He saw the boy's father and spat in contempt; merely a peasant. He saw his mother. *Oh yes,* he grinned, *I'd like to wrestle with her in furs in my* yurta. But the boy was what Tzeven wanted, the Feeble Sun, the key to his destiny.

And now, the boy was biting him till blood oozed and Tzeven, patient as he was, had had enough. He drew on the reins. His horse reared and stopped. Tzeven jumped out of the saddle, shook the tiny bound body off into snow and grabbed the whip.

"I'll teach you how to bite!" furious Tzeven howled while he whipped the boy. "I'll teach you!"

The boy, contorted under the whip, his teeth clenched, never let out so much as a whimper. Only tears rolled down his chilled cheeks. He raised his gaze, his blue eyes skimming across Tzeven's boots, sword, embroidered *deel.* The boy paused on the wolf-skin thrown over Tzeven's shoulders, defying the warrior's small black eyes squinting from under the fur cap low on his forehead.

Tzeven paused and looked at his riders. They did not utter a word; they knew better than to contradict an angry Tzeven. The dog-head cursed and grabbed the boy, jumping with him back into the saddle. The little boy did not

31

bite anymore, but Tzeven did not miss the way he had withstood the whip and measured him toe to head. Not even the experienced warriors dared to defy Tzeven like that.

For a moment, Tzeven recalled the end of the old man's prophecy. Some vague chill possessed him. Because if the boy was like that, what would his mother be like?

"Where did you hide my wolf-skin?"

Yambrek paused, taking Jana by her shoulders. "Jana, don't —"

"Where did you hide my wolf-skin?"

"They took him away, Jana. We can't catch up with them, don't —"

"Where did you hide my wolf-skin?" Jana's voice grew as relentless as ice, and her husband cracked like a twig in the wind.

"Don't you go, Jana! Don't you leave me too!" Yambrek was on the verge of tears and Jana embraced him and held him close to her, his warm breath spilling across her breasts. "I don't want to lose you too. We can't..."

"*Men* can't catch up with them, Yambrek," Jana pushed him away gently and looked him straight in the eye. "Men can't. But *wolves* can. Where did —?"

Yambrek rose and headed for their cowshed. Jana followed. He paused, weighing up: Mishko or Jana. He knew Jana could catch up with the dog-heads. He also knew she would bring Mishko back, he saw it in her green eyes. She was the only one who could do it now, bring Mishko back. But then she would return to the forest, join the pack for good, and abandon her son and husband. He would never see her again, never warm his soul at her fire again, never enjoy her heat again. Just listen at her howling in the icy nights, when the full Moon is crowned with a halo like a saint.

Mishko. Jana. Balanced on a pair of scales.

Yambrek looked at his Jana once again as she stood at the door, lips tight, bloodied by his blood. Then he decided. He pulled Jana's wolf-skin from the hayloft, hidden deep in the hay, wrapped in coarse cloth and tied with a rope. The cow stirred, but Yambrek calmed her with gentle voice, as only he knew how.

Jana took the bundle, untied the knot, unwrapped the canvas, spread out the wolf-skin. She squeezed it in her fingers, raised it to her cheeks, let the soft hair caress her. She was getting drunk on her scent. Then she looked at Yambrek. He was holding an old rusty hoop in his hand, taken from a rotten barrel and thrown aside.

"Hold it, Jana!" Jana shook her head. "Hold it for me, so I can leap through it and turn into a wolf. So we can go together!"

"No, Yambrek!"

"I want to go with you, I want —"

"No, Yambrek, I need you!" Yambrek stopped as Jana brought her wolf-skin to him. "I need you here, so there's someone to find me. To recognise me. Do you understand?"

Yambrek submitted to his wife quietly. He took the wolf-skin from her hands, touched it and raised it to his face, letting the scent of a beast overpower him. He looked at the wolf's snout and ears, remembering them so that he would never forget them.

Jana took off her boots, and then she undressed. Yambrek placed the skin in the hay before her and left for the yard. There was nothing more to say; there was no time, the dog-heads were fast. Jana, fully naked, threw the wolf-skin over her. The wolf's back fell over hers, the wolf's snout covered her face, the wolf's limbs clung to hers. Wildness surged from the wolf-skin into Jana's body, permeating her every pore, taking her entire being over. It touched her very core; the skin became Jana, and Jana became the skin. The woman that had been a she-wolf became a she-wolf once again. Only the awareness of something that could not be delayed, something horrible, stopped Jana from yapping in joy and snarling in passion and howling and announcing to all the world that the beast had returned to her origins.

The she-wolf looked at the man standing at the entrance to the cowshed, the hatchet in his hand. Bloodied; he brought it to the she-wolf's nose. "This is a dog-head's blood. Smell it, to help you follow the trail easier."

For two days, Jana had been following the dog-heads.

Her tireless paws carried her across drifts following the fresh trail. She kept a safe distance. She remembered the tales of the dog-heads' arrows flying far, how they had the eyes of a falcon and hands that never trembled as they drew their bows.

She did not know if they had spotted her, but apparently they had not; she was a tiny black dot using up as little space as several blades of dry grass sticking from the snow, a dry leaf remaining on a thorny bramble twig embellished in frost, a tree. Hiding was taking her a lot of time, but she dared not follow them openly across the revealing whiteness. And it had taken her time to catch a hare she had driven from behind a dog-rose bush. For a moment, Jana wanted to suppress her instinct and let the hare leap to safety. But she could not miss that opportunity; hunger would exhaust her. It had been worth it, she realised, when freshly spilled blood filled her nostrils, and when her teeth tore through hair and bit into flesh of the poor animal, still twitching.

She'd spent a lot of precious time, but she'd never lost the dog-heads' trail. When she could not see them in the distance, she was led by the scents of horses and unwashed bodies; when she could not smell them, the wind would carry whinnying and voices across the whipped plain.

From the moment she had seen them, Jana knew she could not do it alone. Twenty horsemen, all with bows and sabres, some with axes. They would chop her to pieces without her bringing a single one down. She would need the pack. Alone, she was helpless. In the pack, she was almighty.

But then Jana realised not even the pack could fight them openly. The dog-heads were experienced hunters. Jana had seen that many of them had wolf-skins across their backs and saddles. And other skins, yellowish and spotted, skinned from beasts she had never seen. She also recalled tales which told how the dog-heads loved to hunt. They would surround an area and drive out all the game and all the beasts, and kill them all with arrows and spears for sport. And if a lucky beast escaped one of the hunters, the other hunters would whip the man, so it never happened again.

Jana did not want half the pack killed in the open, unless there was no other choice, if that was the price she had to pay to free Mishko... But she saw the riders did not change their direction, always driving their horses into the sunrise. Jana recalled her wolf days. She had crossed the length and breadth of this countryside on her four paws, with the pack, and she knew every tree and stream. She knew where every road led and she was certain the dog-heads were riding to the mountain. In the mountain—covered by snow, chained in ice and cold—they were safe from prying eyes. At least, that was what they thought...

Jana let the raiders gain distance. Then she memorised where she left them—just in case she had to return—and sped away from their sharp eyes, overtaking them and, by evening, reaching the young oaks, sentries on the edge of the large forest that covered the entire mountain.

The Moon was like a night watchman. The pale lantern he held tirelessly above the world led Jana uphill, through the forest which was asleep under the snow. The bare trees were threatening, rising and seeming to enclose her from above; the trunks were dark apparitions, the branches interwoven fingers, gnawed to the bone, tearing at the chilly night sky. She left the dog-headed riders far behind. She remembered the forest well. She smelled the familiar scents here and there. The pack had been in this part of the forest recently. They did not go far, and she would summon them easily.

High in the mountain and deep in the forest, Jana found a fallen oak, reclining down the slope. She had not come there by chance. A remote forest road passed above the fallen oak. The dog-heads had used it when they went to raid the village. Jana smelled their scents along it, days old, followed them and reached the oak. The she-wolf recognised the tree, remembering it standing strong and proud. A storm must have felled it while she was a woman. Falling, the heavy giant had crushed another tree beneath it. All around, thin and fragile shoots rested till spring, when they would continue their race for the sun.

Suddenly, Jana smelt the scent of danger coming from below the fallen oaks and boughs and snow. She approached carefully, stepping softly, taking care that her paws did not fall through the snow. There was a thick bough here, several thinner branches falling across it. Everything was covered by the snow, a shield against frost and chill. Beneath, with dry leaves and ferns, it must have been soft and warm and cosy indeed. Jana carefully tested how firm it was beneath her paws. Not firm at all... If something with a heavier step came this way...

If wolves could grin, Jana would have grinned. She followed the road with her eyes. Yes... *The dog-heads will certainly come from this direction... And we can wait for them behind those trees, hidden from eyes and arrows... And here...* The she-wolf cast another glance and decided. Here, beside the fallen oak, was the right place for an ambush. Now, she had to find the pack.

When she spotted the first pair of embers on the edge of the clearing, Jana's heart leapt with joy. She did not have to call them for long; they replied right away, from everywhere. As soon as she had thrown her head back and started howling from a rock rising above the snow-covered beeches, the whole mountain awoke. Their greeting to a long-gone friend spilled above the bare tree crowns. Joy filled the forest, rising all the way to the Moon, flowing through Jana's innards, freezing blood in the veins of every human being in the countryside.

And now, the pack was here, everybody gathering around Jana. She was surrounded by dozens of wolves. She rubbed her body against theirs, caressed her cheeks against theirs. They rolled and jumped over each other, playful in the snow. She smelled them, soaking up their scents; her old comrades. With sorrow, she learned some were no more. She learned the new scents, too, of wolves and she-wolves whelped while she was a woman. She bared her teeth in jest and bristled the hair on her back and snarled in mock threat, discovering the pack still respected her. And they all greeted her, happy that she had returned after so many years of absence.

Jana told them how she had become a woman. She told them about her man and a son she had with him, about a boy with eyes as blue as the sky above the mountain and hair as shiny as gold. She also told them about the horde killing humans and wolves regardless, about the dog-heads who had kidnapped her Feeble Sun and would soon cross the mountain.

"You shouldn't have left."

The pack sank into silence and moved apart, leaving Jana alone among them. Something resembling a man stepped from the forest into the clearing. He was stooped, dragging a leg, leaning on a knotty cane. He was dressed in ragged, torn, and dirty trousers and a flax shirt, an old cloth waistcoat thrown over them. A horn was hanging from his shoulder; Jana knew he used it to summon the pack. When the creature raised his beastly head, his eyes were ablaze and his wolf snout grimaced, baring yellowish fangs. Jana bowed her head. Not even she could defy the wolf-shepherd at that moment. "You shouldn't have left, Jana, little Jana. And to a human village, of all places. After they took everything away from you."

"What other men took from me, one man gave me back." The wolf-shepherd stopped in mid-stride, and only then did Jana realise how much she was divided between the two worlds. She had never thought about it as she lay in Yambrek's arms. She had never thought about it with Mishko against her bosom. Only among the wolves and before the wolf-shepherd did she realise how much she was a she-wolf. But Yambrek was still in her heart, and Mishko...

"And then some other men took it away again."

"That's why I came, for you to help me."

"And then you'll return?" The wolf-shepherd leaned into Jana's face, his scent hitting her. "Here, where you belong, among your wolves?" All the wolves looked at her, the entire pack, and Jana could only nod.

The wolf-shepherd straightened, satisfied, and faced the pack. He raised his cane and drew a circle above the wolves as he was speaking. "What are we to do, my wolves? It is just that we help a she-wolf in distress. Even if she deserted us, even then it is just. She has a son with a man, and that son is in man's image. But he's the son of a she-wolf and that makes him a wolf cub. What are we to do?"

Tense silence settled upon the clearing. And then all the wolves around Jana and the wolf-shepherd, young and old alike, the entire pack, threw their heads back and howled. And the wolf-shepherd howled with them. Then he burst into laughter and looked at Jana.

"See, Jana, what the wolves are? All as one! And where are those humans of yours, where's that village of yours to help you?" He leaned into her face again, pinning her in the snow with his eyes. "You shouldn't have left, Jana, little Jana."

Day had dawned quite some time ago, but the morning grey was still dragging through the naked forest. Jana was lying in the snow, hidden. She looked around, the wolves were waiting. The wolf-shepherd was behind, leaning on his knotty cane, his horn in his hand. *You shouldn't have left*, his words murmured in the she-wolf's ears, and she recalled that autumn day, years ago...

"Let 'er go! Let 'er go! Let 'er go!" Yells of shepherds jumping to their feet, the scared bleating of an agitated flock and angry barking had followed Jana as she was running back to the forest, carrying a ewe in her jaws. It was dusk. For two days, Jana had been following the flock driven by the shepherds from the south, over karst and rocks, and carried across the slow river by a ferry. For two days, she had been watching, waiting, downwind all the time, so the strong pen-dogs could not smell her. And then she had grabbed an opportunity, a moment of carelessness by the dark shepherds; curses always on their lips, knives always at their belts, clubs always in their hands. She had darted out of the forest like grey lightning and grabbed the nearest ewe. The she-wolf paid no attention to the struggling and bleating of the poor animal kicking with her hooves. She just squeezed tighter.

Back in the safety of the forest—when both men and dogs had halted, hesitating on the edge of darkness—Jana dropped the ewe. The stunned animal tried to rise, but Jana bit into her throat. Hot blood filled her mouth, she drank it and licked more from the gaping wound with relish. And when the ewe died, the she-wolf tore into wool and skin, and feasted on the meat greedily.

It was autumn, not yet the time when wolves raid flocks. But there were no more seasons for Jana, no hunger to drive her attacks. The she-wolf was attacking whenever and whatever she could, as long as it was human. She slaughtered a hunter in early summer. And a logger, whose intestines she dragged across half the grove. And another one. And she bit a woman. She lost count of how many dogs she had slain. Throughout the summer, she was entering the villages themselves, snatching dogs from their chains. Then she would leave their heads on the edge of the forest, to drive horror into human bones. She attacked whenever and whatever she could, as long as it had been human.

The way her wolf and cubs had been slain that spring by men and dogs.

Jana had abandoned what was left of the ewe. Maybe she would return, maybe she would not. There were more sheep where this one came from.

It was night already and the Moon, the old night watchman, raised his lantern above the world. Fallen beech leaves were caressing Jana's paws as she ran through the forest, bloodied, sated, her hatred quenched a bit. She climbed the rocks uphill until she heard the murmur of a waterfall.

Jana reached the shore of a small lake. A rock was rising above it, a waterfall falling down from it. She was coming here often to drink and bathe, to soothe the flame burning inside her. The she-wolf jumped into the lake, letting the water wash the fury and horror and slaughter away. Then the beast stepped out and shook the drops off. With only the old night watchman watching, Jana took her wolf-skin off and turned into a beautiful girl, with green eyes and hair like grain falling down her back. She spread her wolf-skin on a stone and returned to the water. She swam until she got tired, and then she stepped back onto the shore, laid down on the soft grass and surrendered to the calming darkness of dreams.

Something snatched Jana out of her sleep. A sound, a twig cracking. The girl realised immediately that she was not alone. The Moon was high in the sky. A soldier was sitting a few steps from her. He put his helmet aside and removed his chain mail. He placed his sword, wooden shield, and spear next to them. He was watching Jana's beauty, smiling with his blue eyes. Jana did not even think of shame, leaping like a beast caught in her den and reaching for her wolf-skin. But it was not on the stone.

"Give me back my skin!"

"I will not. For nothing in the world," the soldier replied. "You'll become my wife."

Jana cursed and threw herself at the lad; he must have hidden the wolf-skin in the canvas bag behind him. But the lad evaded swiftly and caught Jana by her wrist, drawing her to him. Something in his blue eyes—was it weariness, sorrow, longing?—stopped the she-wolf from biting him.

"Will you slay me, too?"

The she-wolf realised that he had heard of her. She had filled the entire countryside with horror and people must certainly have dissuaded him from going into the forest alone, and at night to boot. But he would not listen. The chain mail, the shield, and the spear meant that he was returning from a war, and the she-wolf would not scare a man who had faced Death herself.

The lad's eyes, his hot breath on Jana's cheek, his strong body against hers, a peasant's hand holding hers... Jana felt her cheeks blushing. She was filled with a warmth she thought had been extinguished forever. The lad's lips neared hers, his breath heavy, broken, beastly. For a moment, the she-wolf and the girl fought in Jana. But when their lips joined in a kiss, the she-wolf and the girl wanted one thing only: to mate with a wolf, to make love to a man, to wash away all the pain and hatred with passion.

And so, years ago, Yambrek Valiavetz had returned from a distant war, bringing a wife with him to the quiet envy of the entire village. And the she-wolf disappeared, never to be seen or heard of again, neither by wolf nor man.

Until this day, of course, in the morning grey, waiting in ambush behind a tree, with the horde about to arrive any moment. She knew they were coming from the howling of the wolves following the dog-heads since they entered the great forest. Once again would Jana the she-wolf spill human blood.

Tzeven's sharp eyes did not miss the wolf behind an oak. He cursed. The animals had been following them since dawn. Tzeven estimated the pack to number a dozen beasts. They were driven by hunger; the horses were tempting prey, but two *arbans* meant a lot of arrows and the wolves knew it. They did not attack, merely howled every so often. The boy was tied up. He saw the wolf, too, but he did not show fear.

Tzeven grinned, but he felt unease growing in him. He still did not know the full meaning of the old shaman's prophecy. How could this boy be the key to his destiny? But the boy's courage and spite meant the shaman was right.

He even ate hot *borts* as if he had never eaten anything else in his life. *The Feeble Sun... Feeble, right!*

And what had the shaman meant when he had warned Tzeven of the boy's mother? What could she do, four days' worth of riding behind them? Still, from the moment Tzeven saw the first wolf, she did not leave his mind. A she-wolf. Yes, that was what the old man had said before he died. *Rubbish*, Tzeven thought, *twaddle with the last breath*. Or maybe not. Maybe the wolves... *Oh, rot!*

The old road led them uphill. It must be the remnant of an empire. Tzeven had heard there were mines in this mountain, but nobody knew where anymore. Tzeven's scout had discovered the road, deep in the forest and passable even under snow. The chances of anybody seeing them, much less of encountering a strong force, were slim. Tzeven was an outlaw; he could barely gather enough men for an incomplete *jaghun* and, although he knew the hundred or so of them could defeat an army ten times bigger, he did not want to try his luck.

Tzeven turned around. The forest was dense here. Everybody was cautious, hands ready to grab weapons. The horses were nervous, too, scenting the wolves. They were still there, hidden from stares and arrows, but there. Maybe they would charge after all. Hunger can drive even the most cautious beast into a desperate attack. Tzeven knew that well.

A bit further uphill, Tzeven saw an old tree felled by a storm, covered with snow. It was atop another tree, both lying downwards on the slope. Tzeven's horse whinnied suddenly, twitched his ears and stopped, wavering. Tzeven spurred him, his hand grabbing the sabre. The other dog-heads took the cue. In a moment, arrows were pointed in all directions. The column was like a hedgehog speeding up the road. Dark stares sought targets in the snow, but could not find them. It seemed the wolves had disappeared. So what was unnerving the horses?

Suddenly, the sound of a horn broke through the forest. Grey beasts darted from behind the trees, and Tzeven cursed above the cries, the snarling, and the whinnying of the horses. *What kind of pack is this?* he wondered. He had never seen so many wolves in one place. *Erlik Khan take them, there are more than fifty of them! And ambushing us!* What dark force was at work here?

Jana sprang from behind the tree like a shot arrow, her body casting the snow aside as she ran for the dog-heads' leader. She spotted Mishko; the bastard had the boy tied before him in the saddle. But the rider drew on the reins and his horse reared. Jana tried to bite the horse's legs but failed, barely escaping the hooves and the blade whistling above her.

Behind Jana were scared whinnying, screams and snarling, teeth going for the throat and slaying. And arrows flying, most missing the swift and agile beasts whose attention never wavered. But one arrow did hit home, and Jana's heart was torn by the painful yelp of an injured wolf.

No time for mourning. The leader's orders overwhelmed the chaos. The riders tried to form a circle, but it did not go as planned. They were not in the steppe but on the narrow road; a slope below, a steep above. *Still, the dog-heads could make the circle,* Jana realised, and then her planned ambush would fail. The pack would never break through a tight group of twenty men with deadly bows.

The wolves saw it in time and charged at the horsemen. Jaws snapped, the wolves were biting at the horses' legs. The poor animals could not obey anymore, and the dog-heads barely kept them reined in. One she-wolf leapt at the nearest dog-head, her teeth tearing at the hand in which he held the bow. The weight of the beast pulled him out of his saddle, and they fell into the bloodied snow. Before the dog-head managed to draw his knife, the she-wolf tore into his face. The dog-head pressed on the horrible wound, blood gushing between his fingers. Jana jumped at him and slew him. Somebody else screamed behind them as three beasts tore another dog-head apart. His horse rolled in the snow, hooves kicking, then rose and galloped down the road.

40

One she-wolf was cut across her back with a sabre. She tried to take cover, but three arrows pinned her against a furrowed oak. All around Jana, a witch-dance of hooves, wolf jaws, arrows, sabres and axes. Curses. Whinnying. Snarling. Cries. Whining. More screams, the wolves charging from all directions. If a rider fought them back with a sabre or an axe, he was safe for a moment. If a rider was pulled out of his saddle into a mash of snow, mud, and blood, he was lost. Death mowed mercilessly, bodies piled on the road and down the slope; slain dog-heads beneath shot wolves; cut wolves under torn dog-heads. Horrified and bitten, the horses ran around. The wolves let them go; they would be easy to hunt one at the time later, in the deep snow, as the pack became hungry.

Her fur bloodied, all her senses saturated in steaming blood, Jana looked for the leader. And Mishko. She found them, cut off from the battle with three more dog-heads. Jana counted five dead wolves around them, five dead brothers and sisters. A dozen wolves and she-wolves joined her.

It was only then that Jana took a decent look at Tzeven. The surrounding slaughter did not scare him one bit. Fury, spite, and determination were in his eyes. He would not surrender. He would not let the horror darken his mind. He intended to break out of the circle of wolves and only death could stop him. Tzeven and his three horsemen shot arrows at the swift wolves. One whistled within inches of Jana's ear. The dog-heads loosed more arrows. A she-wolf to the left of Jana was grazed, whined, but stood her ground. A wolf charged, snapping at the nearest horse. The rider cursed and swung his axe. The wolf escaped the deadly steel by a hair's breadth.

Tzeven shot an arrow, hitting the beast's side, bringing him down and finishing him with another arrow. He cursed, the wolves were all around. It was as if *khagan* himself had trained the damned things to fight! They had broken his two *arbans* into small groups and were slaughtering them. More arrows, one hit. The battle behind Jana was nearing its end. A curse, a scream, and it was finished, just the whinnying of the horses and the whining of a wolf hit.

Tzeven realised the battle was over. More beasts were gathering around him and the last three riders. And they all seemed to look to one beast, a she-wolf. The warrior took a closer look at her, and then he shivered. *Was it possible the bloody old man meant it literally?*

"Let's go!" Tzeven bellowed. Nobody else was left alive, and he had to break through the ranks of wolves. The pack threw themselves at him and his three comrades. The dog-heads were shooting into a whirling mass of bloodied bodies. Some collapsed into the snow, whining, and remained still.

Jana leapt before Tzeven's horse, snapping, scratching, and the animal reared. Tzeven was furious, cutting into nothing. He spurred his mount, but more wolves blocked his way. The she-wolf darted at him again, and the boy, tied up, did not even blink. He did not even scream, let alone cry.

Tzeven and his men brandished their sabres and axes, steel to keep the animals at bay. And then, a passage among the wolves opened for a moment. This could be their chance! "Follow me!" Tzeven commanded.

And indeed, the four horsemen broke through the wolves. The pack sped after them, their paws swifter across the snow than hooves. Soon the wolves flanked the dog-heads. The only way out was over the fallen old oak, and Tzeven lost no time, the horsemen speeding down to it.

Jana followed the four men tensely. She must cut off their retreat, she must... Tzeven cleared the fallen tree, the horse landing on firm ground. *Damn*, Jana thought, *he didn't...* But the next rider leapt right after him and fell through. Snow-covered branches could not hold his weight and they cracked. The horse whinnied, the horseman fell out of his saddle and rolled, breaking branches. And then something large, dark and angry rose up, throwing the snow and broken branches aside. The third and fourth horsemen failed to stop or swerve so that they ran straight into a furious bear, awoken from his winter sleep by the hooves.

Jana's trap closed in a lethal whirl of whinnying, screams, and angry mumbling. With a forceful blow of his paw, the bear broke the neck of one of the dog-heads, then threw his body aside like a rag. The bear caught the other one with his claws and tore his face into bloody ribbons. The dog-head screamed, and then fell under the weight of several wolves. The remaining wolves charged at the last rider. Avoiding his sabre, one she-wolf brought him down. The next moment, he was torn apart beneath a whirling mass of mad beasts. In the meantime, the bear, still half-asleep, did not even try to understand what was going on. He bolted out of his den and ran clumsily into the forest, happy to be alive.

Tzeven remained alone, surrounded, facing the she-wolf. He squeezed the tied boy before him, the boy with eyes as blue as the sky above the mountain and hair as shiny as gold. The Feeble Sun... The sabre in his other hand. The shaman's last words would not leave his mind.

Jana did not hesitate any more. She leapt at Tzeven, bringing him and Mishko down into the soft snow. Another she-wolf darted between them and grabbed Mishko by his clothes, dragging him into safety, away from the hooves, the sabre, and the fangs. Tzeven struck into nothing, and Jana tore at his throat. His blood gushed, spurting across the grey fur, soaking Tzeven's blue *deel*. The eyes of the she-wolf burned in hatred, merciless, just like Tzeven's black ones. The eyes of the she-wolf were the last thing the warrior saw before the darkness took him and the hand with the sabre sank helplessly into the bloody snow. And in the last moment of consciousness, Tzeven finally knew how the boy was the key to his destiny.

Beware of his mother, Tzeven! The she-wolf. Beware of her!

The blizzard was whipping Yambrek, blinding him. The chilly wind found its way under his cloak, the snow fell into his boots. But Yambrek did not stop, staggering towards the forest looming out of the blizzard like a dark wall, only to be hidden again by the snow curtain a moment later.

Jana had brought Mishko home the night before.

Yambrek had been sitting at the table in feeble candlelight, absorbed in his dark thoughts. Eight days had passed since the dog-heads had taken Mishko, eight days since Jana went after them. The villagers were mourning their dead and fixing their roofs; life moved on. Only in Yambrek's house did everything stop.

And then, suddenly, there was scratching at the door. Yambrek started, his hand reaching for the hatchet; there was still dog-head's blood on it. Again, scratching. Claws! That must be the claws! Jana!

Yambrek darted from the bench, opened the door, and stood there. Mishko was in the snow, chilled and dirty. Alone. There were only wolf tracks leading to the door. Yambrek wrapped the boy in his cloak, brought him inside, and tossed some logs onto the fire. Then he rushed out.

"Jana!" Yambrek called into the night. He thought he saw the shape of a beast running into the forest. "Jana!" he called his wife again, but distant howling was his only answer.

At daybreak, while Mishko was asleep—warmed, washed, and fed—Yambrek went for Mara. The villagers would call on her to help with wounds or illness; she'd had her hands full last days. As he was throwing a bag with some bread, bacon, and onions across his shoulder, he told her to watch over Mishko and ask no questions.

"And where are you going in this blizzard, Yambrek?" Mara was not the kind of woman who would ask no questions. "And with the sword, too?"

"I'm going to get Jana," Yambrek replied. Mara nodded. She had heard the howling, the wolves had been close. Maybe she guessed what Jana was, maybe not. Yambrek did not care. People were whispering that Mara was a friend to fairies and were taking great care not to cross her. She would watch over Mishko as if he was her own blood until Yambrek Valiavetz returned from the forest with his wife.

43

The blizzard stopped, the wind got tired. Only an occasional flake was falling quietly on the white snow that covered the countryside with silence. Yambrek shook the snow from his shoulders. He blew into his fists to make them warm. The forest before him was like a threatening army of giants rising from the snow. Who knew what awaited within those trees? And the pack was there somewhere, he'd followed their howling. Through the chill and the wailing wind and the curtain of snow, the howling had led him to the edge of the forest. Perhaps they were watching him that very moment as he stood there, wavering. Maybe all the creatures, the entire forest, wondered with beastly disdain whether fear or love would prevail in Yambrek Valiavetz. Maybe Jana wondered the same thing. And that was the thought Yambrek could not stand for a moment.

And so, Yambrek followed the snow-covered road into the forest.

Surrounded by the trees, Yambrek quickly lost sense of time. No beast was to be heard, only the snow crunching beneath his boots. The pack stopped howling, as if silenced by the blizzard. But Yambrek felt them near.

Dawn was still far away when Yambrek reached a path crossing the road he had been following. He cursed quietly. So far, it had been easy; all he'd had to do was follow the road. And where to now? Which path to follow?

Then Yambrek saw someone squatting by a tree, some twenty paces away. His hand reached for his sword, but he did not draw it. Somebody was indeed there. The figure rose, a knotty cane in his hand. He was dressed in rags, dragging his leg, a horn hanging from his shoulder. When he approached Yambrek, he raised his beastly head. His gaze was burning. His wolf snout grinned, baring yellow fangs.

Yambrek's heart stuttered in his chest. He barely restrained himself from cutting down the creature before him with his sword.

"What do you want in this forest, stranger?" the wolf-shepherd snarled.

"I'm looking for my wife. She turned into a divine she-wolf."

The wolf-shepherd nodded.

"So, you are Jana's man? I told her you wouldn't come after her. She said you would, and I admit she was right. You gave her a nice cub. Only he cost us dearly."

When he had come to his senses, Mishko had told his father everything: about the dog-heads and the wolves ambushing them, about the bloody battle and the bear and how he was not scared, not for a moment, because he knew Mother was among the wolves. Yambrek had laughed at the boy's words, and then he had spotted a spark in his blue eyes, as blue as the sky above the mountain. His laughter died; he had seen the same spark in the green eyes of the she-wolf, the moment before she had run after the dog-heads. He had caressed Mishko's hair of gold without a word, and then he had put him into bed and covered him. A moment later, the boy had been fast asleep. And now was the time to bring his mother back to him.

"Where's my wife?"

"She's here!" The wolf-shepherd blew at his horn. Before Yambrek could blink, he was surrounded by some thirty beasts. "Guess which beast is your wife and she will return to you. But beware," the wolf-shepherd growled. "Should you err, my wolves will tear you apart!"

Yambrek, surrounded by the wolves, looked closely at each of them. At first glance, they all looked the same: the same snouts, pointed ears, burning stares. Teeth. But when Jana had given him her wolf-skin before she left, as soon as she had told him he must recognise her, he had realised that every wolf was like a man and every she-wolf like a woman — distinct in their own way. He was certain he could recognise her in the pack. He must not be frightened by the shepherd's terrible threat.

Yambrek tried hard to recall his wife's wolf face. He skimmed across the pack, immediately discarding some she-wolves, so different from Jana. This one had a scar, that one a torn ear. One was old, Yambrek did not think she would live to see the spring. The pack was waiting patiently. That was not his Jana either, her scent was different and so was her hair under his fingers. The snap of her jaws at his hand running across her neck convinced him that he was right. This one resembled Jana, but no, that was not his wife either, he was certain of that. This one here? Yambrek kneeled before her. The beast calmly let him feel her all over, look at her from all sides. No, she was not the one, either.

The night flowed silently around Yambrek, the wolf-shepherd, and the pack. The worm of desperation began squirming inside him; there were twenty she-wolves in the pack and some really resembled each other. Yambrek rose to his feet, it was dark in the forest. *What if I make a mistake, what if I err?* He looked at the shepherd, his fiery eyes threatening.

Why doesn't Jana give me a sign? Why doesn't she snarl, wag her tail, jump to me? Maybe she dared not, maybe she was afraid of the wolf-shepherd. *Curse him, what power does he have over the pack?*

And then Yambrek paused, recognising the feeling of dark suspicions multiplying. It had been like that in the war, before every battle. Fear. Nothing else but fear. And whomever had conquered it, had lived. Yambrek had learned that lesson well, under blows from swords and thrusts of spears.

Yambrek looked at the pack again, carefully, calmly, bringing Jana's wolf-skin before his eyes: her snout, nose, cheeks, forehead, ears. Her back, sides, legs, tail, trying to recall every tuft of hair. With Jana on his mind, he was looking for Jana in the pack.

And he found a she-wolf among the stirring beasts who was just like his Jana. He looked at her thoroughly, but his resolve remained strong. Their eyes met, his human and her wolfish; his heart beat faster, and something within Yambrek decided for him.

"There, that she-wolf is my wife!"

The wolf-shepherd limped over to the chosen she-wolf and tore the wolf-skin from her. Jana was left in the snow. Yambrek threw his cloak over her nudity. Without a word, the shepherd nodded to his pack. The beasts retreated quietly into the forest. Their shepherd followed, leaving Jana's wolf-skin behind.

Yambrek embraced Jana, kissing her all over her face.

"You made it, Jana, you made it," he whispered through her hair as he wrapped her in the coarse cloak and helped her to her feet. "You made it, Jana, my she-wolf, you brought Mishko back."

And Jana smiled, green eyes glowing in the dark with the gaze of a beast becoming a woman again. Then she picked her wolf-skin up and folded it with care. Who knew when she would need to become a she-wolf again?

"Let's go. The road is long. We must not keep Mishko waiting."

ALEKSANDAR ŽILJAK

The Nekomata

THE NEKOMATA

*M*ukashi mukashi—a long, long time ago—all the cats in Japan had tails. And then, one fateful day in the capital, a cat fell asleep next to a fireplace. Live coals set her bushy tail ablaze. And before anyone could catch her, the poor cat escaped into the yard, wailing, waving the torch of her tail. She ran from yard to yard, through houses and warehouses, leaving a trail of flame behind. Nobody could stop the blazes, and soon the entire capital was on fire.

When the smoke finally cleared and the Emperor saw the city in ashes, he decreed angrily that all the cats in the Empire should have their tails cut off. Since that day, no cat in Japan has a tail.

Save one.

*O*shichi froze. She listened carefully. Yes, somebody was indeed walking the forest path. Oshichi silently put down her armful of dry twigs and crouched. The trees hid her; she was certain the stranger did not see her. She became still, hidden behind a maple tree, its crown ablaze in autumn fire. Taking care that no leaf rustled beneath her, she peeked around its trunk.

Some poor fellow walked the path, dragging his left leg. That was why Oshichi had heard him. He supported himself with a knotty cane. The *mino*—a straw cape—he was wrapped in was old and ragged. His wide *sugegasa*—a woven sedge hat—didn't look any better.

Obviously a beggar, the girl thought. *But what is he doing here in the mountain?* Didn't beggars belong in the crowd, in a city or before an inn, where they could hope for charity? Oshichi had learned a long time ago that things were not always what they seemed and that men were not always what they pretended to be. She decided to stay concealed until the stranger went away, and then run—as fast and as quietly as she could—and notify the clan.

Oshichi took another look. The beggar limped slowly down the path. Suddenly, a dark shadow pounced upon him from an old tree, as silent as a cat. It was all over in an eye-blink. The man didn't have a chance to utter a sound before he was down in the dust, his neck broken by the deadly strike of a fist. Oshichi felt sick. The dark shape rose, adjusted her ninja garb and looked at the girl.

"You can come out, Oshichi-*chan*. He was alone."

Oshichi rose, picked up the dry twigs she had been gathering, and descended the slope. "He could have been just a beggar, Shizuka-*sama*," Oshichi said, unable to hide the accusation in her voice.

Shizuka lowered her scarf and revealed her face, nostrils still flaring in excitement, cheeks burning. She gave Oshichi the stare of a beast that has just quenched its thirst for blood. Then she picked up the beggar's cane, held it firmly, and triumphantly drew out the shiny blade concealed in it.

"There's your beggar!"

The girl lowered her gaze; she had suspected that herself.

"Nevertheless," she muttered.

"Nevertheless what? Maybe I should have let him spy on us?" Shizuka said angrily. The *kunoichi* was twice Oshichi's senior, and the girl could by no means stand against her— or her bloodlust. "You are *kirishitan*, a Christian. We know your tale well, Oshichi-*chan*. We gave you sanctuary, but you are not one of us, so stay out of our business!"

"I understand, Shizuka-*sama*," Oshichi whispered. Shizuka smiled. She brushed aside a strand of silvery hair from her forehead; being almost thirty, she was too young to be grey yet. Just as everybody in the clan knew of Oshichi's cursed destiny, they were horrified by Shizuka's as well.

"Go now, you shouldn't be seen here," Shizuka said gently. Her gentleness made Oshichi shiver. "And tell no one of this. I'll take care of the body and inform Lady Murasaki."

Agoshawk took the blink of an eye to spot a pheasant in a flattened patch of dry grass. The large dark green cock pecked at the seeds peacefully, never suspecting he was being watched by two hunters. The bird of prey looked at her master, begging. He smiled and launched the hawk into the air. The hawk spread her wings, gained speed in several strokes. Cleverly keeping to the edge of the forest, she rushed towards her prey.

The pheasant still suspected nothing. Then he was alerted by the sudden scream of a jay, watching the scene from the safety of the forest. He flapped his short wings and took off, trailing his long tail, to reach the shelter of a nearby thicket. Too late! The hawk caught up with him. A moment later, sharp talons seized the pheasant. Green feathers flew everywhere as the birds tumbled down to the ground. The hawk's deadly hooked beak struck the pheasant just behind his head and he lay still, forever.

"Ha!" Tokugawa Ieyasu yelled. He faced his escort triumphantly. "See? What a bird! What a bird!" Ieyasu ran as though he was a young man and not fifty years old. Soon, the hawk was perched on his arm again, rewarded by a morsel of meat, while the pheasant was passed to a servant.

Ieyasu waited for his hunting companions to join him, and then he waved his servant away. "Nothing better for a warrior than falconry," he said ecstatically. "You learn the military spirit and understand the hard life of the lower classes. You exercise your muscles and train your limbs. You walk and run, indifferent to cold and heat, and you are little likely to suffer from illness. Of course, you two have different exercises." When he was certain the servants could not hear him, he asked, "*Oni no* Hanzo, any news on that new *kunoichi* clan you reported about?"

Hattori Hanzo bowed before his master. He had served him for over ten years, and he knew his passion for falconry—as well as his warrior skills—well. He had to admit the fresh autumn air did him good too. "Apparently, they claim to be from the Koga region, my Lord."

"Weren't the clans from Iga and Koga destroyed by Oda Nobunaga himself, a year before his death?" Yagyu Munenori remarked. He was a sword instructor to the entire clan of Tokugawa and perhaps the only man Hanzo hoped he would never have to cross blades with.

"That makes their impudence bigger," Hanzo replied angrily. It was well known that he was from the Iga province, and he considered the ninjas from Koga to be his fierce enemies. "It is possible they are led by a pupil of Mochizuki Chiyome. And she herself was rumoured to be from one of the Koga clans."

"Whatever is the truth," Ieyasu said, "every *kunoichi* is dangerous. We all know that. Once these female ninjas take root, we'll have to suspect every *miko*, singer, and laundry girl walking down the road. And such actions lead nowhere."

"I concur," Hanzo said and nodded.

"Soon, the time will come when all of Japan will be united," Ieyasu continued, his expression showing clearly under whose banner the country would finally unite. "Peace will reign, and that peace will depend on every *daimyo* being obedient and under our control. It will not do that they should have within their grasp a secret weapon, such as a new *kunoichi* clan offering their services to anyone who pays."

Hanzo and Munenori nodded; that, too, was clear. The clan would have to be destroyed while there was still time. "Do we know where they're hiding?" Ieyasu asked, passing the goshawk another morsel. The bird swallowed it greedily.

"I sent out my best men, my Lord," Hanzo replied. "One man didn't return."

"Didn't return? That... Oh, I see." Ieyasu smiled.

"So, we know where they are!" Munenori exclaimed. "What are we waiting for?"

"Patience, Master Yagyu, patience," Ieyasu said gently. "No doubt enough samurai will defeat any ninja clan. The great Nobunaga proved that. But can we be certain we would kill them all? Do you see the problem?"

Munenori thought of it. Hanzo himself was indeed proof enough that somebody will always escape, somebody who could later plot revenge. And anybody with reason would fear a ninja revenge. "What shall we do then?"

The hawk on Ieyasu's arm studied the clearing carefully, looking for new prey.

"Suppose we eliminate the woman leading them without anyone suspecting us?" Hanzo muttered suddenly. "Should she fall victim to dark forces..."

"You will not frighten a *kunoichi* with superstition," Ieyasu remarked.

"I'm not talking about superstitions." Hanzo looked at the other two. "We need a true *bakemono*, a demon."

"That's a dangerous game," Munenori said with unease.

"And how will you do that, *Oni no* Hanzo?" Ieyasu asked.

"I have a hawk of my own, my Lord," Hanzo said, grinning mysteriously. "I just have to let her fly."

O shichi wiped the sweat from her forehead and once again mentally ran through all the chores Lady Murasaki had given her that day. The firewood was chopped, the floors thoroughly scrubbed, the *futon* aired and folded neatly in the corner. She was certain Lady Murasaki would be pleased. She carried out every chore her mistress gave her diligently: she would fetch water, clean her house, wash her clothes, and so earn her meals and the shelter that the clan gave her.

Like all the other dwellings in the village, Lady Murasaki's house was a common peasant house under a thatched roof. Although she knew nothing about Lady Murasaki, Oshichi was certain her mistress was used to much, much more. But years of exile and hiding, of which she had heard vague rumours from other girls, were showing. Only a six-fold screen—painted with a scene of a lonely rider riding through mountains, closely watched by a goshawk on a pine bough—testified to Lady Murasaki's better days. It was rumoured that injustice had forced her to replace the comfortable life of a baron's wife with the path of a warrior. Three *naginata* stood on a stand by a wall, sharp sword-like blades on long shafts. The stand on which the *tachi* rested was empty; Lady Murasaki went nowhere without her sword. Unlike the plain swords the other *kunoichis* carried, her sword was a real samurai one, its black lacquered scabbard embellished with a golden flowering cherry branch.

53

Oshichi stopped in front of the *naginata* stand. She listened, turned around, and only when she was certain she was alone, did she reach for a *naginata*. She removed the sheath and looked at her reflection in the blade. Then she gripped the shaft with both hands. She felt the weight of the deadly weapon. She assumed the fighting posture, the way she had seen other girls do in training. She struck, swung, leaped back, swung again, steel whistling as Oshichi cut down an imaginary foe. Then she decided it was enough. She returned the *naginata* to the stand. They never let her practice with anything deadlier than a staff. She was not one of them: those were Shizuka-*sama*'s exact words.

Oshichi felt dejected. She was aware that the clan would never accept her as one of their own. She was eternally grateful for the shelter they had given her, but she was hurt by the derision with which some *kunoichis* looked down on her. If it wasn't for Lady Murasaki, they might have chased her away from the village. Or worse. Oshichi knew that secrecy was of key importance to any ninja clan. Dead mouths do not speak.

Oshichi studied the screen thoughtfully, admiring the skill of the artist who had illuminated it. Should a stranger visit Lady Murasaki's house, the screen alone would be a telling sign she was not a peasant woman. Oshichi wondered if it was wise to keep something that so obviously did not belong in the house. Shouldn't a *jonin*, a clan leader, be more cautious? The girl shivered before the lethal gleam in the hawk's eye, before its sharp beak and deadly talons. She wondered if the bird warned her of some vague threat? Or was the bird itself a threat? *Nonsense*, she thought.

There was a wooden wall behind the screen. Suddenly, Oshichi noticed that a panel in the corner protruded at the bottom; just a bit, not even as much as half the thickness of a sword blade. She had not noticed that before—but then, it wasn't something that could be noticed in just a brief glance. The girl examined the panel closely. *Maybe it dried out and bent*, Oshichi thought. *Or maybe...* The girl pressed it lightly, and a swing door opened ajar to reveal a hiding place, big enough for one.

This was the second secret that Oshichi had discovered while cleaning Lady Murasaki's house. Last summer, she had stumbled upon a secret passageway that led into the forest right behind the house. She had not been surprised; she knew that ninja houses keep many secrets. Hiding places. Passages. Tunnels. Sometimes a whole hidden room, all inside a plain peasant house.

Oshichi was about to close the door, thinking she had been here too long, when she heard voices in front of the house. It was Lady Murasaki and Shizuka. She could not escape! And if they found out she'd discovered their secret...

Not thinking, the girl bolted into the hiding place and shut the door behind her, just at the last moment.

"Oshichi-*chan*!" the girl heard Lady Murasaki calling. "Oshichi-*chan*! Hmm, she's gone... Oh well, since she did her chores, I guess she went home."

"Nevertheless, Lady Murasaki, she should have waited for you," Shizuka said angrily. "She doesn't show enough respect!"

It was hot in the hiding place. Oshichi started to sweat. But she knew she must not utter a word. She heard the *futon* being unfolded onto the floor.

"You don't like her much," Lady Murasaki stated.

"She's not one of us," Shizuka replied. "She wants to be, but she's not."

"She wants to be? Didn't you teach her anything?"

"All right," Shizuka admitted, "she can move quietly in the forest. And I must admit a *bo* suits her better than I expected. Should any scoundrels attack her, she'll know how to defend herself with a long staff. But, Lady Murasaki, she's *kirishitan*. Can we send her on any of our missions? What if she's caught? Will she swallow poison or cut her belly to evade torture? Suicide is a sin to the Christians. Frankly, I don't know why we're keeping her. She's a risk!"

"You forgot you were a risk too," Lady Murasaki scolded Shizuka. "You didn't know anything either when I took you under my wing. You forget that. Your dislike of Oshichi surprises me really. The way you watched your children cut to pieces, and the way she had to watch the samurai cut her parents down, back when Toyotomi Hideyoshi was conquering Nagasaki... You two have more in common than you wish to admit, Shizuka-*san*."

In the silence behind the wall panel, beastly faces floated before Oshichi's eyes, crazed looks filled with hatred, bloodied swords. Flames devouring, smoke whirling above the streets. Father's body; Mother broken above him, screaming as she was impaled on spears, screaming and yelling and cursing, struggling, twitching and then falling, finally, lifeless.

"Maybe we should find her a husband," Lady Murasaki said pensively.

"Maybe we should find *ourselves* husbands," Shizuka replied in bad mood.

"Do we need husbands at all?" Lady Murasaki asked, and both women giggled.

Then Oshichi heard a kiss. Clothes rustling. It was well known in the clan that Lady Murasaki and Shizuka-*sama* were intimate together, and they were not the only ones, Oshichi knew. She blushed, listening to the hushed sighs. She was sweating. She untied her *obi* and let her worn out *kimono* slide down her arms. She imagined Lady Murasaki and Shizuka naked, embraced, kissing. She touched herself. She bit down on her sash so that no sigh would escape her lips. She heard Lady Murasaki and Shizuka surrendering to each other, unaware that they were not alone in their lovemaking, that Oshichi was also being carried by the tide of passion with them, until they all burst in fireworks of sweaty pleasure.

It was much, much later that Oshichi dared to open the door slightly. She sneaked out, silent as a mouse, and it was only when she put on her *waraji*—straw sandals—that she froze. Miraculously, the women had not noticed the extra pair. If they had...

She escaped into the chilly autumn night with trepidation in her heart.

Oshichi was not surprised when she saw Lady Murasaki standing in the middle of the road, obviously waiting for her. She must have sneaked after Oshichi, silently taking a shortcut through the forest. Oshichi could not tell if she was angry. She came to her mistress and bowed.

"Do you know your mistake, Oshichi-*chan*?" Lady Murasaki asked her gently.

"*Waraji*." Oshichi swallowed. It had been silly of her to think she could fool Lady Murasaki for a moment. "I hoped you didn't..."

"Don't underestimate me. True, my sandals were next to them, but I can count."

"Then why did you not look for me?"

"Because Shizuka-*sama* should not know about that hiding place. Shizuka-*sama* didn't notice the *waraji*; sometimes, she's too confident for her own good. And then she misses important details."

"It is not for me to judge Shizuka-*sama*." But despite her words, Oshichi could not help it. She knew that Shizuka would beat her up for such impudence if she ever found out. "Forgive me, Lady Murasaki, I..."

"It's all right, Oshichi-*chan*. It's a warning for me. If *you* discovered the hiding place, then it's not much of a hiding place."

"Errr... Lady Murasaki... If that is so... Then you should know that the secret passage is not so secret anymore. I mean..."

Lady Murasaki laughed in the dark.

"You notice well," she remarked with satisfaction. Then she smiled at her once again, a bit mischievously. "I hope you had a nice time in that little place."

Oshichi lowered her head, cheeks burning. She wanted to stutter an excuse, but when she looked up again, Lady Murasaki was not there anymore.

So quiet, the girl thought. Like a spectre.

For three days and three nights, Hattori Hanzo rode the hidden roads, not acknowledging thirst, hunger, or fatigue; he would stop only to replace an exhausted horse with a fresh one. Just before the dawn of the fourth day, he stopped on the edge of a deep, mist-shrouded valley. Birds were waking up in the tree tops; it was time to start foraging for food while there was still some, since cold mornings heralded chill and starvation. Hanzo was looking east impatiently. The sky was turning red; purple and gold were scattering the darkness. And then, the Sun emerged from beyond the horizon. Hanzo shielded his eyes with his hand; it was painful to watch it rise above the world.

Hanzo turned and looked at the other side of the valley, towards the peaks rising from the mist. The mountain forest was ablaze with the Sun beaming upon it. Suddenly, it was as though a giant *katana* had cut the hill and slashed a gorge that swallowed the sun. Hanzo smiled. A moment later, the gorge was not visible. But Hanzo knew where it was anyway, so he spurred his horse and rode down into the misty valley.

It was early morning, the Sun driving away the last streaks of mist, when Hanzo entered the hidden gorge, barely wide enough for a mounted *bushi*—warrior—to pass. He was riding slowly through the moist darkness, squeezed between the vertical cliffs. Here and there, a shred of blue sky could be glimpsed high above. A chilly stream murmured around the horse's hooves. Then the gorge widened into a valley surrounded by steep rocks overgrown with a blood-red creeper. Hanzo looked up and saw a shrine chiselled in stone high up on his right. A narrow path led to it which was impassable on a horse. The path was easy to defend. The shrine was a secret, impregnable fortress, hidden from prying eyes.

Hanzo stopped his horse, dismounted, and whistled. A ninja dressed in dark blue leaped out from the bush and ran to his master, twigs and creeper hanging from him. The ninja bowed, and Hanzo passed him the reins. If the camouflaged sentries, invisible even to the sharpest of eyes, did not recognize him the moment he had emerged from the gorge, he would not have reached even this far. "Watch my horse," Hanzo commanded before he headed for the fortress.

"You came, Hattori Hanzo, you cursed one," said a blood-freezing voice, greeting Hanzo from the darkest corner of the dungeon. A guard grabbed his *bo* to punish the impudence, to stab into the body which was hidden in the dark, but Hanzo stopped him.

"As pleasant as usual, Otoyo," Hanzo said mockingly. Chains rattled in the damp darkness. Eyes flashed, like the eyes of a giant cat. Unspeakable hatred poured from them. "And after all we've done, feeding you well and giving you shelter..."

"Come closer, so I can thank you, wastrel!"

Hanzo sighed and nodded. It was like this every time he came. But today, he had no time.

At Hanzo's nod, the guards grabbed the chains and dragged the prisoner into the flickering light cast by the tallow candles on the wall. She was thin, but Hanzo was aware of her true strength. Dirty tatters were all that was left of her *kimono*. Hanzo caught the stench of an unwashed body; when he was away, nobody dared to come close enough to splash her with water. An animal stare burned through the long, dishevelled hair hiding her face. A beast, Hanzo knew, a beast in human form.

"Hattori Hanzo, damn you!" the beast yelled in a hoarse voice as four guards dragged her across the stony floor. "You scum!" the girl cursed, spitting, hissing, struggling. Two men kept her at a distance, jabbing at her with the tips of their staffs and hitting her across her back. Another guard stood ready with a *naginata*, the blade pointed at her, just in case. "Wastrel!"

Hanzo merely nodded, and the guards grabbed Otoyo and restrained her within an instrument of torture. The plans for it had come from across the sea. A system of winches, ropes, and pulleys moved it. *Infernal device*, Hanzo thought while the guards were securing the girl's arms and legs between thick bamboo culms. Two guards stood next to the device.

"Damn you," Otoyo wailed, struggling to free herself.

"Will you listen to me?" Hanzo pushed dirty strands of hair away from her face. A straw blade fell across her nose. Hanzo took it and threw it away.

If she wasn't what she was, Hanzo thought sadly, *she'd be beautiful.*

Too bad she hated so much, too bad she did not understand... "This leads nowhere. Will you—?"

Otoyo glared at him defiantly and spat at him. Hanzo merely shrugged and wiped the saliva from his face. Then he nodded and the guards turned the winches. The ropes groaned and the culms creaked, squeezing Otoyo's arms and legs in a bamboo grip. The beast screamed in pain, and then she clenched her teeth, her face contorted.

"Will you listen to me?" Hanzo asked again.

"I'll kill you, Hattori Hanzo," Otoyo hissed through her teeth. Tears ran down her cheeks. "I'll kill you and I'll spill your guts, Hattori Hanzo, damn you!"

Hanzo nodded, and Otoyo screamed as the culms bent her arms and legs further. Hanzo nodded again. The guards turned some more. Otoyo yelled, her body bent, her eyes wide open. The bones in her limbs were at breaking point... And then Hanzo commanded the torturers to stop. The girl was breathing shallowly, tears in her eyes.

"Can you feel that moment, Otoyo?" Hanzo whispered in her ear. "The moment every torturer worth his name aspires to, when your bones are at the breaking point. Can you feel it, Otoyo, in your limbs? It takes but the slightest turn, Otoyo, to crack your bones like twigs. Are you listening, now that you've finally stopped yelling, Otoyo? Are you listening carefully, *nekomata*?"

Shizuka finally stopped running. Hot blood streamed through her body, drummed in her ears, beating in time to the rhythm of her heart. Sweat broke through her dark blue garb. She had spent the whole afternoon running through the forest. And she knew she could run for as long again, should need arise.

She remembered well the day Lady Murasaki had taken her under her wing. And she also remembered when Lady Murasaki had started training her; Shizuka could barely run a *cho* or two without panting hard and feeling pain in her legs. *Well*, she thought, smiling with satisfaction, *those days are behind me now.* They had died with her slaughtered husband and butchered children. Now, she was as strong as a beast, as fast as lightning, as evasive as the wind. Invincible.

Shizuka stood on the rock, feeling the moss-covered stone under her feet. Before her, the ground fell away into a deep ravine. A tree had collapsed across it that spring, brought down by a storm, and was now being slowly overgrown by creeper. Shizuka listened to the forest, becoming one with the world surrounding her. A stream murmured in the ravine, swollen with rains. Chilly breezes whispered in the treetops. The *kunoichi* heard every ruby leaf falling down; the calls of tits searching the branches for the last insects; the far cry of a jay; the stamping of a hind's hooves; a hidden *tanuki* napping in a bush.

Suddenly, Shizuka felt something that did not belong in the forest. She froze, listening tensely. Those who knew the secret paths could penetrate the clan's sanctuary unseen. When she was not going there herself, Shizuka would regularly send a girl to check if anybody had passed through the ravine. Even the most cautious intruder would leave a trace, and Lady Murasaki had taught them how to spot such traces.

But no. Apparently nobody was following the stream from what she could hear. Nevertheless, some threatening premonition gripped Shizuka. Somebody, something, was close, hidden in the forest. A samurai? A chance traveller? A beast? The woman held her breath, listening. Slowly, slowly, she reached for her sword. She stopped. Perhaps it was nothing, maybe her senses had deceived her—

Shizuka turned around swiftly. A girl was standing at the foot of the rock, fully naked. Thin, but strong-looking. Her head was bowed, her long, shiny hair hiding her face. Perhaps some scoundrels had dishonoured her, and she had managed to escape before they slaughtered her. But the girl's bearing showed no fear. Maybe some stray village fool then? But the nearest village was far away. Besides, she was clean and tidy; if she was the victim of violence or a village fool, wouldn't she look worse than a miserable beggar?

"Who are you?" Shizuka asked sternly.

The girl lifted her head, pushing the hair back from her face. She looked at Shizuka. Something flashed in her eyes, filling the *kunoichi* with dread; something mean; something Shizuka had never seen in her life, although she had witnessed enough hatred and fury in her time. Something beastly.

"I am Otoyo," the girl snarled, "and I came to kill you."

"Ha!" Shizuka laughed and gripped her sword, driving away the growing unease. "Well, if you say so. I wonder how you plan to do it."

For a moment, Shizuka considered catching her alive. She carried nutshells in her jacket, filled with *metsubushi*: a mixture of fine grit, ashes, ground pepper, and nettle hairs, all designed to blind the enemy. After that, it would be easy to subdue her. At worst, a *shuriken* or two in the girl's legs would stop her without killing her.

On the other hand, another voice said inside Shizuka, *where are we going to be if we allow any fool to threaten us with death?*

Otoyo stepped onto the rock, keeping her eyes on Shizuka. Her supple moves made Shizuka realise that Otoyo was strong and swift, despite her famished look. *Who was she?* Shizuka shivered before the flash of bloodthirsty hatred in the girl's eyes. Those were not the eyes of a human being, she realised with fear, and drew her sword. She was facing a *bakemono*, a monster.

Otoyo ran up the rock, charging bare-armed against the warrior woman who held a sword. Shizuka raised her weapon and charged, intending to cut her down. This had to be resolved in a single strike!

And then the running Otoyo turned into a giant cat: fully white, with two tails, her left eye silver, her right golden. *Nekomata!* Shizuka realised. *A monster!* The cat howled in a way Shizuka had never heard a cat howl before and threw herself at the woman.

60

"You damned thing!" Shizuka cursed, and she cut at the monster with her sword, but the *nekomata* evaded her strike with incredible speed. The blade sliced into empty air. The cat leaped and brought Shizuka down, pinning her against the rock. Strong paws drove air from her lungs. The claws tore through her clothes and into her breasts. Sharp fangs grabbed her throat and ripped it apart, without Shizuka uttering a whimper. Blood poured into the cat's mouth and she drank it greedily.

"You damned..." Shizuka cried through the blood filling her mouth. She tried to throw the cat off her, to kick her away, but the beast butchered her, draining the life out of her. Shizuka's resistance weakened with every draught of blood the *nekomata* drank. Finally, the *kunoichi* surrendered. The sword dropped out of her lifeless hand and clattered down the rock.

Otoyo rose above the pale, dead, drained body. Silence reigned in the forest, as though every living thing had fallen quiet before the bloodshed taking place on the rock. The *nekomata* licked the blood from her lips, legs, paws. She slurped with satisfaction and mewed, as though she asked to be petted, finally fed after years of starvation in the dungeon. Her eyes shone brightly. She lay next to Shizuka, her prey, and licked her fur, cleaning herself after a successful hunt. Then Otoyo mewed once again and turned back into human form.

A moment or two later, a naked Shizuka was standing on the rock.

Yuki moaned under a merciless blow across her back and then collapsed helplessly in dry leaves, a sign of her final surrender.

"You think you'll be spared if you whine?" Shizuka grinned with disdain. Oshichi felt she was being crueller than usual. "Is that what you think? Get lost!"

Yuki rose and returned to her place in the circle, staggering. She fell with a painful grimace, massaging the spot on her thigh where Shizuka had struck her with the tip of her staff, thus bringing her down. Shizuka stood, surrounded by the seated pupils. Her gaze swept across them all.

"Don't fool yourselves! If you're discovered, you'll face an enemy bodily stronger than you. Only if your *will* is stronger than his, will you win!"

"And maybe baring our necks would suffice?" Ofusa heckled. Her suggestion meant an open invitation. Girlish giggling and teasing broke through the forest at the suggestion they outwit their foes using feminine wiles.

Shizuka watched them all without blinking. "And what if you meet somebody who prefers boys?" she said in a cold voice. The laughter died, as though cut with a *katana*. "Or a true *bushi*, a samurai fully devoted to his master? What then? Such a man will not hesitate before your *daiji na tokoro*, that important place. Don't overestimate your looks! Better trust in this!" Shizuka swung her staff. "Oshichi-*chan*!"

Oshichi reached for her *bo* and faced Shizuka without hesitation.

"Tell us, Oshichi-*chan*, what does your Iesu Kirisuto preach? Turn the other cheek, if I'm right?" The woman circled Oshichi, a predator ready to pounce on her prey. Oshichi did not take her eyes off Shizuka. She knew Shizuka was challenging her, trying to make her angry and provoke an attack which she would then deftly evade while her staff found its way to some key point on the girl's body. Oshichi had learned that painful lesson a long time ago. "Didn't help him, did it?"

"No." Oshichi shook her head. "That's why he is now enjoying the eternal life."

"Ha!" Shizuka laughed. "You telling me I'm wrong?"

"Yes and no," Oshichi said cautiously. "We agree on one thing, Shizuka-*sama*: if one must die, let it be by the hand of someone truly greater."

Shizuka laughed again before looking at Oshichi with a deadly gleam in her eye. Her *bo* suddenly sprang to life and darted towards the girl. Shizuka aimed straight for Oshichi's face, her whole body behind that thrust. Instead of blocking it, which would lose her precious time, Oshichi did what Lady Murasaki had taught them all. She deftly evaded and hit Shizuka's right wrist with her staff. Shizuka clenched her teeth, her face twisted with pain, but did not utter a sound. She continued her assault and nearly hit Oshichi in the belly. Again, the girl skilfully evaded the thrust; she leaped back, swung, missed, leaped, blocked the attack, darted aside, evaded again, all the while being pursued by a seemingly unstoppable Shizuka. The staffs merrily sang their warrior song, whistling through the air, clashing in frantic rhythm, like percussions. Above all that was the fast breathing of two warrior women in the heat of the battle, the rustling of dry leaves, and stifled cries when a thrust broke through and hit its target. Too fast for the eyes of an ordinary mortal, the two opponents attacked and retreated, struck and evaded. Leaves flew under their feet as they danced their deadly dance, surrounded by the tense stares of the other pupils. Oshichi bent, Shizuka's *bo* whistled above her head, and then she whipped up a bundle of leaves unexpectedly with her staff and threw it into the woman's face. Shizuka leaped back, staggering, barely remaining on her feet. Her attention dropped only for a moment, but it was sufficient for Oshichi to get her chance for victory. The girl charged at Shizuka, swung her staff and momentarily loosened her grip. The staff's momentum carried it through her hands. Just before the impact, Oshichi tightened her grip again and drove the tip of the staff forcefully into Shizuka's left shoulder. The woman screamed at the unbearable pain that coursed from her shoulder into her arm. She almost dropped her staff, and

Oshichi pressed forward, skilfully driving her *bo* between her legs and bringing her down into leaves with one strong sideways lash. Oshichi leaped back, ready for any counterattack.

Shizuka rose, helping herself up with her staff. The circle around them was silent. It was not easy to defeat Shizuka, and Oshichi was the last one expected to do so. Shizuka merely measured the girl from head to toe.

"You're learning," she said in a barely audible voice. Something in her stare filled Oshichi with dread.

"You're learning," she repeated louder. "Maybe you will become one of us after all, Oshichi-*chan*."

Something jerked Lady Murasaki out of her sleep. She remained still, listening carefully in the chilly night illuminated by moonshine, breathing as though she was still asleep. By listening to someone's breathing, an experienced ninja could deduce if someone is really sleeping or merely pretending. Her *tachi* was within her reach, she always slept that way. An owl was heard in the forest outside. Did she imagine it, or was somebody sneaking around the house? Slowly, imperceptibly, under her blanket, she went for her sword with her hand. Suddenly, a quiet, drawn out mewing was heard in the dark.

Neko? A cat? Lady Murasaki thought. Where did a cat come from? No girl here kept a cat, and the village was too far from other people for one to wander through the forest.

Lady Murasaki rose.

And frowned.

Five or six steps away from her, Shizuka knelt, fully naked, eerily lit by the moon. She stared at Lady Murasaki.

"Shizuka-*san*! What is the meaning of this?" Lady Murasaki asked sternly. Shizuka had her own house, and Lady Murasaki certainly did not like unexpected night visits.

"Forgive me, Lady Murasaki," Shizuka said quietly. Something in her voice was not right; Lady Murasaki detected a hint of treachery. "You did me no wrong. But through you, I shall have my revenge!"

Shizuka sprang on all fours towards Lady Murasaki. Before Lady Murasaki could reach for her sword, Shizuka had turned into a great white cat with two tails, her left eye silver, her right eye golden. Her eyes flashed in the moonlight and she leaped on the stunned Lady Murasaki and pinned her down with her strong paws then lunged at her neck. Lady Murasaki grabbed the hair of the monstrous cat, tearing out entire tufts, but in vain as the beast sucked her blood, and sucked, and sucked. Soon, Lady Murasaki surrendered helplessly, becoming faint, her eyes emptying, while the beast had her fill of hot, salty blood.

"Remember well!" Lady Murasaki said, pointing at her followers. "Five weaknesses! And five needs!" She was sitting before them, Shizuka to her right. The girls were focused on what Lady Murasaki was teaching them. "So, the five weaknesses: laziness, anger, fear, sympathy, vanity."

She was pale, and Oshichi wondered what was going on, whether she was ill. For the past several days, she had looked weak, exhausted. She had gotten up late. She was wearing a scarf around her neck, although it was not that cold. Sometimes she would lose herself, as though she did not know what she had just said.

Lady Murasaki paused, gathering strength to continue.

"The five needs: security, sex, wealth, pride, pleasure. We can use each of these human weaknesses and human needs. Or, the other way around, we can fall victims to each of them. Because, unless we control them, they are at the same time *our* weaknesses and needs."

Lady Murasaki fell silent again. Oshichi thought she would collapse in front of them. What was wrong with her? She looked at the other girls. They did not miss that something was wrong either. Only Shizuka looked calm, not giving away any hint that she was aware of any changes in Lady Murasaki's bearing.

Lady Murasaki opened her mouth to continue but then she closed her eyes and swayed. Oshichi and several girls jumped up to help her, but Shizuka was closer, so she steadied her. Lady Murasaki took a deep breath, opened her eyes, and straightened herself.

"It's all right," she muttered, pushing Shizuka away. And when she saw the worried looks of her followers, she frowned and motioned them to sit back down. "You worry too much, I said. I'm all right, let us continue."

Oshichi decided that she had rested long enough. She rose and took her *bo*. Threading her way softly, she followed the foaming stream in the ravine, swollen with autumn rains. Oshichi leaped nimbly from stone to stone. Above her, a woodpecker was chiselling at a bough with its beak, looking for grubs under the bark. The ravine was not unfamiliar to her; the girls patrolled it regularly, watching lest someone uninvited sneaked in that way. Oshichi looked carefully for any traces of potential intruders.

A tree had fallen across the ravine that spring. It had been uprooted by a storm and was now being overgrown by a red creeper which tumbled from the bole like a cascade of blood. A tall and mighty rock rose above Oshichi. The girl recalled Lady Murasaki again. She was getting worse day after day. This morning, she had not left her house at all. Shizuka-*sama* had said calmly— much too calmly—that their mistress was exhausted and merely needed some rest.

"As though she doesn't care," Yuki had murmured quietly as they were breaking up, and Oshichi had agreed with her. It looked as though Shizuka-*sama* was the only one in the clan who was not even a little worried about Lady Murasaki's unexplainable illness.

And what if it was something serious? Oshichi wondered, a chill in her heart. She looked at the tree collapsed across the ravine. What if Lady Murasaki...? No. It was too awful to even think about. What would happen to them all, to the clan? Every girl had a story of her own. Oshichi had been orphaned because of her faith. Some girls had suffered hard lives, selling themselves for money, or being forced to steal. Lady Murasaki had offered them all shelter and given purpose to their lives. With her gone, the clan would disperse; they would all be left to themselves again.

And only Shizuka-*sama* seemed completely indifferent, as though nothing was happening.

For the first time, some undefined suspicion arose in Oshichi. Shizuka-*sama* did not seem herself anymore; no longer was she a woman compensating for her pain with disdain and barely concealed cruelty to anyone weaker than herself.

Suddenly, Oshichi heard leaves rustling in the deep shadow under the rock above her. She gripped her *bo* tighter and looked more carefully. A *kitsune*—a fox—apparently finding a meal. *A fox?* Oshichi wondered. *Out in broad daylight?* Curious, Oshichi stepped towards it. The fox heard her and raised its head, unafraid, regarding her with its amber eyes.

"Run!" Oshichi yelled. "Go away, *kitsune!*" Driven by her shouts, the fox ran into the forest, no doubt to return as soon as the girl left.

When she climbed a bit higher, Oshichi saw there was something under the leaves. Flies buzzed. And when she smelled the stench, a wave of nausea washed over her. A corpse! She saw clearly the dark blue fabric—torn and ripped apart—in the leaves, just like the fabric used to make ninja garb. Carefully, barely restraining herself from vomiting, Oshichi took several more steps forwards. Gritting her teeth, she pushed the leaves aside with the tip of her staff. The corpse was decomposing in the moist earth, the face eaten away down to the skull. White teeth grinned at her, eye sockets watched her with the stare of someone who knew the final truth. Only the *kunoichi* discipline, which Lady Murasaki had taught her, stopped Oshichi from screaming when she recognised a strand of silvery hair.

Breathing deeply, shaking, controlling her horror and suppressing the urge to run screaming straight to the village, Oshichi crossed herself and said a quiet prayer for Shizuka-*sama*'s soul.

Leaning against a young tree, Aguri threw up; her stomach could not bear the nauseating sight and stench of the decaying body. Horrified, Yuki and Ofusa looked at Shizuka's body. They both gripped their swords. Ofusa faced Oshichi, almost accusingly.

"What is this supposed to mean?" she asked in a trembling voice.

"That Shizuka-*sama* is dead," Oshichi replied calmly, gathering strength. Lady Murasaki needed her. Every night, her mistress, her benefactress, was facing something horrible; alone every night, she was growing helpless. She needed Oshichi to remain strong.

"But—"

"*Baka*!" Yuki hissed through her teeth. "Fool! Don't you understand? Shizuka-*sama* was killed by a *bakemono*! And now the life of our mistress is at stake!"

"What are we waiting for then?" Aguri snarled, drawing her sword.

"Stop!" Oshichi stepped in front of her. She had thought it over as she was running to fetch them. She knew it was no time for rash moves. "Stop, all of you. You think we can fight that monster in broad daylight? What if she turns others against us?" Oshichi stared around at Yuki, Ofusa, and Aguri, her best friends, the only ones she could really trust. She had brought just the three of them to see what was left of the real Shizuka. "Who knows what she's capable of doing? And she's certainly holding Lady Murasaki under some spell since our mistress doesn't complain about her illness herself."

"Hmm..." Ofusa paused. "You're right there, Oshichi-*chan*. But what is that monster doing to Lady Murasaki?"

"We all see that she's paler with every new day," Aguri said thoughtfully. "Maybe... Maybe that *bakemono* is drinking her blood." The girls looked at each other uneasily. For some reason unknown to them, a demon haunted their mistress. They knew her death would be the only outcome. "But why?"

"It doesn't matter now. Frankly, how much do we know about Lady Murasaki anyway? Who knows what enemies she had made and where? It's best we lay an ambush for that monster tonight," Yuki suggested. "We'll keep vigil, hidden around Lady Murasaki's house, so that when the demon shows up, busy with her evildoing—"

"I'll keep vigil with you," Oshichi said, grabbing her staff.

"No, Oshichi-*chan*." Yuki faced her. She was the oldest of them. "You did your part by warning us, but you can only use the staff. And this time, it won't be enough."

Once more, the next morning, Lady Murasaki did not leave her house. In a calm voice, Shizuka informed the entire clan that their mistress did not feel well again, and that she had ordered the girls to devote themselves to their usual chores and duties. And that was it.

As soon as the girls started breaking up, grumbling quietly, Oshichi took Yuki, Ofusa, and Aguri aside.

"Well? What happened?" she whispered impatiently, glancing over her shoulder. Yuki looked down with embarrassment. The other two girls kept silent, as though they had failed their mistress.

"Well?" Oshichi pressed.

"I'm ashamed to admit," Yuki said reluctantly, "we fell asleep. All three of us."

"What?" Oshichi almost yelled. "How—?"

"That cursed thing must have cast some spells," Aguri said, hushing her. "I never felt so sleepy in my life. Never!"

"I think so too," Ofusa agreed. "I didn't feel right in my head either."

"Rubbish!"

"No, Oshichi-*chan*, it's not rubbish! You know we can all go without sleep for days if needed. The *bakemono* is casting spells around the house, making us fall asleep before she haunts Lady Murasaki."

"What are we going to do, then? Maybe to look for an *onmyoji*?" Aguri suggested. "They should know how to deal with witches and demons."

"There's no time for that!" Oshichi objected. "First we must find one, then bring him here secretly, and by the time he determines what it's all about... I'm afraid Lady Murasaki will not last that long. We'll have to do it on our own."

Oshichi lowered the knife in her hand and looked at her village in the valley below; small, humble houses under thatched roofs, small fields with paths between them. The day was drawing to its end, darkness was creeping into hidden corners of the world around her. A chilly evening calm descended from the hills, spreading through the forest protecting her clan, the clan of Lady Murasaki. Here and there, a bird called out before settling at last for the night.

The girl sat under an old maple tree, on the soft carpet of fallen leaves, leaning against the trunk. She felt the bark against her back and drew strength from the tree. She needed to be calm and concentrated on what was awaiting her that night. She surveyed the entire valley; she could see almost every house, only a few were hidden by the tree tops. Smoke rose from some, girls had lit candles in others. Soon, the village would fall asleep. Soon, a demon in the shape of Shizuka-*sama* would start its bloody descent.

Oshichi set to sharpening the end of a wooden stake with her knife. The other end was already sharpened. Next to her, eight *shurikens* rested, each made of two stakes tied into a cross. The girl recalled Shizuka-*sama* driving her away with disdain when the girls were practicing throwing the real steel *shuriken*. And she remembered Lady Murasaki calling her aside later and showing her how to make a *shuriken* out of stakes. At first glance, it was clumsy and blunt, large and heavy. And it certainly could not be driven halfway into a tree with a single throw. "Did you plan to fight against trees?" Lady Murasaki had asked her with a friendly smile. "You have chosen yourself mighty opponents. A human body is frailer."

Oshichi was not one of them. They had given her shelter, but she was not one of them. Even Yuki, Ofusa, and Aguri, the only ones in the clan that truly accepted her as a friend, did not have enough faith in her to take her with them. She was not one of them. And not even Lady Murasaki could do anything about that—except to secretly teach her some useful tricks.

Oshichi crossed the last two stakes and took a piece of string. The cross reminded her of her faith and prompted her to mutter, "I didn't pray much to you lately, Iesu Kirisuto, and I don't wear your cross around my neck. At best, they'd mock me. And if evil men should catch me... You could say I denied you in fear. And you'd be right. Should you say that I follow the wrong path, that I follow the wrong leader, a mistress who teaches me how to fight and kill and plot, you'd be right too. But, Iesu Kirisuto, when was the last time you walked this land? There's nothing here but fighting, killing, and plotting. And for us, the poor ones, only misery, starvation and death. Lady Murasaki alone saw us as human beings, she alone took us as her equals, although we aren't, not by a long shot. She made a clan out of us, she created something we could belong to. She teaches us hidden knowledge and secret skills. She shows us how to cast away fear and weakness, and be strong. Without her... Without her, we'd be nothing again, hungry and despised and forsaken. We'd be scattered, blown away by the wind. She took me into the clan, even though she knew that I prayed to you, Iesu Kirisuto, even though she knew what happens to those who hide your followers. Doesn't that make her a bit closer to you? If so, Iesu Kirisuto, help me tonight. Help me save Lady Murasaki, help me vanquish the *bakemono* haunting her. And if you won't, Iesu Kirisuto... Then go to Hell!"

Oshichi tightened the knot, satisfied with the *shuriken* she had just made. She sighed, stored her *shurikens* under her jacket, rose, took her *bo*, and followed the steep path down into the village, heading for Lady Murasaki's house.

It was already dark when Oshichi reached the back of Lady Murasaki's house. Yuki was keeping vigil in the shrubs across the road from where she had a good view of the entrance. Ofusa and Aguri were at their places too. But Lady Murasaki's house was at the very edge of the forest. When she had still been alive, Shizuka-*sama* herself had said that Oshichi could walk through the forest very quietly; without a single leaf rustling under her *tabi*, without cracking a single twig, invisible behind a tree, hidden in the bush—these were the skills that Shizuka-*sama* and Lady Murasaki *were* willing to teach her. Oshichi passed half a *jo* behind Aguri's back, like a silent shadow.

Hmmm, she thought, *if that's the way you guard your mistress, the* bakemono *doesn't need spells.* With such thoughts, she slid quietly through the secret passage she had discovered.

Lady Murasaki was asleep. Her breathing was barely audible, the candle snuffed. Throughout her illness, the false Shizuka would not allow anybody to keep vigil next to her. And Lady Murasaki herself, doubtless under Shizuka's spells, told everybody not to worry but to do their daily chores and training. And so, undisturbed in the dark, Oshichi snuck into the hiding place in the wall, behind the screen, and shut herself silently inside.

She took a bamboo carrying case from her jacket. She opened it and scattered the contents on the floor: *hishi*—dried water chestnuts—each with three or four wooden spikes protruding from it. A ninja would scatter them before pursuers or use them to block a passage. Oshichi knew how painful it was to step on them. She took a piece of rag, wrapped it around her face and then bit it tightly as she sat down. She clenched her teeth, her eyes filling with tears of pain caused by the spikes. But she knew it was the only way to save Lady Murasaki. Shizuka-*sama* had said it herself: the enemy will always be stronger in body than you. So, she would be stronger by will. The pain, unbearable at first, penetrated her and spread through her legs to become omnipresent and continuous. It became a background to her thoughts and thus something bearable. Now, all she could do was wait.

She did not know how much time passed. The night was dragging by silently. Suddenly, Oshichi felt her eyelids growing heavy, her thoughts escaping her. She felt something both relentless and enticing dragging her into a deep sleep. All she had to do was surrender and close her eyes. Fall asleep like a baby. Sleep... Luring her. To sleep... *Sleep*...

But the sharp spikes piercing her thighs would not let her droop. As much as sleep invited her, the pain kept her awake. *Close your eyes*, she heard a quiet voice telling her. *Sleep, child, sleep!* But how to fall asleep when lightning flashes of pain raced through her body? To sleep... *Dream*, baka *Oshichi, silly Oshichi, foolish little girl, close your eyes, sleep!* But the pain kept Oshichi awake, enabled her to endure. Sleep—

No, you damned thing, you will not break me down! Oshichi thought with determination. *The pain will not allow it, the spikes are here to hold me, to guard me, hundreds of small allies helping me defend my mistress!*

Finally, the pain prevailed. Oshichi was fully awake, the voice gone, her eyelids were not leaden anymore. She had broken the spell. It was only then that she understood what her friends had faced. She asked them for forgiveness for doubting the strength of their loyalty.

Oshichi gripped her *bo*. She knew that the monster was close, sneaking to the house, hidden by its curtain of spells.

She thought she heard something. She listened more carefully; feet were treading softly, softly across the floor. And then she heard quiet mewing. Her throat tightened, she felt fear possessing her. Mewing? What was that? Slowly and quietly, Oshichi opened the door of her hiding place.

She peeked carefully around the screen.

She froze.

A monstrous cat was leaning above Lady Murasaki, huge and white with two tails. She bit Lady Murasaki on her neck. Oshichi heard her greedily swallowing blood. Her mistress was lying with her hands limp, helpless to resist. Without thinking, Oshichi reached for her spike *shuriken*.

"I told you to sleep, *baka* Oshichi!" the cat snarled. She raised her head and looked at Oshichi with mismatched eyes, the left one silver, the right one golden. Blood was dripping from her mouth and she licked it away.

"Leave my mistress alone!" Oshichi retorted.

"Or else?" The *nekomata* grinned.

Oshichi drew a *shuriken* and threw it. The *nekomata* evaded the missile and the *shuriken* clattered into the corner. Without hesitation, the girl grabbed another. In one leap, the cat was on Oshichi, and she swung the sharp weapon like a knife, cutting the beast across her chest. The *nekomata* hissed in pain and leaped back. Oshichi threw the *shuriken* after her. It flew into empty space.

"*Baka!* Fool! You think you're match for me?" the monster growled. But the *nekomata* had become more careful. She did not leap any more but instead was circling Oshichi, twisting her two tails. Her eyes shone in the dark; hatred and the anger of an infuriated beast poured out of them. "You think you will kill me with that staff of yours?"

Oshichi realised her enemy was telling the truth. She held her *bo* before her, ready to strike should the cat charge. But the staff would not be enough. Then her gaze came to rest on the *naginata* on the stand. If only the beast was not between her and those sharp weapons.

The girl threw her third *shuriken*. The *nekomata* evaded it with lightning speed, as well as the fourth and the fifth; it was only when Oshichi darted across the floor, grabbed a *naginata*, tugged off the sheath, and pointed the lethal steel at her that the monster saw through the feint.

"Is that so?" the *nekomata* snarled. "Suddenly you have mastered *naginata-jutsu*? As far as I recall, Shizuka didn't put anything deadlier than a staff in your hands."

Oshichi charged, the blade pointed at the cat. The *nekomata* evaded the strike, spitting. She scratched at the blade with her claws, almost tearing it out of Oshichi's hands. But Oshichi retreated and attacked again. The *nekomata* retreated, then leaped, only to barely evade being impaled by Oshichi. The blade sliced through the air as the girl stabbed and swung the weapon, trying to land a blow. At one point, the *nekomata* evaded a thrust and the blade tore through the illustrated screen, cutting the rider in half, plucking the hawk's eye, cutting the pine. Oshichi had no time to mourn the beauty ruined while the *nekomata* tried to paw the *naginata* out of her hands.

And then, suddenly, the cat wailed painfully. Her left hind leg was cut, blood soaking the white fur. Lady Murasaki, her throat bloody, collapsed back to the floor as if dead, exhausted by the single strike she'd made with her *tachi*.

Oshichi attacked more fiercely now that the beast was hurt, but the cat swung her paw and broke the *naginata* shaft with one forceful blow. The blade clattered across the floor. The girl grabbed another *naginata* just as the entry door slid aside and a dark shape appeared, a *shinobigatana* in her hand. Oshichi recognised Yuki's profile. She was awake; maybe the spell had been broken when Lady Murasaki wounded the monster.

"Call for help!" Oshichi shouted. "Alert the village!"

Yuki paused for a moment, and then she ran into the night, shouting, "At arms! At arms! To Lady Murasaki's! All at arms!"

The night was swiftly filled with cries. Girls from the nearest houses headed for Lady Murasaki's house. The first torches to arrive illuminated the white cat. The beast spat angrily. Another few moments and her retreat would be cut off by Lady Murasaki's furious clan. Unless—

"You plan to escape through the rear exit?" Oshichi saw through her intentions immediately. "You won't, damn you!"

The *nekomata* pierced Oshichi with her stare. Unflinching, the girl held the *naginata* pointed at her, denying her passage. But the *nekomata* had to choose between one girl and enraged *kunoichis* armed to their teeth with swords, *naginata*, *kusarigama*, nets, and spears. That was no choice at all.

Her whole body tensed, pain flashed through her eyes, and then, as though she had springs in her legs, the *nekomata* leaped—and turned into Otoyo!

Oshichi screamed, surprised by the lightning-fast transformation, and jumped enough for the naked Otoyo to grab Lady Murasaki's sword.

"Get out of my way," Otoyo hissed, raising the *tachi*. Her two eyes flashed at Oshichi from beneath long black hair.

"Who are you?" Oshichi asked. "And why did you attack Lady Murasaki?"

Girls were gathering outside. Yuki was telling them what she had seen. Ofusa and Aguri urged others to storm the house. Some girls hesitated, uncertain as to whether they could oppose such a demon.

"I am Otoyo. I was sent by that confounded Hattori Hanzo to kill your mistress. But in such a way that made it clear that the deed was done by dark forces, so as to scare and scatter your entire clan. Only if I carry out my mission can I stand before him to kill him," Otoyo finished with a scream filled with unspeakable fury. Oshichi shivered before such hatred.

"*Oni no* Hanzo knows about us?" Lady Murasaki whispered behind Otoyo. She rose, sweat breaking out on her forehead. She was pressing her hand against the wound on her neck.

"Both he and Tokugawa Ieyasu, and Yagyu Munenori as well. Your heads are of no more value than mine," Otoyo retorted with contempt. "And now, silly girl, get out of my way or I'll cut you!"

"No!" Oshichi replied with determination, keeping the *naginata* pointed at her. "I will not—"

"Let her go, Oshichi-*chan*!" Lady Murasaki moaned.

"But—"

"Let her go! You don't know how it is to fall into *Oni no* Hanzo's hands. Let her go."

Oshichi hesitated for a moment and then, when Lady Murasaki nodded silently, stepped aside, still keeping the *naginata* pointed at Otoyo. The crowd outside was growing; soon the whole village would be here. "And you, Otoyo, find another way to have your vengeance. Now, go!"

Otoyo paused, then lowered the sword. She bowed to Lady Murasaki.

"*Arigato,*" she said through her teeth, clenched in pain. "Thank you. And you, *baka* Oshichi, were a worthy opponent. Your clan should be proud of you!" Otoyo drove Lady Murasaki's *tachi* into the floor and, dragging her left leg, silently disappeared through the secret passage into the night, followed by Oshichi's confused stare.

"**B**ut why, Lady Murasaki?" Yuki asked, puzzled. "Why did you let her go?"

Lady Murasaki was sitting facing her pupils, barely recovered from the *nekomata*'s night depredations. Oshichi was sitting on her right. She knew the answer already.

"Because she saved us," Lady Murasaki explained, "and because she can still be of use to us."

"But how?"

"Thanks to her, we are now aware that Tokugawa Ieyasu knows about us, and that Hattori Hanzo took upon himself to destroy us. We have been warned of our enemy's intentions in time. Besides, if Otoyo is free, maybe she will kill *Oni no* Hanzo before he launches another attack on us. She's the only one who can reach him. And, most importantly, thanks to Otoyo, we know that I failed." The girls were silent; none of them dared say a word. "The essence of every ninja clan is the secrecy of its existence. And Tokugawa Iyeasu knows about us. That is my mistake. Now we can only think on how to avoid annihilation."

"But," Ofusa objected, "she killed Shizuka-*sama*!"

Lady Murasaki sighed sadly. "True. One of us was lost. But," she looked at Oshichi, "we got another. Without Oshichi-*san*, we'd all be lost. Otoyo herself admitted that. And there's no greater praise than that given by your enemy!"

Oshichi bowed to Lady Murasaki. She felt the stares of the other *kunoichis*. She had saved Lady Murasaki, had saved all of them indirectly, and the clan had finally accepted her. Not as an orphan they were sheltering, but as one of them.

"I've been thinking what to do," Lady Murasaki continued. "Should Tokugawa Ieyasu decide to send an army against us, we're lost. We can either scatter, or leave together and go somewhere else. Start anew."

"But where?" Ofusa asked. "Here we have—"

"Here we are exposed, Ofusa-*chan*," Oshichi interrupted her. "We know well how Oda Nobunaga destroyed the clans from Iga and Koga. We must not allow their fate to befall us. We cannot face samurai in the open battle."

"Where, then?"

"North," Lady Murasaki announced. "Into the forests. Away from this turmoil. Until we are forgotten." Lady Murasaki smiled. "Until we grow stronger. North, it's the only place we can go. For the time being."

A girl was sitting on a bench, a shady spot under a cherry tree, before a tumbledown resting place at a crossroads. She was dressed in a plain blue *kimono*. She held her hands modestly in her lap. As she studied the travellers passing by, something cat-like would flash in her eyes, as if looking for prey. Two samurai. A peasant woman with a hoe across her shoulder. A palanquin carried by two bearers.

And then, a lonely samurai caught her attention. He was dressed humbly with a modest bearing, but the girl didn't miss his stare. Those were not the eyes of an ordinary traveller. The samurai was observing his surroundings, memorising every detail, missing nothing. The girl realised she was facing a ninja in disguise, on a mission.

Her eyes met the samurai's. She smiled at him, shy and seductive at the same time. He did not miss that smile, much less her beauty. He paused, as if thinking it over, and then headed towards her. He stopped before her and bowed.

"Can I sit here?" he asked.

The girl smiled and moved up a bit. The samurai sat next to her.

"A hot day," he murmured, wiping sweat from his forehead.

"Indeed, Sir," the girl replied. "It's hard to travel. Especially for a solitary girl."

The samurai looked at her. A more open invitation could hardly be imagined. He decided he could spare some time to satisfy one of the five needs.

"I agree, it is always easier to travel in twos."

"And safer," the girl added. "Especially if accompanied by someone skilful with a sword. By the way, I am Otoyo."

"I am Fuma Kotaro," the samurai introduced himself. "Shall we rest a bit, Otoyo-*san*, and then, if we are both travelling in the same direction, shall we start off together? It would not do for the dark to catch us on the road."

"Oh, Kotaro-*dono*, next to you, a girl would have no reason to fear the dark."

Tokugawa Ieyasu indeed fulfilled his dream and united the entirety of Japan under his sword and banner. The firm and righteous rule of his clan brought the Great Peace to the country. Still, Lady Murasaki's *kunoichis*, hidden in the dense northern forests, were not without a job to do. There was always a *daimyo* curious to know what was his neighbour doing and what he was plotting. There were always rivalries to be resolved by somebody's sudden death. And occasionally, even Ieyasu's heirs unwittingly used the services of seductive, untraceable, deadly *kunoichis* trained by Lady Murasaki, Oshichi, and their successors.

Yagyu Munenori continued to teach the Tokugawa clan swordsmanship. His lethal skills were scrupulously kept alive by his successors, and the fame of his school was to be carried through the entire country.

And Hattori Hanzo?

It has never been confirmed, but it was rumoured that *Oni no* Hanzo met his end at the hands of a ninja called Fuma Kotaro, not long after this tale of ours took place. Nobody was surprised by those rumours; it was well known that the two of them were feuding.

Nobody can tell anything about the final destiny of Otoyo, the *nekomata*. Perhaps, once her hatred was quenched, she found peace after all, maybe even happiness. Or maybe she remained a cursed soul, a demon, a two-tailed cat stalking victims along remote roads by night. Who knows, maybe she's still alive. Who can say if monsters really die or whether they continue to live, just like a famous samurai, while there's someone to tell a tale about them, while their name is not swept into oblivion, like a leaf swept by the cold autumn wind?

Dondo harai. With this, there is no more!

Elsbet and The Book of Dragons

The street was narrow and steep. Elsbet's footsteps echoed on the cobbles it was paved with. Old houses leaning over the street looked down onto Elsbet as if they were about to tumble down and bury her. Tall walls clad with ivy and creepers guarded the yards from prying eyes, the tree crowns giving welcome shade as Elsbet reached the last house.

This dwelling was just like the others, with two floors and a sagging roof. Ivy cascaded down the front wall like green hair, around the heavy wooden gate with a bronze door-knocker, a massive ring in a lion's jaws. The old horse chestnut in the yard behind the wall was in full bloom, the sweetish scent of white flowers making Elsbet drowsy. Somewhere above her, a blackbird quietly warned his nestlings to lay low as an unknown intruder arrived.

Elsbet paused to regain her breath, hugged the portfolio of drawings she was carrying, and removed a lock of hair, the colour of golden wheat, from her forehead. After gathering her courage, she knocked three times with the door-knocker. It was only then that she noticed the gate had neither handle nor keyhole.

Several moments passed, seeming like eternity. Elsbet knocked three more times, and then the gate opened with the loud click of some hidden mechanism and admitted her into the yard.

Elsbet entered and looked around. There was no one but her in the yard which was running wild with undergrowth; the gate had opened by itself.

Why not, after all? she thought as the gate closed by itself, too. Ivy crept across the ground, climbed the scaly bark of a horse chestnut, growing over the walls, giving way to woodbine in a sunny corner. Rioting rose shrubs were budding red and pink. Next to the old horse chestnut, a young sapling struggled for its place in the sun. A paved path led to a walnut tree in the opposite corner; there was an old wooden bench beneath it, ivy creeping up along its legs and spreading across the backrest.

"Are you planning to stand there all day?" The severe voice startled Elsbet. She lifted her gaze. Stony stairs led to a terrace overgrown with jasmine, but there was nobody on it. Elsbet heard a broom sweeping inside the house. "Well, come up!"

Elsbet climbed the stairs and paused before the door which stood ajar. She was about to step into the house when all of a sudden the door opened wide, and the broom leapt out before her. Nobody held the broom, it was sweeping the hallway all by itself, dancing across the wooden boards and driving dust straight at Elsbet. She screamed, and the broom stopped that very instant, leaning against the wall.

"Come in, come in! Down the hallway, to the end." Elsbet obeyed cautiously, keeping her eyes on the broom, ready to bolt should it move again.

The door before Elsbet opened and she entered a large study. Thick shelves were bending under books, flasks, jars, mortars. Elsbet could only guess what was hidden in an old bookcase. A massive table was pushed under the window, volumes stacked on it in several heaps, tipping dangerously. Old scrolls had been placed on it, rolled up or spread out and held by anything heavy enough to keep them from rolling back. A petrol lamp, extinguished. A skull. *God*, Elsbet thought with a shiver, *why always a skull?* An inkstand, open. A large white quill in the hand of a man sitting, his back turned to Elsbet.

"Well, come closer, girl!" Outside, in the hallway, the broom resumed its sweeping. Elsbet approached the man. He had a cloak thrown over him, reaching to the floor. He was immersed in his writing, the quill gliding across paper, but the trail of ink it was leaving disappeared instantly, leaving the paper apparently empty. The hand paused, the face lifted, and Elsbet saw, for the first time in her life, Edigius: reclusive, mysterious, and unapproachable. The Great Edigius: renowned, famous, and esteemed. More legends were told of him than of all the other wizards in the town put together.

His face was elongated, with a pointed chin and a high brow. His cheeks seemed somewhat hollow, giving him a slightly haggard look, but otherwise he had a healthy complexion. His thin lips rose in a smile. Elsbet found it patronising, and she was not certain that she really liked it. His nose was aquiline, giving him a dominating appearance, and Elsbet would have found him predatory were it not for the piercing, lively eyes beneath thick eyebrows, studying her in a curious but friendly manner from behind thick glasses.

Good grief, she thought, *he must be blind without them.* His hair was jet black, streaked with silver. Nobody knew how old Edigius was exactly, but he must have been old, judging by the tales.

"So, you are the one who illustrated *Charms, Spells, and Curses of the Animal World*. Hmmm, I imagined you differently." The wizard's voice was warm and pleasant, soft, friendly, reassuring. As he spoke, his hands made complicated and, Elsbet hoped, random motions through the air.

"Oh. And how did you imagine me?" Elsbet raised her eyebrow, curious.

"You know—plain, possibly plump, perhaps wearing glasses, no sport for flirts, breaking her solitude with art. On the other hand, I'm the last to object the company of a beautiful young lady." Elsbet was well aware of her beauty, aware of all the looks that ran over her figure and pretty face, the locks cascading over her shoulders, and her eyes the colour of a mountain sky, clear and fresh. Still, she felt her cheeks blushing. She saw in Edigius's smile that he did not miss her reaction and that annoyed her somewhat.

"You liked the book?"

"No, for Heaven's sake! No, no, and no!" Edigius's angry outburst scared Elsbet and she stiffened. "Who in his sane mind can like anything Tempesta wrote? Twaddle and rubbish! If his book wasn't dangerous, it would be ridiculous!" The wizard reached for Elsbet's portfolio, his outstretched hand waiting impatiently for her to hand it over. "The only reason that volume of cabbage leaves will not sink into much-deserved oblivion are your illustrations, Miss!"

Edigius unbound the portfolio and spread it open, leafing through several sheets before pausing on one. He took it in his long fingers and studied it from a distance. "You lithograph yourself?"

Elsbet nodded, not without pride. "Myself. I paint and lithograph. All from nature—"

"Ha!" Edigius interrupted. "From nature, indeed!"

"I assure you, Sir—"

"My dear child," the wizard leaned towards Elsbet, penetrating her with his stare, "let us consider, for a moment, this basilisk here. You've never seen a living basilisk. If you had seen it, with your experience—or rather *in*experience— you would now be a fistful of ashes and not chit-chatting here with me.

"The reason I summoned you, after all, is the skill with which you breathed life into this," Edigius looked significantly at Elsbet from beneath his glasses, "*stuffed* specimen. I know you had no source to copy it from and I know—since I know what Tempesta has—that you painted it from his pitiful exemplar. Yet it feels so alive in posture and surroundings. Unfortunately, Tempesta has also never seen a living basilisk—although he dares to pass comment on it—because if he had, he'd point out to you that the basilisk's comb and wattles are, in nature, vividly red and not pale pink as depicted here. Am I right?"

Elsbet did not reply, and a victorious sparkle flashed in Edigius's eye. Then he mellowed somewhat.

"Come, come, don't be sad! With Tempesta, you did the best you could and made the least mistakes. Let's say it was a good exercise. Would you now care to devote yourself to a serious assignment?"

"S-Serious assignment?" Elsbet stuttered. Tempesta's book had taken her almost a year of daily toil.

Edigius pushed his chair back. He grabbed a knotty staff and leaned against it as he rose. His robe opened for a brief moment and Elsbet saw that his right leg was like a rooster's—scaly, yellow, with sharp nails and a spur. He did not miss her horror, and his stare suddenly grew hard.

"Sometimes, charms go wrong. The consequences can be very unpleasant. Does this bother you?"

Elsbet wanted to apologise, but she realised just in time that it would make him even more angry; he would take her apologies for pity.

"Does it bother *you*?" she asked.

Edigius's stare turned mild again. Visibly limping, he walked to the bookcase. "As you can see, it's hard to walk on a rooster leg. I don't know how roosters manage." Edigius opened the door of the bookcase, took out a thick bundle of paper and handed it to Elsbet. All the pages were blank. Apparently blank, Elsbet realised. "I invited you here to illustrate my *Book of Dragons*. All from nature!"

"Dragons? From nature...?"

"I'll pay you well. To say nothing of the fame awaiting you. I know you're living with your ailing mother and younger brother. I also know that your means are not plentiful, so you had to sell your skills to a ne'er-do-well such as Tempesta. I assume he didn't pay you much, did he? And only after you'd reminded him plenty of times?"

"But dragons! I mean..."

"Yes, there are risks. Those afraid of risks shouldn't have been born at all. Decide for yourself. You may waste your time with various others like Tempesta and swallow dust in their Sunday-fair cabinets of wonders. Or you may come with me, see things others don't even dream of, and create something to be remembered by for centuries! That's what I'm offering you. Well?"

"There he is!" Edigius whispered into Elsbet's ear. She, too, heard a dry twig cracking and carefully lifted her head from behind the shelter provided by a fallen oak, collapsed unknown winters ago and covered in soft green moss. Above them, disturbed jays—the watchmen of the forest—cried out. Elsbet spotted one from the corner of her eye. A wren flew out of a deep creek bed and disappeared quickly into a hazel bush behind Elsbet and the wizard. A woodpecker above them ceased drumming. A blackbird fell silent. A wood mouse froze in dry leaves, several feet from Elsbet's legs which were stiff after her long, motionless vigil.

Only leaves rustled and twigs broke as a thirty-foot-long scaly body threaded between oaks, through the forest, panting, sniffing, pausing only to lean over the creek which was swollen by spring rains.

The golden forest dragon quenched his thirst with the clear water. Elsbet lifted her pad and began sketching the dragon's shape in quick pencil lines. A slim body on strong legs, toes armed with curved claws. A long tail with a leathery rudder on its end, lashing at the leaves. A powerful neck, stretched out as the animal was drinking. A large head tapering into a hook-like beak of a bird of prey, nostrils inhaling early morning air and scents of the forest. Sharp teeth that never let go, once they'd grabbed hold. A long tongue, stirring something ribald in Elsbet. Fiery eyes that didn't see her as she drew them. She held her breath, enchanted by the beauty of the beast before her, and at the same time scared by that predatory stare and those strong wings, folded in rest, that could lift him through a whirl of leaves and twigs to pounce on the two of them, helpless behind the old oak.

Elsbet did not miss a single detail, her eyes darting from the pad to the dragon and back, capturing him with her pencil as he drank, and again, as he lifted his head, his attention caught for a moment by the distant trampling of a roe's hooves. Elsbet filled in the details of the head, scales bordering his mouth, teeth, eyes, eyelids. Her pencil became blunt so she put it down in the leaves next to her and quickly took another, already sharpened. She worked the wings out, membranes stretched between the long, long fingers. She drew tears in the membranes; the golden forest dragons—so Edigius stated—lived a long time, and this one had seen a lot indeed. Elsbet studied him more closely, finding healed injuries from old battles. A scar across his ribs. Another one on his left hind leg. Several smaller scars on his neck and a larger one, probably made by a bite. And scales of a glittering golden sheen, dappled by the lace of light and shadow from rays of the Sun breaking through the treetops. Elsbet drew everything, and the dragon became alive on the paper, as alive as in the forest before them.

Edigius smiled with satisfaction, watching every move of the beast, squeezing his staff, ready to cast an invisibility spell should the dragon spot them. *I chose well*, he thought, *that fool Tempesta had no idea of how great a talent he worked with.*

Suddenly, the dragon lifted his head and reared, water dripping from his jaw, nostrils flaring as he detected a new scent.

"He smelled us?" Elsbet whispered nervously, holding her breath, ready to put her pad away.

"Be still," the wizard merely whispered back. His hand on her shoulder gave her some comfort as he looked around tensely, trying to find out what it was among the mighty oaks that had alarmed the dragon.

And then, another dragon came out from between the trees. It was of the same stature and proportions but somewhat smaller, and its scales were yellowish-brown without the golden sheen.

"A female?" Elsbet asked.

Edigius merely nodded, and Elsbet, without even being told, turned to a new sheet and started sketching the newcomer quickly. The female spread her wings and approached the male cautiously, the creek bed between them. The she-dragon was apparently reluctant to cross the bed, as if it represented a border. And then the male spread his wings in all their magnificence and, holding them wide, crossed the creek and approached the female. She was tense, ready to leap upwards at any moment if she needed to escape those merciless jaws and deadly claws. But the male did not charge, quite the contrary. He approached the female slowly, lowering his head next to hers, smelling her and gently touching her beak with his.

Elsbet quickly sketched the movements of two dragons, body postures remaining frozen in a series of rough drawings. A touch of beaks, brief, cursory, and then a longer one, male sliding his beak down her jaw. The female relaxed, stretching her neck and tail, lowering her wings to the ground. The male kept caressing her head with his, and then his tongue darted out and licked her cheek. The female returned the gesture, and Elsbet felt herself blush as she drew the two dragons licking each other with long tongues, caressing each other with cheeks and beaks in a play that was growing ever more passionate. Although she tried to watch the scene before her with the cold eyes of an artist serving science, she became embarrassed upon seeing the dragon's erection. The beast snorted excitedly, nostrils flaring, eyes burning with the passion that possessed him. The female was just as hot, the male's tongue causing the heat of love to blaze up in her, and she finally lifted her rear and held up her tail.

And as Elsbet changed her pencil, the male mounted the female and entered her after several impatient misses. He wrapped his tail around hers and wound his neck around hers. He rubbed his head against hers, covered her wings with his. He glittered golden as the sunlight fell upon him. Elsbet forgot herself, her pencil stopped mid-line as she stared at the golden forest dragons mating with a lot of snorting, blowing, panting, snarling, thrashing of wings and scattering of leaves, completely unaware of anything around them during those several minutes of love-dance. And when the dragon, roaring, discharged his seed, Elsbet unconsciously pressed the pencil down so hard that the soft graphite broke. That startled her out of the trance she had sunk into while witnessing the uninhibited passion of love.

When the dragons separated, the wizard gave Elsbet a sign to indicate it was time to head back. After two hours of walking, with the Sun high in the sky, it was time for them to rest in the quiet of a forest clearing.

Elsbet took a wicker bottle of dark red wine out of a knapsack, placed it in the grass next to Gouda cheese, rye bread, and a pair of *Jaegerwurst*. Edigius took out Elsbet's drawings on the sketchpad.

"Very good. I know of no one who'd get anatomy and posture that accurately. From nature, indeed!" he said, nodding as he leafed through the pencil drawings and those made in haste with pastels in an attempt to get the basic colours of the beasts. Edigius was sitting opposite Elsbet, his legs beneath him, covered carefully by a long, dark brown cloak. His knotty staff, which he'd used as he limped through the forest, was at hand.

"The colour will be a problem," Elsbet objected. Edigius looked up from the drawings. "Golden scales are not easy to reproduce."

"I feel you have some solution." The wizard laid the sketchpad next to him, took a clasp-knife from under his cloak and opened it. He cut the bread, passing half to Elsbet. Hunger pushed the morning's excitement aside and Elsbet took a small bite from her portion, as was appropriate for a lady, barely restraining herself from biting very indecently into the bread. The sausage was excellent, the cheese was just as good, and the wine had just the right bouquet.

"Are you familiar with *The Monograph of the Family Trochilidae*?" she asked.

"Hummingbirds? Yes, I've seen several framed plates." Edigius drank a sip of wine straight from the wicker bottle. The only glass in the knapsack was meant for Elsbet. "Do you know how they did that?"

"Of course, although they keep details secret. In any event, they painted on gold. I'd have to make some tests..." She trailed off, lost in thought.

"Well, since the issue of gold—"

Edigius stopped mid-sentence and Elsbet turned around. A man had stepped from behind a tree, dressed in leather breeches, knee-high boots splattered with mud, and a waistcoat which had been thrown over a dirty shirt. A rapier hung from his belt and a morion was on his head, dented by a powerful blow. He held a knife in his hand, seemingly playing with it. He was unshaved and unwashed. Elsbet's heart stopped when confronted by the glimmer of lust in the dark stare that lingered on her.

At that moment, another man appeared on the other side of the clearing, followed by one more, cutting off Elsbet and the wizard's retreat. They were armed, too, one of them even carrying a pistol, but they did not draw their swords. Elsbet realised immediately with whom they were dealing. The forests were full of bandits who stole from peasants and robbed travellers—and did much worse things, according to the rumours... Should the men-at-arms arrest the bandits, they were summarily hanged. But Elsbet and Edigius were left on their own, deep in the forest, away from roads or any help. Panic crept into Elsbet. The wizard sat still, merely picking up his staff with a slow move of his hand and squeezing it tight.

"Pardon us, impolite and filthy after a long journey," the first highwayman began, "for interrupting your undoubtedly deserved meal in such a rude manner. But, you see, we were passing this part of the forest and we heard the word 'gold' spoken several times. And when we saw the well-laid table..."

The second bandit bowed mockingly to Elsbet. "And so, I'm sorry to admit, since you mentioned gold so many times, we assumed you must have it. So, if you'd like to, you know, share it with us poor ones..."

"And suppose you pretend you didn't see us and continue your own way, gentlemen?" Edigius said in an icy voice. His mouth was drawn in a thin line, his eyes narrowed behind his glasses.

"Perhaps the fair lady would like to contribute something to our cause?" the second bandit went on, ignoring the wizard.

"You think the wench has gold?" the first one asked, grinning.

"Sure! With golden hair such as hers, I bet she hides a golden fleece too!" All three highwaymen burst into laughter; they were looking at a profitable and entertaining afternoon. The fingers around the Edigius's staff turned white from the force he was squeezing it with. Anger boiled in him, and Elsbet wanted to stop him. She'd witnessed several brawls and she knew his chances—given his short-sightedness and mismatched legs—were almost nil against the three armed robbers, who were likely highly skilled in their filthy trade.

"Cover your eyes, dear child," Edigius said mildly to Elsbet.

"Now, that's enough," the first bandit snarled before he charged at Elsbet and the wizard. Edigius lifted his staff and drew a circle with it above Elsbet's head. Elsbet shut her eyes tightly and covered them with her palms. She heard the wizard speak some incantation or curse in a language she had never heard before. The words filled her with some inexplicable horror. And then three flashes burned into her eyes, even through her closed eyelids and palms, three bright white daggers threatening to blind her. When the flashes faded into the darkness behind Elsbet's eyelids, she opened her eyes fearfully.

Edigius laid his staff next to him, reached for the wicker bottle with a shaking hand and took a large swig of wine. Where there had been bandits a moment before, there were now only piles of dirty clothes and weapons.

"What happened to them?"

From beneath the first bandit's shirt, a toad crawled out, large, brown, covered in warty glands oozing acerbic secretions. Cold toad eyes studied Elsbet and the wizard for several moments, and then the amphibian waddled off slowly. Elsbet looked at the wizard.

"They refused to listen to reason," Edigius said, shrugging his shoulders.

"And what will happen to them now?"

"Nothing. They'll live out their toad lives. Unless, of course, you feel like kissing toads."

E lsbet and Edigius arrived at the inn late in the afternoon. During their long walk through the forest, Edigius was silent. Elsbet watched him, worried. He was dragging his disfigured leg, leaning against his staff, while beads of sweat broke out on his forehead and his breathing grew strained. When she first suggested, in a casual manner so as not to annoy the wizard, that they pause to rest, he just waved her away with his hand. The second time, he stopped, bent over, and inhaled the forest air deeply for several minutes before he continued. The third time, he almost collapsed into a layer of leaves. Elsbet hurried to his side to steady him. He looked at her with a strange mixture of embarrassment, anger, and gratitude.

"If we stop once more, I won't easily be able to continue," he muttered, leaning against her outstretched arm.

Before the gate of the inn, Edigius let go of Elsbet's arm. He took out his handkerchief and mopped the sweat from his forehead. Then he straightened his hair, cleared his throat, and entered. He greeted the maid with a voice that tried to be cheerful. The maid carried a bowl of beef broth to a noisy company at a table in the corner. Edigius took the creaking stairs to the floor where he and Elsbet had rented rooms. She followed him tensely as he climbed, ready to come to his aid if he needed it; she noticed new beads of sweat on his forehead.

Elsbet escorted the wizard to his room. He took out his key and tried to insert it into the keyhole but failed. Elsbet didn't even ask his permission; she took his key and unlocked the door. Edigius stepped into the room then he staggered, his staff falling out of his hand. Elsbet dropped her sketchpad and grabbed the wizard, his weight almost dragging her down, but she was strong, and she laid him, exhausted, onto the bed.

"What's going on?" she asked, scared. "What's happening to you?"

Edigius just smiled, exhausted. "Nothing, dear child, that cannot be attributed to the strain of transforming three bandits into toads. Charms and spells are exhausting, you know... Especially when the body's not young anymore." Elsbet helped the wizard take his cloak off. She unbuttoned his clothes, took a shoe off his healthy foot, unwrapped the thick cloth around the rooster one. Then she covered him, adjusted his pillow, lifted his staff from the floor, and placed it within his reach. Finally, she took off his glasses and laid them on the night table. "I see you know how to tend to a sick person..."

"My mother," Elsbet whispered. "When she'd feel particularly ill. Although, your medicine helps, she feels much better now."

"I'm glad to hear that. And now, let me rest... Go back downstairs, that broth smelled fine and if you hurry..."

"And you?"

"I'd love to, but I can't go anywhere like this. Go, Elsbet, don't worry..."

Elsbet nodded, took her sketchpad and placed it on the table, and then closed the door silently behind her. Edigius shut his eyes, breathing deeply, withdrawing into his body which had been squeezed dry, looking for the remaining atoms of strength to gather them into a new spark to kindle. He lost any sense of time, and then the door opened loudly, snatching him from the tired trance he had fallen into.

Elsbet strode into the room, escorted by the maid carrying a large, full tray in her hands. After two plates of broth, some sweet bread with marrow, and several pieces of boiled beef, Edigius felt better. He was tired, but he felt better. He opened his mouth to ask a question but Elsbet was faster, answering his unasked question while clearing the dishes.

"Apparently, everybody was much relieved when word spread that there are now three toads more and three muggers less in the forest."

Edigius laughed and then surrendered to exhaustion. Within a few moments, he had sunk into a deep, refreshing sleep.

"That's it! That's a good pose! Now, just hold still." Elsbet caught the lines of Edigius's face in quick motions of the pencil, just the basic shape. After that, she brought it to life, shadowing out cheeks and mouth and nose. She detailed the eyes behind the glasses, which were studying her with interest while she was absorbed by her drawing. The morning sun shone on the wizard's forehead, erasing the tense exhaustion that had been carved into it the day before. At breakfast, the wizard had felt almost fully recovered, but Elsbet nevertheless declared him unfit for further travel. Therefore, all his protests notwithstanding, they agreed on a day of rest in the forest, some ten minutes of easy stroll away from the inn. Elsbet and the wizard found a quiet spot, a small clearing in which several trees were felled.

"I didn't thank you for last night," Edigius said. A nuthatch called behind Elsbet's shoulder, the small bird climbing down the oak bark, searching for grubs. The metallic call of a titmouse replied from the crown. Elsbet lifted her gaze from the drawing for a moment. She had kept vigil over the sleeping wizard till late in the night. When she could no longer resist the fatigue creeping over her, she had fallen asleep, doubled up in an armchair, covered by a blanket, remaining at his side in case he needed her.

"I should thank you. I'm not sure I'd have enjoyed the attentions of those three."

"Oh, that." Edigius wanted to wave the matter away with his hand, but he stopped himself at the last moment to avoid spoiling the pose. "Did you really think we were in any danger?"

"And then, of course," Elsbet continued, drawing, "if you hadn't persuaded me to accept your offer, I'd never have had an opportunity to spy upon a pair of golden forest dragons."

"So, that's what's bothering you," Edigius teased gently. "I noticed you didn't remain indifferent..."

Elsbet did not reply, concentrating instead on the almost finished drawing. A few more pencil strokes, necessary to correct a lock of the wizard's hair, then she lifted the drawing and showed it to Edigius. "There, it's done!"

He looked at it silently for several moments, then smiled and nodded, satisfied. "It turned out well. Yours is needed now."

"*The Book of Dragons* is your book."

"And yours, Elsbet. There won't be any book without you." Elsbet did not reply. She opened her portfolio, put the portrait in, and then closed it and tied it back up. Edigius watched her rise from the stump she was sitting on. He reached for the staff to help himself up, but then Elsbet had suddenly stooped down and kissed him on his mouth. She straightened immediately, afraid he would get angry. She was confused by her own actions; she did not know what had seized her, what had driven her to that kiss.

Edigius's breath was caught in his throat. He brought his fingertips to his lips, as if he wanted to hold Elsbet's kiss there, stop it from disappearing, preserve that unexpected warmth.

"God, I'd almost forgotten what that feels like." The pain in Edigius's eyes cut Elsbet, the spark of pain and suffering and distant memory of something horrible flashing across his mind and then immediately extinguishing itself. Supporting himself with his staff, the wizard rose. His cloak revealed his rooster leg for a moment, wrapped in thick cloth. "It was when I earned this." He pointed at the leg. "A war of the wizards. Maybe I'll even tell you about it one day, although it's better that you don't know. That's when Marika got killed. My wife..."

"Couldn't you help her? It's rumoured that a wizard such as you—"

"Oh, my dear girl." Edigius laughed bitterly. "You think it works just like that? Presto-abracadabra! And the dead may rise?" The wizard stepped closer, standing right before Elsbet's face, the darkness in his eyes terrifying her. His voice was hard. Elsbet had never heard it like that—full of anger and helplessness and pain, a voice that filled her with dread. "There are such spells, you know, dark magic for healing even a dead body. And they speak the truth, Elsbet, I am a wizard powerful enough to cast them... I know, because I cast them successfully."

"But then why..." Elsbet fell silent, realising the horror of what Edigius had done a long time ago, desperate above his wife's dead body. "Her soul..."

"Yes, dear girl, I see you understand." The wizard nodded, his voice breaking down into a whisper. "Merely an empty shell. As beautiful as when she was alive, yes. And alive, she could have been called alive in some way. She went where I commanded her, sat where I made her sit, ate whatever I put onto her plate. She'd lay down where I told her to. I even—"

"Enough! Don't go on! Forgive me, I didn't mean to..."

"All you see is power! Magic! Spells! Arcane knowledge! But none of you mortals are aware of the dangers or the impotence. Even I wasn't aware of it until I tasted it myself..."

"I shouldn't have—"

"You don't understand, Elsbet, you cannot understand, you haven't seen those eyes! Empty, completely empty, residing in a living body and yet without a spark of life. The last thing I remember... The last thing before I broke that shell... For twenty years, those hollow eyes are all I remember Marika by." Edigius took Elsbet's hand and brought it to his cheek. Than he kissed it and let it go. "You have nothing in common with her. Marika had brown hair and hazel eyes. She was also shorter than you and moved in a different way, she laughed differently too... You really have nothing in common. Except the kiss. God, I thought I'd lost it forever. Forever! And you returned it to me, Elsbet."

The bodies laid scattered across the rocky ground, turned to charcoal in burnt fescue grass, the stench of incinerated flesh driving Elsbet to vomit. She clung to Edigius, the warmth of his hand calmed her, but the beast could not be far away, and maybe it was watching them at that very moment, hidden behind some of the stony towers rising above the hollow.

"The good news is that he's spent his fire for the next day or two." As far as the wizard and Elsbet could tell from the position of the bodies, the men had scattered the moment the dragon attacked them, each in his own direction. But to no avail, as the beast caught up with them and torched them from above, one by one. In the hollow, they had been fully exposed.

"And the bad news?" Wind drove the clouds above towering peaks. Exultant, Elsbet had spent half the sheets in her case drawing barren rocky turrets and towers, pointing white against the blue sky, changing, as if under a spell, with every turn of the path, every stop, every new view. Smiling gently, Edigius had warned her to leave few sheets of paper for the dragon too. It had taken them a whole morning to reach the hollow; they'd left the shade of beeches, maples, and moor grass behind them hours ago. From a spring, they had refreshed themselves with cool clear water and filled their flasks before continuing their climb to the peaks.

"That he's very, very angry." Edigius clenched his staff. Elsbet already knew he was focusing all his power into it, ready and at hand should they need to face the enraged monster.

"Who were these people?" In the grass next to Elsbet lay a broken rifle. A partisan, its spearhead blackened, its shaft splintered, lay a few steps away, next to a charred hand clenching a sword. Nothing had helped against the furious dragon belching flames from above.

"Perhaps some brigands. It doesn't matter, they entered his domain. And so did we, for that matter." Edigius faced Elsbet. "Now, listen well, Elsbet. When I say, drop down to the ground and don't move. Do you understand? Whatever happens to you, don't move." She nodded, the wizard's voice allowed no objection. "Now, let's go!"

The climb they'd made was in vain, a wasted effort. There was no way they could sneak up on the dragon now, and should he spot them, angry as he was, he would attack without the slightest hesitation. Quiet and swift retreat was their only chance. Back to the abandoned shepherd huts at the edge of the hollow: small, stony, crumbling ages ago, overgrown by junipers. They had to hide there till nightfall. Dragons do not like to fly after sunset, and should Elsbet and Edigius reach the forest under the cloak of darkness, they would be safe.

"C'mon! There's no more time to lose." Edigius kissed Elsbet and pulled her arm. She followed him across the grass without a word. The rooster leg slowed the wizard, his fastest pace being merely a wobbling gait and it was only thanks to his staff that he did not stumble and fall between the stones. Elsbet moved to his side, offering her shoulder as support, and his hand grabbed it with gratitude, as his fast, fitful breath spilled down her hair and nape. And then, a dark shadow swooped across them, with barely audible whistle of wings cutting the air.

Where did he come from? Elsbet wondered. *So quiet... Like death.*

"Hit the ground!" Edigius screamed, and pushed Elsbet away. She fell into the grass, hitting a stone painfully with her elbow, dropping her case as she rolled on her back. She saw the mountain dragon above her. He was huge, more than hundred feet long! And powerful. A bronze glimmer licked down his neck and body and long tail. Wings spread to the fullest. Jaws agape, teeth as sharp as knives. A flaming stare that knew no forgiveness and showed no mercy. The beast turned in the air and dived at them. The wizard lifted his staff and drew a circle above his head, mouthing an incantation Elsbet could not understand. The dragon steered with his tail, getting closer and closer, as precise as a buzzard diving at a rabbit, while Edigius finished his spell and, a moment later, Elsbet saw no more.

Suddenly blind, she was possessed by panic welling from the deepest core of her being. Elsbet could barely control it with what little reason she had left. Of course she could not see! Edigius had cast an invisibility spell, and light was passing through her and her eyes, not affecting them, as if they were not there. As long as the spell lasted, Elsbet and Edigius were invisible. And while blind, all they could do was lie in the grass, stay still, and wait for the puzzled dragon to fly away. It was useless for them to run for shelter in the huts; they would only break their legs on the rocks—

The plummeting mass dropped on Elsbet suddenly, cutting short her thoughts and breaking her body like a straw! Something sharp cut and tore her flesh, bones breaking like twigs as the beast stomped and plucked. Elsbet screamed and screamed, and there was a cry and a curse, and another cry calling her name, and then just the screaming. It must have been her screams, but she did not recognise that voice. She wasn't Elsbet anymore, she was merely a rag doll in the hands of a naughty child. Then there was nothing left. Just the victorious roar of an angry beast that destroyed all intruders, and the flapping of wings fading in the distance as the wind drove the clouds above the peaks.

Dark. Black. Pain... Pain? Where was the pain? She did not feel it. Only darkness. Black. Spell? It wore out.

Elsbet tried to open her eyes but could not. How much time had passed? She did not know. Maybe an hour. Maybe a day. She had no way of knowing.

He would not be tricked, the dragon. He was clever. He had remembered where Elsbet and the wizard had been the moment they disappeared. It had been enough for him to carry on his assault, to dive upon them and stomp blindly, to whip with his tail, and bite, and slash with his claws. He could not have missed.

Elsbet tried to move, but her body felt as if it had gone from her control. She wanted to open her mouth, but not even a rattle would come out. She realised she was chained, imprisoned in a shattered shell, another body among a dozen burned that day. Dark. Black.

Somebody dropped to his knees next to her, his hands holding her. She recognised those hands, she knew them well and loved them. She loved the way they had embraced her in the night and held her and caressed her. Now, those hands lifted her body, inert, crashed, lifeless. Just like the dead. Dead? No, not dead, merely imprisoned and helpless. Fingers removed blood-soaked locks of gold from her brow, gently caressing her cheek. She knew those fingers, she knew them well and loved them. She loved the way they had teased her in the heat of the night, and explored her, and walked naughtily through her bush where it was not decent. Edigius clung to Elsbet's body, shaken by mute sobs.

The darkness around Elsbet turned even denser; a whirlpool of nothingness grabbed her mercilessly and sucked her in like a river eddy. *Help me*, Elsbet called to the wizard, or rather tried to call but could not. She could not so much as sob to show him she was still alive and not like Marika. She was still there, clutching at that torn body, hanging on by the last thread, but still hanging.

And the wizard, broken, held Elsbet, covered in blood. He saw her wounds and felt her broken bones. Terrified, Elsbet realised he would not even try to bring her back to life. She gave no signs of life, and Edigius believed she was dead, killed in a gust of unbridled dragon's fury. He had no courage to try and summon once again the powerful charms that could heal even a dead body. He had no strength for that, after what had happened with Marika. He could not face another empty-eyed shell without will.

Edigius laid Elsbet back into the grass. She felt his lips on hers, his kiss, his warm breath. She rejoiced at those lips, she knew them well and loved them, loved the way they had kissed her at the dawn-break, kissed her across her entire body, enflaming anew the heat in her.

"Forgive me, Elsbet," the wizard whispered into her ear. "I shouldn't have brought you here. Forgive me."

Elsbet wanted to scream in her helpless anger. Edigius rose to leave her in the grass, beneath the peaks which would protect her for eternity, those stony guardians rising towards the sky. *Don't leave me alone*, Elsbet screamed without voice, crying, locked in the dungeon of her broken body as the dark poured from all sides and suffocated her. Only a tear managed to flow down her bloodied cheek.

The dark was like murky water closing above the drowning Elsbet. The eddy would not let go, and Elsbet surrendered, exhausted. And then, with the last figment of consciousness, she felt the hands grabbing her anew and shaking her, and she heard the wizard's curse, mad at himself, as he wiped the tear from her cheek with disbelief. She felt Edigius's fingers, all ten of them encircling her face, ten fingertips, ten warm spots on her cheeks. The heat of magic burst through her skin, the power penetrating and tearing and scattering the black like the first rays of sunrise. Life force flowed from Edigius into Elsbet, channelled by ancient arts, their roots lost in oblivion, and skills that only the great magicians learn to master to the fullest. The heat was an offered hand of salvation pulling Elsbet out of the dark.

Embraced by magic, Elsbet refused to surrender and struggled for breath. Power flowed through her body, filling her entirely, returning her to life, healing her wounds; first those that were most severe, most dangerous, most deadly. Who knew how long the recovery would last, but Edigius caught her and would not let go. And, with a sigh growing into a joyous scream of living and love and creation, Elsbet returned, led by the magician's power into the glittering light of *The Book of Dragons*.

The Law of the Sea

"For God's sake, Raul, don't do it!" Mercedes screamed, facing a knife-point aimed at her.

"Don't try to stop me!" Raul snarled through clenched teeth. His mouth cracked, skin sunburnt, hair matted; he was dripping with sweat. It must have been a week since the last rain. *Or more*, the girl realised, not taking her eyes away from the knife. How long ago had it been, for how many days had they allowed themselves merely a sip or two of tepid rainwater, squeezed out of the torn sailcloth?

And only a mile away were white sands washed by waves, and tropical greens; palms above the beach and a lush jungle covering the entire island. A paradise, almost within reach, luring and enticing. All it took was to jump into the water and swim across the reef, following the siren call of wind rustling in the tree crowns, the murmur of the sea on the beach, and the calls of the birds in the sky.

"You know you won't make it," Don Jorge said, trying to reason with Raul. "Luis tried, and you saw what happened to him. We all saw…" Don Jorge stepped towards Raul. The knife flashed, pointing at Don Jorge's chest and he stopped. Ramon and Juan kept a safe distance, not even thinking of coming to Don Jorge's aid. Mercedes knew only Don Jorge could stop Raul. Only he could snatch the knife from his hand, overpower and pinion the crazed youth. But Don Jorge did nothing, merely watched the blade. Mercedes saw in his dark eyes that he would not even try to stop Raul; Don Jorge was not the man that would forgive a knife aimed at his chest.

"Don't you try, you hear me?!" Desperation, thirst, hunger, and the Sun mercilessly burning for days had filled Raul's eyes with madness. Mercedes knew there was no more help for him, no way to reason with him, no way to persuade him. Raul would have killed anybody who tried to stop him. Finally, he grabbed the rope and swiftly, with the skill of a sailor, descended the rat-lines to the surface of the sea, some fifteen feet below. He stopped for a moment, but only a moment, and then he let himself into the water and started swimming in strong strokes.

Followed by tense looks, Raul was a good distance from the mast when Mercedes spotted the first dark shape in the deep. And the second one, and the third. "Raul!" she screamed. "Raul! Come back!"

But Raul paid no attention to her screams, unaware of anything but the inviting land; unaware of the swift, lethal shapes gaining on him. They smelled the fresh prey and nothing would drive them away. A triangular fin cut the calm surface for a moment, followed by another one. The young woman's eyes filled with tears as she called the youth's name in a hoarse voice. Don Jorge merely stood there, lips tight, while Ramon prayed silently. Juan remained doubled up against the mast, eyes tightly shut, hands covering his ears, in the vain hope that he would not have to see and hear the horror that all four knew was imminent.

Raul kept on swimming, briskly, madness making up for the strength drained away by the Sun. Then he leapt suddenly, as if hit from below by some invisible fist. He cast a horrified glance back at the safety of the mast he had abandoned. Then he disappeared beneath the sea, dragged down by the savage force of relentless jaws. The water where he'd been became coloured by blood. Raul surfaced for a moment, thrashing frantically, beating at the bloodied water, trying to drive the monsters away. But nothing could stop them anymore, nothing could make them go—their nostrils filled with salty blood—and the jaws bit. Raul screamed and screamed and screamed as the sharks tore piece after piece of his flesh away in an orgiastic feeding frenzy. Mercedes covered her ears so as not to hear the screams which broke above the reef and the lagoon, reaching all the way to the island, flushing the snow-white birds and making them take to the wing.

And then it was over. Raul had been pulled underwater and he did not surface again. Only the blood remained, spread by the currents. Mercedes fell to her knees without a sound while Ramon and Don Jorge crossed themselves, helpless under the indifferent heat of the sun.

The monster inhaled, filling her lungs with air, and dived. She pushed herself into the deep with her flattened tail. The prey rested on the surface, perhaps ten of her lengths away. She spotted it and began stalking it with sinuous movements of her body, intending to attack it from below, from where it would not notice her before it was too late.

She saw the ominous shape against the blue of the sky, the body with heart-shaped fins on its end, the head armed with arms. The monster knew that a giant squid was dangerous prey that would never surrender without a fight. But the squid above her suspected nothing, merely resting on the surface, lulled by waves, its arms swaying feebly.

She approached it until she was quite close and still the squid did not sense her. Sometimes the squids on the surface were sluggish, as if sick or dying. The monster did not know the reason for that, but she remembered the fights with them in the deep, in the eternal darkness where the Sun never reached: the battles of life and death, the arms wrapped around her body in a steel squeeze, the strong beak trying to bite, tear, dismember.

The hunger drove such memories away, the hunger pushed her into an attack and the sea serpent flicked her tail, hurling herself at her prey. She bit at the squid and jerked, trying to shred it. And the squid, which a moment ago had resembled a carcass, suddenly went berserk. Feeble arms were feeble no more, instead becoming a living trap entwining around her and squeezing her strong body in a relentless bone-crushing hug, driving air out of lungs, trying to stop the heart from beating. The serpent coiled, her bite never relaxing, and dragged the squid into the deep, into the whirlwind of two mortal enemies, locked in a merciless fight. The arms, the serpentine body, the jaws, all mixed in dense clouds of ink. There was no quarter given nor taken; only one was to come out of this battle alive.

Finally, the strong jaws and sharp teeth managed to tear the squid apart and the sea serpent devoured her prey greedily. Soon, nothing remained of the squid, merely a morsel or two for remoras, the faithful companions of the monster.

Eat or be eaten. The strongest survive. The law of the sea.

After a night of horror, the hurricane had finally torn the ship loose from her anchor and thrown her against the reef like a cockleboat. The sharp rocks pierced the mighty galleon, the water burst in, and the ship, dragged by the weight of her precious cargo and cannons, started to sink.

A scene out of Hell opened before Mercedes, six hundred crazed souls invoking the Virgin Mary in their helplessness. Their shrieks were swallowed by the demonic howling of the unbridled wind, drowned by the infernal thunder of waves, all while the savage sea crashed, tore, and dismembered. In a flash of lightning, the young woman saw an overloaded rowboat pushing off from the galleon. Somebody screamed for the Almighty as the sailors at the oars struggled to move away from the condemned ship that could not be saved. A moment later, a billow lifted the boat, hurled it against the side of the ship and smashed it, everybody in it disappearing into the foam. Mercedes's ears were pierced by the screeching and cracking and breaking of timber as the foremast fell, crushing everyone beneath it under the weight of yards, sails, and shrouds. The sailors tried to launch another boat. Strong arms driven by horror wrestled with the sea, defying the savage storm, but in vain. A new billow swept across the deck, tore the boat away from under them, and threw sailors and passengers overboard. The hungry sea ate the fragile bodies.

Lightning was tearing the sky apart. Mercedes turned, whipped by the wind which was throwing her wet black hair into her eyes, and looked for Doña Antonia; the panicked crowd separated them. She found her mistress praying, pressed against the mast. Pedro, her six-year-old son, clutched at his mother's skirt and wept, sobs shaking his tiny body. Mercedes wanted to embrace them both; Doña Antonia has always been kind to her. She wanted to console them, but after the next flash they were gone. She tried to find the captain; she still hoped to find salvation in his thundering voice and firm stare. But the captain was gone too; the sea must have taken him already.

All that remained for Mercedes was to find hope in words devoted to God. *But God's not listening*, she decided in blasphemy, *He abandoned us.* Or perhaps He had not; perhaps the storm and all the madness around her was God in His true image—angry, furious, merciless. Yes, that must have been it. He was punishing them—who knew why—but He was punishing them, and there was no salvation. A new wave rose above the ship, and Mercedes screamed as the might of the water hit her, driving air from her chest. Mercedes surrendered to the will of the sea, somehow at peace with her destiny. She did not know how, she did not understand, but it was as if she had found her own oasis of tranquillity—amidst the bellowing of the hurricane, the screams of the damned, and the moaning of the galleon—to which she succumbed with relief...

Somebody's strong hand grabbed her, not letting go, not allowing her to give in. Another hand and she was dragged through the seafoam, through a whirl of corpses and ropes and sea and flashes, then pulled up onto the rigging. The galleon sank. The sea closed above the ship's deck, her hull hitting the bottom with all its weight and settling there.

The monster felt the storm rising above her. She felt it speed and grow, fed by the Sun and the Ocean, maturing into a behemoth that started towards the sunset, carried by trade winds. She remembered such storms well, she recalled the darkness torn by flashes, the foaming sea whipped by winds, and the unbridled elements before which only the deep offered shelter.

But the sea serpent also remembered ships caught in the unleashed fury. Wooden shells capsizing, sinking and breaking to scatter their precious cargoes. Plenty of bodies, lifeless, helpless, on their way into eternal darkness. And many bodies on the surface, screaming, screeching for help, struggling in vain, clutching at a piece of mast or yard, or praying for salvation in fragile boats. The monster never discriminated, she devoured them all with equal relish.

The serpent particularly remembered a ship, overloaded with bodies in her ripped and flooded innards; black bodies, many black bodies, tied, shackled, chained in heavy manacles. And she had never forgotten their screams, the screams of terror before her gaping jaws and sharp teeth which never let anyone or anything escape. The monster also recalled the man driven to fury, madness in his eyes, whipping her, yelling and cursing, trying to drive her away. But in vain. The monster had noticed that his body was white and that he was not chained, that he did not have manacles around his legs and arms. Somewhere in her animal consciousness, the serpent realised—in some way and for some reason incomprehensible to her—that the one with the pale body had chained those other dark bodies, making them almost motionless and fully helpless before her hunger. And somewhere in her beastly consciousness, the monster had been almost grateful to him. She had feasted well during that storm.

The storm that was rising above the sea now was growing, maturing into true horror. The serpent decided to follow it across the ocean.

Six had survived. Captured on the maintop, with the galleon resting below, gently embraced by the sea satisfied with the offered sacrifice. Mercedes, a maid without a mistress. Raul and Luis, sailors without a ship. Ramon, an emigrant hoping for a new start in the new world. Juan, an assistant to a rich trader who now rested somewhere in the wreck with all his merchandise. And Don Jorge: the dark one. The slaver.

Mercedes had perceived him as the dark one the moment she saw him. His hair was jet-black, his pointed moustache neatly trimmed and his goatee streaked with grey, his piercing eyes missing nothing. He was dressed immaculately, his movements were feline. He had measured the young woman from head to foot. She'd shuddered at the flash of lust in those dark eyes. Mercedes had heard from her mistress that others onboard feared him. Strange rumours had spread about him: that he had been everywhere and done a lot of things. It was said that he was second to none with a sword and unstoppable with a knife. And he was cruel, Doña Antonia whispered. All these stories were being told by the passengers in low voices so that he would not overhear them by chance. But Don Jorge had been the one to snatch her from the sea, Raul coming to his aid, so that they both pulled her out of the water onto the maintop.

Now, only four of them were left on the top. Luis and Raul had tried to reach land; they had both been torn apart by sharks, without getting far. The cruel killers had circled the wreck while the bloated bodies floated around for days. Many corpses remained trapped under the deck, and there was no end in sight to the horrible feast.

It must have been around noon. The Sun was merciless. The sail cast the only shade; they were all sheltering in it. Far out on the horizon, dark clouds were gathering.

"There's going to be a storm. Maybe," Don Jorge muttered.

"Thank God, rain," Mercedes replied. The storm meant wind, it meant lightning, waves, savage sea, but it also meant rain. She wondered once again how long it had been since the last rain. What little they had gathered from soaked sailcloths was nearing its end. It was as if God was toying with them, letting the Sun squeeze them dry like sponges, to the last drop, and then sending them rain to soak them and keep them alive for the next few days. The same way that He had sent them a bird on the third day, a large one: white, snow-white. It had merely watched them, fearless, until Don Jorge drew out his knife. With a knife, he was unstoppable.

"Not good," Don Jorge stood, staring at the horizon, studying the clouds. And then he shielded his eyes with his hand, as if he was straining to see something far out. He remained that way for several moments, and then he cursed and mumbled something incomprehensible.

Mercedes rose to her feet. "A ship? Is it a ship?" she asked in a voice filled with hope. Ramon and Juan rose, too, searching for a sail, any sail. They would have even rejoiced at the sight of Englishmen, but the sea was empty. All that they could see were the distant clouds.

"No, it was not a ship." Don Jorge shook his head. "I was deceived. Just the Sun flashing on the surface." They all sat back into the shadow, but Don Jorge was thoughtful, silent, holding a *higa* in his fingers, a talisman against evil spells. It was the first time Mercedes had seen him like that; she did not even know that he had a *higa*, a small ivory pendant in the shape of a hand where the thumb was stuck between the index and middle fingers, mockingly defying curses.

Maybe he saw something, she thought. *But what? Or was he losing his mind too?*

The hot day was drawing on and on. Mercedes was watching a white bird soaring in the sky, high above their suffering. For a moment, the girl hated the bird with all her heart. And then, with a rush of guilt, she asked it to forgive her, because she did not really hate it. What she really wanted was to *be* like that bird, free, her wings spread, to rise above all the pain in this suffering, God-forsaken world. Ramon and Juan snoozed in the shade and Mercedes closed her eyes. The only salvation for her exhausted body was in sweaty sleep.

"She's back, that damned thing," Don Jorge muttered to himself. Mercedes did not indicate that she'd heard him. She was afraid to ask him anything. He had been silent throughout that entire afternoon, thoughtful, the *higa* clenched in his fist. He had risen several times and observed the sea carefully, as if expecting to spot something. Then he would sit down again, without a word, and Mercedes began wondering in earnest if the scorching heat had finally obscured his wits.

Later, when she awoke, Ramon was sitting on the edge of the maintop platform, absentmindedly watching the sea. Juan was leaning against the mast, conserving what little strength was left in him. Don Jorge was scanning the horizon. The clouds had scattered; there were more days to wait before the next rain came.

And then Don Jorge turned to face the rest of them. There was some strange glitter in his eyes, as if he had come to a fateful decision. "Tomorrow we swim to the shore!" he announced.

"That's madness," Ramon objected from the edge of the maintop. "You saw what happened, we all saw. The bloody sharks won't let us!"

"Nevertheless, tomorrow we swim. Can you swim, girl?" He had never addressed Mercedes by her own name; she was always just 'girl' to him, as if it was beneath his honour to address a maidservant by her name. Mercedes nodded. She had learned to swim when she was a child.

"You must have gone crazy," Ramon exclaimed, pointing at the sea surrounding them. "You think you'll escape them? You think any of us can escape? We'd only be going to certain death when all we'd have to do otherwise is wait to be rescued! Anyway, we're too weak to swim across."

"Then you will die," Don Jorge snarled. He looked at them all. That look made Mercedes shudder. "The law of the sea: only the strong survive."

"Look, Don Jorge," Juan tried to be amiable, "we should have reached Habana by now. They'll know there has been a storm, believe me; they'll start looking for us. You know well enough, just as I do, that we were carrying quicksilver. And you know well enough what no quicksilver means—no gold and no silver. They *will* come looking for us, rest assured. We just have to be patient."

"We're not safe here anymore." Don Jorge shook his head. "Even if they find the ship, we won't be on it. Tomorrow, we swim."

The monster was a little disappointed. The storm had passed, unleashing its anger on the helpless archipelago, and the serpent had not been able to feast on bodies scattered from some crushed and sunken ship with its broken masts and torn sails. She soothed her hunger with a marlin; even the fastest fish in the ocean was not fast enough to escape her jaws.

An island and a reef were close. The shore and shallows filled all the monster's senses: the wind in the tree crowns, the beach washed by the sea, the calls of the birds up in the sky. Then currents brought the serpent images of horror and death: the ship that had hit the bottom, the scattered bodies, but also many others, still imprisoned inside the vessel. And the sharks feasting.

The serpent raised her head above the surface, just for a moment, but enough to see the mast pointing out of the sea, and the sail on it, and someone on the maintop. Meagre prey, barely worth the effort.

The monster dived down to the reef, surprising a school of fish. She drove them into a large living mass, moving, whirling. She did not let them scatter but instead charged, snatching one fish at a time until she was sated. The law of the sea.

Mercedes flinched in her sleep then opened her eyes. It was dawn, the rising Sun colouring the world in flames. Don Jorge stood above her, naked to his waist, a knife in his hand. His eyes filled her with horror, they had the look of a demon from the depths of Hell; his hollow face was burning in the fire of sunrise.

"He's mad!" Mercedes screamed. "He's gone mad, help!" But Ramon and Juan were tied up on the planks, helpless.

"They won't come to their senses for some time," Don Jorge snarled.

With lightning speed, Don Jorge grabbed Mercedes before she could escape and pressed her down with his strong body, ramming his knee between her legs. His left hand caught her right one and pinned it down. Mercedes drove her left hand into his face, scratching, nails tearing at his cheek, leaving bloody trails, but Don Jorge merely laughed and secured Mercedes with rope, tying her hands behind her back. Then he stopped, breathing heavily, passing his fingers across the wounds she had inflicted. He rubbed the blood between his fingers and then he wiped them casually against his trousers.

"You, girl, you are not weak. No, you will live!" With a madman's glee in his eyes, Don Jorge threw himself at Mercedes, baring her breasts. He stopped for a moment, enjoying the sight, and then he tore and cut off all her clothes. When she was left completely naked, he took his trousers off. "I've seen women like you before. I've trapped them and broken them myself. And I knew right away which one will survive to serve well, and which one we'll throw overboard mid-way."

Don Jorge spread the young woman's legs. Mercedes clenched her teeth as he penetrated her, ramming his fingers into the flesh of her buttocks, his lips ravaging her breasts. She did not scream, did not call for help, did not sob. She merely clenched her teeth while the beast was satisfying itself with savage thrusts. Tears ran down her cheeks. She cried, humiliated and filled with helpless rage at the monster that was taking possession of her; she was helpless to resist, helpless to withstand the blasphemous passion stirred in the heat of the dawn. Mercedes cursed herself and her tortured sweating body, her will crashed within it like a mussel within its smashed shell. When Don Jorge finally emptied himself into her with animal groans, she came too, betrayed by her own flesh.

"You needed it too, didn't you?" Don Jorge remarked as he was rising. Mercedes spat into his face, willing the hatred in her eyes to burn him to cinders.

"Curse you!" she screamed in her shame and helpless fury. "Curse you to Hell!" Don Jorge reached for his knife, and Mercedes froze in terror. But he merely cut her ropes and laughed. "Oh yes, I judged you well. Just the right one for a new life in the new world!

"Now, listen to me well, girl." Don Jorge took his shirt and tossed it to her. "Take this and put it on. There may be paradise over there, but you're no Eve. And the skirt would only drag you to the bottom. Now, go down and enter the water, slowly. And swim to the shore. The less you splash, the better."

"And them?"

Don Jorge stooped, grabbed Mercedes's face and kissed her on the mouth, a long kiss, passionate with desire. "They're weak, they won't survive."

"And me?"

"Honey, compared to what I did in my life, what happened with you won't even be mentioned when I step before St. Peter." Then Don Jorge took his *higa* off and hung it around the young woman's neck; the little mocking fist fell next to her golden crosslet. "You'll need it more than I do. It won't help me where I'm going. Now, go! And whatever happens, don't look back, just swim!"

Feverishly, Mercedes put Don Jorge's shirt on and descended the ratlines. Holding the rope, she cast one last look at the maintop and Don Jorge on it, then she slowly entered the water, careful not to make the slightest wave. She let go of the rope, pushed herself off, and started swimming cautiously to the shore.

Mercedes never looked back, just kept swimming, and then she heard a splash behind her, as if something had fallen from the maintop into the sea. She turned and saw Don Jorge lifting a body; it must have been Ramon's, he was bulkier than Juan. And she saw the knife flashing as it sliced the throat, saw blood splattering down the body. Don Jorge threw it, lifeless. Two splashes and the blood out of two cut throats... That would certainly draw the sharks, attract them so strongly that they would forget about her. They would not even notice her if she swam only quietly and persistently. That was what Don Jorge had planned, that was how he had bought her time to swim across the reef. Slaughtered lives in exchange for hers, curse him!

The sharks gathered around the mast. Mercedes saw the triangular fins, the sea boiling as the creatures, attracted by the blood, threw themselves at the offered flesh with relish.

Then, suddenly, a head burst out of the foaming sea, a head that looked as if it came from Hell itself. A shark struggled in its jaws. The head was huge; it looked bigger than a human body to Mercedes. And the jaws... Strong enough that not even a shark which could have cut Mercedes in two could escape them. And behind the head, the body, repulsive, scaly, snake-like, with a torn and ragged fin along its back, dark coils stretching through the agitated water as the monster devoured a shark before snatching up another one.

And then Mercedes realised that Don Jorge's bait was not for the sharks. He must have spotted the monster the day before, for a brief moment only, too brief to warn the others. That was the reason why he had been so moody that afternoon, playing with the *higa* between his fingers and rising every so often to scan the sea with his eyes. He knew that the monster was here and that—just like the sharks—it would not allow them to swim across to the island.

Mercedes would never have imagined that the sea serpent before her could be a reality and not just a fable told by sailors at inns as they boasted drunkenly in the company of women. And Don Jorge must have encountered it before; who knew, maybe while he had been sailing along the African coast, hunting slaves for the New World, or somewhere along the shores of America while he was delivering survivors to be sold. Yesterday, he had seen it again, and he knew it was no apparition; he knew that the monster was real, and that it would not spare them. That was why he had slaughtered Juan and Ramon, as bait for the monster, as a sacrifice to the merciless jaws that now tore a third shark apart, while Don Jorge looked down from his vantage point at the slaughter beneath him.

Then Don Jorge noticed Mercedes was not swimming.

"Swim on! Swim!" he screamed with all his voice. "Swim, Devil take you!"

The sea serpent surfaced and coiled around the mast. If she had not known that Don Jorge was above her, he had announced himself. Don Jorge stood, knife drawn, at peace with his destiny, knowing well enough that there was no salvation. The monster rose above the maintop; they would not have been safe up there, and Don Jorge had known it – just as he had known that someone had to be sacrificed to the pitiless serpent. And he was alone, facing her, naked, with just a knife in his hand.

"Swim! Swim and don't stop! And remember, a new life in the new world!" Don Jorge shouted, and Mercedes turned her back to the terrible sight and swam on. She crossed the mighty reef wall, the corals beneath her were like the sharp fingers of an ancient giant. They had crushed the ship, and now they were reaching for her. She kept on swimming until a scream broke above the sea, inhuman, savage, the angry scream of a beast snatched by a beast.

Mercedes turned. The sea serpent was squeezing the mast with the coils of her body. Don Jorge was in her jaws, bloodied by the sharp teeth, helplessly striking with his hand, but the knife could not penetrate the thick scales. Finally, his body surrendered to the steel clench of the monstrous jaws, and he collapsed. Don Jorge was dead, a destiny he knew was coming after all the crimes he had committed.

The mast broke under the weight of the monster, the shrouds snapped and everything fell into the sea. The sail covered the serpent as she let go of the broken mast and disappeared in the foaming water, Don Jorge in her jaws.

Silence returned above the sea; the serpent was no more. She had dived into the deep. Mercedes did not lose another moment. She turned towards the island and kept on swimming, entering the calm of the lagoon. She was tired, her exhausted body a knot of pain, but something kept driving her, giving her strength to answer the call of the wind in the tree crowns, the murmur of the waves on the beach, and the calls of the birds in the sky. The sharks were gone, scattered by the sea serpent. The monster was gone, too; perhaps she had disappeared in the deep or was still coiling somewhere around the once proud galleon, but she did not follow the young woman. Mercedes reached the shallows, and when she felt the soft sand under her feet, she sobbed in relief.

And as she staggered up the white beach, still unheated by the Sun, she recalled Don Jorge's words. A new life in a new world. She collapsed onto the sand, eyes filled with tears now that she knew what he had wanted, why he had raped her, and had then given her the chance to stay alive. He could have tried to swim to safety himself, with similar odds, she realised. Instead, he had sacrificed himself, hoping that he had left a part of him in her.

Only the strong survive. The law of the sea.

The last survivor lay on the beach while the white birds soared in the sky high above her. She gathered strength to rise and go looking for water. The last survivor... Maybe not, she corrected herself, her belly caressed by the fine weaving of Don Jorge's shirt. Maybe the last *two* survivors.

ALEKSANDAR ŽILJAK

The Aeolomancer

"Sell me a wind, woman!"

Katka shivered—not too obviously, she hoped. She kept stirring the soup with a ladle. She was cooking for tomorrow. It was summer, and the days were hot, too hot to cook. Evenings were the time to do it, when it was cooler. She tasted the hot soup with the tip of her tongue. *Good indeed*, she decided and removed the pot from the fire. She covered the pot with a lid, wiped her hands on her white apron, and looked at the stranger.

"You hear what I say? Sell me a wind!" Mingan was sitting at the table, not taking his eyes off Katka. He threw a leather purse on the table, several gold coins scattered from it, jingling. Katka saw doubloons, gleaming in the light of an oil lamp. The pirate studied her with his leaden-grey eyes under strong eyebrows. His aquiline nose and thin lips gave him a predatory look. He was grey-haired, too young to be white with age. His hair was neatly clipped, his moustache and goatee carefully trimmed. He was muscular, wearing dark trousers tucked into high boots and a white unbuttoned shirt, its sleeves rolled up. His hairy chest showed. He had laid his tricorne on the table. He had placed his *shamshir* with its ornate scabbard and ivory handle within easy reach. Katka did not miss the knives pushed into his boots, one in each, and a revolver, tucked into his purple silk waist sash.

"What will you do with a wind, Sir?" Katka asked. The doubloons were cursed coins, she knew, minted from gold that had been dug up and then stolen in blood across the ocean, from the mountains reaching all the way to the clouds and vast jungles. And whatever Mingan wanted, she had heard enough about him to know it could only mean more blood.

"I need it to defeat the Golden Armada." Mingan grinned. A beastly gleam flashed in his eyes. Katka trembled. "I need a wind, woman, you hear? A storm to sweep the corvettes, to scatter the frigates, to bring down the treasure ships from the sky."

"That requires a strong wind indeed, Sir."

At least as strong as a bura, Katka thought. *Perhaps as strong as a hurricane.* She had never summoned a hurricane.

"Don't tell me you can't do it." Mingan leaned back in the chair. "You're an aeolomancer. You summon winds. I know well that you raised the *bura* that smashed the Serenissima fleet against the cliffs of Krk. Never before and never since have people seen such a *bura*. How much did the Captain of Nehai pay you, woman?"

"Some things are not done for money, Sir," Katka lied, unconsciously wiping her hands on her apron. There was blood on her hands. The entire fleet sent by La Serenissima against Senj, with all hands. She had not heard of anybody surviving.

Mingan pointed at the purse. "There will be more, woman. This is just to show you that I mean it."

Katka raised her gaze and crossed her arms with determination. "No, Sir. I don't sell wind anymore."

Mingan measured Katka from head to toe. After several moments, he just shrugged. He rose, picked up the gold coins, took his *shamshir*, and put his tricorne on his head. *He gives up so easily?* Katka wondered. She had expected angry persuasion and threats. Mingan headed for the door to leave. He opened the door and stood there, framed by the stone doorway. He faced Katka.

"You have a daughter, right? Fourteen, fifteen years old? Life is before her, you should think about her future."

Mingan walked out into the night, leaving Katka standing next to the table, pierced by fear, holding herself so as not to fall down.

"Who was that, Mother?" Rashelka asked. She descended the stairs into the kitchen, dressed in a nightgown. Her brown hair was dishevelled, traces of disrupted sleep in green eyes that were just like her mother's.

"An evil man, my daughter. He wanted me to sell him a wind." Katka took off her apron and hung it on a hook next to the stove. *Bava* was blowing gently outside. Dark sea. Clear sky. Katka closed the green-painted shutters tight. She shut the windows, too. She wanted her house properly secured tonight.

"What did you tell him?"

"I sent him away," Katka smiled and caressed Rashelka's cheek. "I don't think he'll come back," she lied. She locked and barred the door. She yawned. Cooking had tired her. And Mingan? Perhaps she should go to the port master and report him. Or should she simply keep quiet? Mingan's sinister reputation had spread far. But Mingan was usually pillaging across the ocean, by the shores of Brasilia and all the way north to the West Indies. Nobody ever spotted his airship in the Adriatic Sea, nobody offered prizes for his head in these skies. What was he doing here? Did he fly all the way across the ocean just for her? Who knew if the port master would believe her? And would he do anything, even if he did?

"Come, Rashelka, it's time to sleep. We must take to the oars tomorrow, to check the fish traps."

Katka lay in her bed. Despite her fatigue, sleep would not come; Mingan drove it away. She stared into the darkness, remembering Senj and the Fort of Nehai, and small dots in the sky, the invading air fleet. She had been seventeen, already a mother, and already wearing the black of a widow. Katka closed her eyes and memories rushed in, still vivid and horrifying after all those years...

Katka stood on the wall of Nehai, madness in her eyes, arms spread towards the sea. The wind was throwing her hair across her face, carrying away her black kerchief. *Bura* was in her fingers. Katka wove the wind as if working lace from the island of Pag.

Using her hands, Katka brought the *bura* down from the Velebit—the breath of the stony dragon asleep above the coast—and made her whistle above the fort, howl in the pines beneath the walls, roar over Senj and all the way to the cliffs of Krk. Frightened people were taking shelter in their houses of stone, closing their doors and windows. Shutters slammed, roof tiles smashed. Once unleashed and summoned from her mountain throne, the *bura* knew no mercy, carrying away innocent and guilty alike.

Katka was flogging the sea with wind, whirling *fumarea*, blurring the horizon. Above the sea, a grey reconnaissance corvette struggled to stay on course. And then a squall hit the airship and tossed her, breaking her wooden frame like a spoiled child tearing a toy apart. Her back broken, the airship tumbled down, then an explosion and fire engulfed the entire corvette. Tiny dots were falling from the flames—the crew, greeted by the calls of gulls as they jumped to their deaths, escaping the heat of burning hydrogen and the explosions of gunpowder and grenades.

More grey airships were in the distance, approaching. They must have seen the flames, but the corvette's demise did not stop them. La Serenissima— Venice—had raised her fleet against the Fort of Nehai. Corvettes and frigates and ships of the line, armed with machine guns, cannons and grenades, to deal with the impudent *uskoks* of Senj and their Captain. Katka waited for them to come closer and then barehanded, she cast gusts at them, each stronger than the last. The engines ran at full steam, but the unbridled *bura* was stronger, whipping at the ships, scattering them, breaking their battle formation and smashing them against each other. Explosions and flames as far as the eye could see; from the walls of Nehai, the sea and the cliffs looked as if they were made of fire.

The Captain looked through his telescope as fires devoured the pride of La Serenissima. When it was all over, when the sky above the Velebit was free of invading airships, he roared a laugh of victory and shouted to his men, and they cheered with joy and celebrated and fired shots in the air. On the walls, an exhausted Katka fainted, suddenly overwhelmed by all those distant deaths, and the *bura* stopped—once there was no one to drive her—as suddenly as she had started.

Later, when Katka came to her senses, somewhere within the protective walls of the Fort of Nehai, a leather purse greeted her from a cabinet next to her bed. It was full of looted Venetian *scudas*. A purse of silver coins for the *bura* that had destroyed the cursed Venetians.

Because Katka was an aeolomancer. Katka sold wind.

Until the deaths she had brought that day with her own hands made her realise the true price of her power.

Ascream tore Katka out of her sleep. *Rashelka!* The name burst through her drowsy mind. She jumped out of bed and rushed out of her room. In the gloom, dark shapes were dragging Rashelka down the stairs. She was screaming and struggling, but strong hands would not let her go. Then her screams fell silent, her mouth covered by a palm.

"Let go of her, you trash!" Katka bellowed, and she ran after them, wind growing in her hands. And then, something hit her across the back of her head, and she collapsed to the floor, stunned, helpless, on the edge of fainting. She felt someone lifting her. She recognised those hands through the dark, that smell of a wolf. Mingan dragged her downstairs into the kitchen and then outside. Somebody was in front of the house.

"Shall I burn it?" that somebody asked Mingan. It looked to Katka like he was holding a grenade.

"No, Wayne," the pirate replied, dragging Katka through dry grass. "Nobody heard the screams, the nearest house is half a mile away. But fire might cause people to come out and investigate. Let's go, everybody back to the *Embolon!*"

Night air cleared Katka's mind a little. She discerned the dark shape of an airship against the star-strewn sky; it seemed as big as a corvette, more than two hundred feet long. Rashelka was already onboard. Mingan pushed Katka through the entry hatch on the side of a long gondola. Somebody's hands grabbed her and dragged her down the narrow passageway toward the tail. Mingan and Wayne boarded after her; the pirate barked a command and the ship jerked up before steadily climbing. Katka heard the engines running: the steam in the cylinders, the chains transmitting power to the propellers driving the airship up.

Katka shook her head, pain was hammering inside it. She clenched her fists, feeling the wind gathering in them, surging, flowing into her fingers, tingling under her nails -

"I don't think so!" Mingan leaped after her and grabbed her hair, tugging on it painfully to break her concentration. He yanked her head up. Their eyes met. "We're at one hundred feet already. It might not seem much, but have you ever jumped from that high with a burning airship above you?"

Katka sank helplessly back down, letting the wind dissolve from her fingers back into her body. Mingan nodded. They understood each other well.

"That's better," he muttered. "As long as you're onboard, you can't touch us. Otherwise, you and your kid will fall with the *Embolon*, got that?"

Rashelka rose from a mat and looked through a porthole. The sea was spreading below her. She did not see a single ship on the sea nor a single dirigible in the sky. Neither did she see any island or distant land. No birds either. It seemed they were flying at three or four, maybe even five thousand feet. It was rare for any airship to venture higher.

The confining cabin in which she had awakened must have been a storage closet of a sort, emptied just for her. Bare shelves lined one wall. A metal chamber pot had been left for her in the corner. Including the sleeping mat covered by a flax sheet, there was barely space enough for turning around. The sliding door was closed. Rashelka tried to open it; of course, it was locked. *What did I expect?* she thought.

Suddenly, she heard footsteps. The lock clicked. The door slid aside. Mingan entered the storage space. He was carrying a cotton shirt, loose trousers, and fabric slippers. He measured Rashelka from head to toe, and then he threw the clothes and slippers on her mat.

"There, put these on," he ordered. "So nobody gets any funny ideas should they see you in the nightgown."

"Where's my mother?" Rashelka leaped after Mingan. The door slid shut and she hit it with her fists. "I want to see my mother!" she yelled. The click of the lock was her only answer. Rashelka grabbed the pot, hit the door with it, once, twice. "You hear me? I want to see my mother! Open -"

A curse. The door unlocked and slid open. Mingan stormed in, his face contorted in anger, and slapped Rashelka. She staggered; the pot fell out of her hand and clattered into the corner.

"I need you alive, girl," Mingan snarled. "But there are different ways one can be alive. Got that?" Rashelka nodded, her cheek stinging.

"Glad we understand each other," the pirate growled before slamming the door and locking it again.

Rashelka threw a curse after him. Then she took the chamber pot and used it in the way it was meant. She took her nightgown off and put the trousers on. She tightened them with a waist-string. The shirt was too big for her so she tucked it into the trousers, rolled the sleeves up, and put the slippers on. She sat back on the mat.

Her stomach growled with hunger. She wondered when would they bring her something to eat.

"**W**hat did you do with Rashelka?" Katka hissed.

"She is where she belongs," Mingan replied nonchalantly, finishing his supper. "She doesn't sleep on bare planks, I gave her clothes, fed her, emptied her pot, she's under lock and key so nobody touches her. What else do you want?"

"Perhaps to be returned home, Sir?"

Mingan roared with laughter. "Oh, you're good, woman!" He was watching her and nodding. "I see I won't be bored with you."

Katka was sitting in a comfortable upholstered chair facing Mingan, in his cabin at the rear of the gondola. Sunset was burning through the starboard windows, painting the cabin in gold. *We're flying south*, Katka deduced. What was there in the south? Or perhaps Mingan planned to cross the ocean at its narrowest. She would not ask him anything.

The captain's cabin was accessed through a wooden sliding door. The pirate's bed was alongside the starboard wall, drawers beneath it. A narrow clothes closet was next to the headboard. A toilet with a sink was positioned in the corner, separated by a folding screen. A desk was alongside the port wall, charts spread on and above it. A barometer hung on the wall above the desk. A chronometer, a sextant in a box, a compass, and folded charts were all on the desk. Books on a shelf. The mouthpieces of voice tubes. There was a heavy antique-looking globe next to the desk. Arms, repeating rifles, three revolvers, and a flare gun were padlocked. Katka doubted those were the only weapons onboard. Besides, she had never fired a shot.

On the table where they sat—surrounded by windows giving them a view of the sunset above the sea—were expensive plates made of the finest Bohemian porcelain, silver cutlery, and crystal wine glasses. Bare chicken bones and some potatoes were the only leftovers of the meal, and a splash of wine. Mingan had dragged Katka from her locked cabin and then dumped her into a chair at a table that had already been set. Her nostrils had twitched at the aroma of roasted chicken and potatoes. She was hungry. So hungry that she forgot about everything else. Even Rashelka. She realised with anger how easily she had succumbed to the pirate's hospitality. She did not fail to notice a wooden club within reach of Mingan's hand, next to the knife and fork. Nevertheless, she did not resist when the pirate poured her the first glass of wine.

Mingan wiped his mouth with a napkin and pushed the plate away from him. He poured himself another glass of wine. He offered Katka one too. She waved it away. She had drunk too much. She wanted to rise.

"Sit down!" Mingan barked.

"But Rashelka -"

"I said she wants for nothing! Don't worry, I'll walk her from time to time. Although, the less my gang see of her, the better. You'll manage."

"How long shall we travel, Sir?" Katka knew it would take at least five days to cross the ocean east to west. Less in the opposite direction, depending on the winds.

"As much as it takes. Depends when the Armada starts."

Katka sat back in the chair. "It must be a special convoy if you went all the way to the Adriatic Sea to kidnap me."

"It is." Mingan grinned. "More gold and silver than you can imagine. Your job is to stir the storm, to drive away and destroy the escort. Then, you will bring the treasure ships down, or at least damage them. My *bombardellas* and machine guns are not enough to attack the Armada openly. They'd sweep us from the sky before we got within firing range. But you will have to obey me, got that? I don't want them brought down over the high seas."

"But how will you recover the treasure, once the ships are down?"

"That, woman, is my worry."

Mingan pushed the chair behind him, rose, and approached Katka. She did not like the gleam in his eyes. He touched her cheek. She pushed his hand away, but there was nowhere she could go. Mingan touched her cheek again.

"How old are you, woman?"

"That... That is something a well-mannered gentleman does not ask a woman, Sir," Katka whispered. Mingan's palm on her cheek would not give her peace.

"But I *am* asking you."

"Thirty. Last May."

Mingan nodded. "You gave birth young. Almost a girl."

"I was also married young, Sir—and widowed."

116

Mingan laid his hand on Katka's left breast. She pushed his hand away furiously.

"I had a good supper," Mingan snarled, "and the wine was good. And now I want a woman, to warm me up."

"Let me go, Sir, let -"

"Or should I go for Rashelka? Perhaps she would be more willing, who knows?" Mingan grinned. "And send you to entertain the crew? What say you, woman?"

Mingan laid his hands on Katka's breasts again. He was kneading them through her coarse shirt. Katka did not try to push his hands away this time. She closed her eyes, and took a deep breath through her teeth. *Happy*, she thought before submitting to Mingan's fingers on her nipples and to the rhythm of the engine driving them south across the ocean, *just keep him happy. For the time being.*

Rashelka peeked through the porthole; the airship was resting peacefully just a few feet above the water. The sea was calm; they had settled in the deserted bay of an island that rose into a high volcanic peak. The Sun-scorched grey soil was covered by tough plants struggling to survive. *Islas Canarias?* Rashelka wondered.

An unusual vessel was anchored away from the airship, her hull somewhat plump, of a horn-like stem, with eyes painted on her iron-spiked bow and folded lateen sail set on a forward-raking mast. Suntanned sailors were transferring a large bundle covered with burlap and tied with a strong rope from the strange vessel onto the *Embolon* boat. Mingan was overseeing them personally. A sailor scooped a pail of water from the sea and spilled it over the bundle, wetting whatever was inside. Rashelka was puzzled. *What could it be?*

When the bundle was finally loaded, Mingan threw a purse to the captain of the vessel. The man caught it, measured its weight in his hand, opened it and looked inside before smiling with satisfaction. He waved to Mingan while his men rowed back to the *Embolon*.

Ten minutes later, Rashelka heard Mingan's heavy steps as well as the tread of his men following him, straining as they were carrying the heavy bundle along the passageway.

"Careful," Mingan warned them. Rashelka heard keys jingling, a door sliding aside. *The cabin next to mine*, she realised.

"C'mon, on the floor! Unwrap her!" Mingan was giving orders.

Unwrap? Whom? Rashelka heard an inhuman scream, the sound of struggling, thrashing on the floor, curses.

"Hold her, Goddamit!" Mingan bellowed.

"Watch it!" somebody else yelled. "Don't let her loose!"

"Hold her!" Mingan repeated. "Good, that's it! Let's go, put 'er in the water!" Rashelka heard water splashing and then hinges screeching and clanking, as if a heavy grate was being lowered, then chains jingling and the sound of a lock being secured. Then came the sound of flesh hitting the glass, fast and fierce.

"Damn, she'll smash it!" somebody said worriedly.

"No, she won't," Mingan replied. "She'll calm down. Hmmm... I've got an idea."

Rashelka heard Mingan's boots as he rushed out of the cabin and stopped before her door. Keys jingled then the door slid aside noisily, pushed by a frantic hand.

"Come here!" Mingan grabbed Rashelka by her arm before she could make a sound. "Looks like you won't be dead weight after all." Mingan dragged Rashelka out of her cell and brought her among his men. Four of them were lined up along one wall of the cabin. Along the other side...

Rashelka held her breath. A large box, a bit larger than a coffin, had been placed along the other wall. It was made of glass panes in a steel frame. The whole box was sealed and watertight, covered with a heavy iron grate, locked with a padlock. And in it...

The creature inside the tank seized the bars above her with her right hand and shook the grate, once, twice. In vain. She glared at them savagely. Her green eyes spelled murder; she would kill them all if she could. Then her eyes paused on Rashelka. As if she sensed that the girl, too, was a prisoner on this ship, her gaze softened and she relaxed a bit. She removed a lock of black hair from her face. Rashelka could not look away from her face, which was just like the face of any other girl, and her strong body turning beneath her navel into... *the grey body of a dolphin*, Rashelka realised. She had a small dorsal fin and a tail, just like a dolphin.

A womanfish! That damned Mingan had caught a womanfish and was now keeping her imprisoned in that confined glass cage and -

"She's your responsibility now," Mingan said, startling her. "You feed 'er, you change her water. You'll get a bucket and a hose. And fish. Got that?" At first, Rashelka did not answer, still stunned by the unusual creature before her. "Got that?" Mingan yelled, and he shook her.

Rashelka merely nodded. Who knew why Mingan needed the womanfish, but she realised that maybe she had an ally before her.

The *Embolon* was cruising the sky, driven by her steam engine. Rashelka looked through the porthole; the ocean beneath them spread as far as the eye could see. She saw a small dark spot in the distance and smoke rising from a funnel. It must have been a paddle steamer sailing east. Had they spotted Mingan's airship? Had they recognised her as a pirate dirigible? After all, who knew whose colours the damned Mingan hoisted.

Rashelka returned to the womanfish who had eaten the mackerel she had given her. "More?" Rashelka asked.

The womanfish just nodded, and Rashelka took another fish by its tail and lowered it through the grate. The womanfish took it with both hands and bit into the head. Rashelka studied her as bones were crunched between the strong teeth.

"What does Mingan want from you?"

The womanfish looked at Rashelka with her green eyes.

"I think I know, my daughter," Katka murmured. She sat on a folded blanket, leaning against the wall as she watched Rashelka feed the womanfish; the unusual creature had quite an appetite. It was the fourth mackerel she was devouring.

"What did you say, Mother?"

"When the Golden Armada airships fall..." Katka lowered her voice almost to a whisper. Rashelka sat next to her. The womanfish appeared to have pricked up her ears as well. "When they fall, they'll tumble into the sea. The shallows, I guess, perhaps a lagoon or some shallow cove, but still. After that, the treasure chests will have to be recovered from whatever remains of the ships." Katka and Rashelka looked at the womanfish.

"But those are heavy chests. She's not that strong," Rashelka objected.

"It's enough if she just dives to them and attaches the rope. Then they can pull them out with an engine, using pulleys. I've seen men from Nehai recovering machine guns and cannons from a Venetian ship that way."

"They also had a womanfish?"

"No." Katka smiled. "They paid some sponge-divers."

"I wonder if she understands us," Rashelka whispered into her mother's ear.

"I hear you and understand you," a slightly rustling voice replied through the grate. Katka and Rashelka started and looked towards the womanfish. She smiled at them, their embarrassment apparently amusing her. "I am Nirveli."

The *Embolon* was floating above the spreading white cloudscape. The Sun on the azure sky was piercingly bright, making Katka blink. The clouds below them veiled the ocean. Mingan was observing the sky above the clouds with his telescope, looking for a reconnaissance corvette, ready to order the ship to dive into the clouds at any moment. The helmsman held the course. Two more spotters on the bridge were watching the sky. The machine gunners stood tensely behind their multi-barrelled weapons.

"Nothing in sight," one of them reported. Mingan looked at him and nodded. The Armada was close, he had told Katka the evening before. He had well-informed spies, Katka was certain. He knew when the Armada had departed, which course they had taken, where they would be and when. And now, he was patrolling the sky above the clouds, waiting for them.

"Lower Branduff!" Mingan commanded.

"Aye, aye!" was heard from behind. Katka watched as three men took to their stations in a hurry. One of them—Branduff—buttoned his jacket up to his chin, and then he put on his leather aeronaut's helmet and gloves. Goggles protected his eyes. The other two were preparing the car; it resembled a small airship, painted pale grey (harder to spot, Katka realised), some twelve feet long, with a single seat behind a small windshield. Branduff sat in the car, strapped himself in, and gave them a thumbs up. The other sailor pulled a lever and the floor below the car opened. He pulled the second lever and the car slid from its cradle, suspended on a steel cable. The sailors took to the winch. They lowered the car slowly through the floor and beneath the airship, into the clouds. Little fins on its end stabilised it in the slipstream; it followed the *Embolon*, hanging beneath her.

The car disappeared in the clouds. Katka glanced at the chronometer. Some twenty minutes passed before the clicking of a telegraph register was heard. The car was connected to the bridge by a telegraph wire. That way, a spotter could report what he saw while the *Embolon* remained safely above the clouds. Mingan tore a piece of paper tape, read what Branduff had signalled, and commanded the sailors to stop lowering the car. He typed something back and received an almost immediate reply.

"Now, we wait," he said as he caressed his grey goatee.

"If that scoundrel thinks he will force an abducted womanfish to do as he pleases, he's very wrong," Nirveli hissed with anger as she stirred restlessly in her cramped box. Water splashed through the grate and spilled onto the floor planks. "As soon as he releases me back into the sea…"

Rashelka looked at the blue sky through the porthole. They sailed above clouds that spread as far as the eye could see. The shadow of the *Embolon* swept across the whiteness below. *What is Mother doing?* she wondered. Mingan had burst in and taken Katka without a word. Hours must have passed, and she still had not returned.

"And if your mother is as powerful as you say," Nirveli went on, "how come you haven't freed yourselves already?"

"But how?" Rashelka replied, desperation in her voice. "If she destroys the airship, she'd kill us too!" The girl sat gloomily next to the box. The days on the airship seemed like an eternity spent waiting, locked in the confined cabin with a mysterious sea creature.

At least I'm not caged, she thought.

"I think… I think Mingan is using me to make Mother obedient."

Nirveli studied Rashelka carefully, thinking it over, then nodded. She pushed back a lock of hair from her face angrily. Rashelka looked back at her. Mingan certainly did not kidnap a womanfish without knowing how to deal with her. "I'm afraid he'll find a way to make you do whatever he says too."

The late afternoon Sun painted the clouds gold. Hours had passed before the telegraph jumped to life again; the register started printing dots and dashes on the paper tape. Mingan pulled it, reading as the code was revealed, his lips moving mutely. Behind him, his crew stared intently. Then the message came to its end, and Mingan tore the tape off and raised it triumphantly.

"The Golden Armada, lads! It's here!" he shouted. "Three treasure ships!"

"As many as three?"

"Three, I tell you! So says Branduff, and he has the eye of a falcon! The *Santissima Madre*, the *Algeciras*, and the *San Juan Nepomuceno*. And the escort is spread five miles long and three miles wide."

"The *San Juan Nepomuceno*… That's a lot of cannons," a machine gunner said.

"And a lot of treasure!" Mingan replied, grinning, a gleam to his leaden eyes, as if he was about to snarl. He looked at them all, cheering them on with his stare, beckoning them to follow.

Katka watched the gold-madness spreading among them, passing from one to another like plague. She watched the glitter of gold and silver and gems clouding their minds. *If they were not like that*, she knew, *they would not be what they were.* And then her eyes met Mingan's. She was the source of his confidence, the key to the bloody riches in the three large airships. She was his secret weapon.

"The usual battle formation?" Wayne asked, as if he wanted to scatter the spell possessing the pirates. Wayne was Mingan's second-in-command, the pirate captain's most trusted man. He was the man who had wanted to burn her house down.

"By the book." Mingan nodded and looked at Katka. "Box formation, fifteen hundred feet high, with three corvette finger-fours as vanguard." Mingan studied the chart pinned on the wall and read the tape once again. He was nodding. "Just what our informer told us. Devil take him, that greedy swine was worth every doubloon he squeezed out of me. They're cutting across the sea toward the Grenadines." Mingan tapped the chart with his finger.

"Course oh-five-seven," he ordered the helmsman, and the helmsman obeyed and turned the steering wheel. The nose of the airship headed starboard, the whole ship speeding ahead as if she herself was lusting for blood and treasure.

"Support?" somebody from the crew asked.

"Nobody to come to their aid anymore," Mingan answered. "Habana is far away. The Santo Domingo and Maracaibo detachments will be grounded by the hurricane. And we'll jump them above the Grenadines; there are reefs and lagoons there. Shallows." Mingan looked at Katka. She shivered before the bloodthirsty gleam in his eyes. "That's where you come in, woman. That's where I need your wind."

"What if the English cut in? They're near," Wayne asked.

"Ha!" Mingan grinned. "The English protect the Spaniards? We only have to be quick lest *they* rob them first!"

Suddenly another message came in. Mingan and Wayne looked at each other. Mingan read the tape, his lips tight. He frowned.

"What's the matter?" Wayne asked.

"Funny," Mingan muttered. "Another airship. Out of formation, appearing briefly below the clouds, three miles behind. And she entered the clouds right away, too fast for Branduff to see the type."

"Perhaps a ship from Paramaribo," Wayne suggested, "although she's too far west. Who can it be?"

"She's not Dutch, you can bet on that," Mingan murmured, watching the sky above the clouds through the window. Then he shrugged and faced Wayne. "Maybe she's just passing by. We stick to the plan and shadow the Armada."

"The Joy-of-Sea?" Rashelka asked, whispering. Her face was next to Nirveli's, separated by the grate.

"A pearl," Nirveli whispered. She did not dare speak louder. In the evening, Mingan had burst into their cabin, cursing, pushed Rashelka out into the passageway, and locked the door behind her. Rashelka had heard him talking to the womanfish in a quiet voice, nearly a whisper, so she could not discern the words. He had exited after a quarter of an hour or so, grabbed the girl by her hand and thrown her back into the cabin. The womanfish had been quiet, clinging to the grate, lost in her thoughts. She had not uttered a word throughout the evening. Only after the pirates had brought them supper—a bowl of porridge for Rashelka, three mackerels for Nirveli—and left them alone, and when Rashelka had made certain that the *Embolon* had settled into its night watch routine, had she dared to ask the womanfish what Mingan had said to her.

"The greatest pearl human eyes have ever seen." Nirveli showed her clenched fist, indicating the size. Only their breathing and the monotonous sounds of the steam engine driving them across the sky could be heard in their cabin. "The Spaniards looted it from our Queen seventy summers ago. In the waters of the island you know as Jolo."

"I don't know where that is."

"The Pilipinas," Nirveli hissed.

"But that's the other side of the world!" Rashelka objected. "Another ocean!"

"Another ocean to you, perhaps. The one and the same ocean to us," Nirveli replied. "They stole two pearls from us. And they killed many of my sisters. The Tear-of-Sea was lost in the abyss of the trench ploughed next to the Pilipinas. No one can reach it now. Maybe for the better, it was an evil pearl. We thought the Joy was also lost for good. We spent years searching for it. But it found its way here. If Mingan is to be believed, the Spaniards were hiding it in a vault in the city you call Lima. And now, they're taking it across the ocean."

And then Nirveli grabbed Rashelka by the collar of her shirt. The girl felt the hot womanfish's breath as she whispered in her ear, "I must return the Joy-of-Sea, you hear? I must return it to our Queen! I must bow to Mingan. The Joy-of-Sea is the pay he promised me."

"And you trust him?" Rashelka tore herself away from the womanfish's hand angrily.

Nirveli's eyes shone with deadly glitter. She nodded and grinned. "It doesn't matter. What matters is whether Mingan trusts me. So, I'll be obedient to him—until the pearl is in my hands."

Katka dreamed of the Tower. The octagonal tower; they had left it behind, across the ocean, in hot Athens. The Tower of the Winds with eight wind deities sculpted in stone. The north wind god Boreas; the north-easterly Kaikias; Apeliotes blowing from the east; the south-eastern Euros; the south wind god Notos; the south-western Lips; the westerly Zephyrus; and the north-western Skiron. The winds of the ancient Mediterranean sailors, turned to stone a long time ago by somebody's chisel.

The eight winds did Katka dream of, and herself at the top of the Tower of the Winds, the mistress summoning them and selling them. And she dreamed—sweaty and struggling for air in the stifled cabin—of Mingan, the wolf. He was laughing, even as he was whipped by the eight winds. He defied them and laughed, madness in his eyes, a knife against Rashelka's throat. The shiny blade rested above her jugular vein. It would take but the slightest movement to make blood gush forth, to cast her bleeding body lifelessly before his boots. Katka did not doubt his threats for a moment.

The airship was carrying Katka across the ocean and the winds of the New World blew through her now. She felt them in her dream, throbbing through her body and coursing through her hands, tempting her to try them. The *knik* and the *matanuska* and the *taku*, winds of the Alaskan winter. The fierce *squamish* raging in the fjords of the British Columbia. The strong sharp barber, carrying freezing sleet across the sea of ice. The nor'easter storming off the coast of New England. The warm dry *chinook* descending the slopes of the Rockies. The savage tornado ravaging the prairies. The strong, hot Californian *diablo*, the Santa Ana, and the sundowner.

She felt the violent summer *chubasco* thundering along the west coast of Central America, and the *coromell* blowing from the sea in the Golfo de California. The hurricane-strength *cordonazo*, the Lash of St. Francis, whipping the west coast of Mejico. The dry cold *norte*, and the furious *papagayo* and *tehuantepecer*.

The *bayamo*, roaring along the southern shores of Cuba, bringing rain. The Puerto Rican *brisa* and the Cuban *brisote*, and the squally *brubu*. The trade winds, swelling the sails of the conquistadors. And the hurricane itself, the unbridled beast born along the shores of the Dark Continent and spiralling and travelling—driven by the trade winds—across the ocean to unleash its wrath over the coasts of the Americas.

On the beaches of Brasilia, the *abroholos*, a summer squall. Far south, past the mighty Rio de las Amazonas and vast rainforests, all the way to the grasslands and snow-capped peaks of the Cordillera, and the shores on which millions of birds call and thousands of seals wallow; the cold, showering, stormy *pampero*; the hot, dusty, stifling *zonda*; the wintry *suestado* bringing agitated seas and rains, sometimes even snow; the strong, dry *terral*, the *puelche*, and the *virazon*. And—on the very southern tip of the Americas, in the Estrecho de Magallanes—the sudden *williwaw*.

And Katka longed for the winds of her Adriatic Sea, the sea she had come to with her late parents from the hilly Bohemia when she was three years old. She had taken it for her own, and its winds had embraced her in return. The early morning *bonaca*—the calm—when the sea was as smooth as oil, a bass leaping from it with a loud splash. The *bava*, just a breeze blowing gently above the water. The *maestral*, blowing away sweat from the forehead on a sultry day. Katka loved the *maestral*, raising and going to bed with her. She also loved the *levant*, the short-breathed east wind, bringing sudden snow, and the *ponent*, the west wind crisscrossing the sea. Katka enjoyed the southern *jugo* too, driving the dark clouds and making waves, smashing them against the rocky coast, making foaming water surge and then pour down the cliffs. The *lebich* and *tramontana* were her friends, too, all the small boats seeking safe haven before them. And the *bura*! Cold mountain breath, carrying the sea dust in gusts, that would not let you walk, howling in pines, bending cypresses, whipping olive trees. And Katka standing firm, embraced by the *bura*—just a breeze to her—and laughing as the *bura* whistled in her hair.

Katka dreamt of the winds of the ancient sailors. She listened to the winds of strange names. She longed for the winds of the sea she grew up by.

And in her dream, the hurricane was howling ever louder. The beast was being born. It would not fall back, no matter how much Katka hushed it down. It claimed and demanded, spoilt, hungry, bloodthirsty. It made Katka put a leash on it to sell it to an equally hungry monster, laughing above the body of her Rashelka.

The sea had gone wild, crisscrossed by the roaring winds. Through the tattered clouds two thousand feet below, waves dozens of feet tall were smashing into each other. From the gondola, it looked to Rashelka like snow-capped mountains were colliding. The blue was laced with foam, the artwork of an insane lacemaker. Rashelka craned her head up, the wall of clouds whirled miles high, an amphitheatre surrounding the eye of the storm. And in the centre of the hurricane, the *Embolon*. She sailed in peace amidst chaos, sunlit, driven by her steam engine; Katka was the source of the storm that was roaring and trampling, tearing and devouring everything in its path.

Katka stood in the middle of the bridge, her eyes closed, her hands hanging limp by her sides. Her mouth moved silently, as if she was speaking to the hurricane without voice, just by thoughts. The gathered pirates, pale, watched her with horror in their eyes, in reverent silence. It was only then—surrounded by the wall of clouds, angry sea beneath them—that they realised the full awesomeness of Katka's power. The helmsman clutched the wheel, afraid the airship would escape his grip and be swallowed by the clouds. Wayne, ordered by Mingan to keep Rashelka at gunpoint, lowered his pepperbox revolver. He was saying his rosary, praying for absolution after making a pact with the Devil herself. Only Mingan was grinning, his leaden stare full of madness, exhilarated by the hurricane surrounding them. When the storm passed, he knew, there would be nothing left of the Golden Armada.

Rashelka knelt, her eyes darting from her mother to the storm outside and back. She knew the way Katka summoned the wind. She used to call it when they were left becalmed on the sea, their sail limp, or to drive away the scorching heat, or when clothes left hanging needed to dry faster. But those were all breezes, old friends always ready to help. Now, before them, Katka was taming a monster, controlling it, telling it whom to pound to pieces and whom to merely whip.

"Look!" Wayne shouted suddenly, pointing up in horror. Rashelka looked. A frigate hit the western wall of the storm. The wind tossed her some five hundred feet down, like a toy, then hurled her up, at which point her wooden structure could not take the forces anymore, and the airship disintegrated. The hydrogen exploded, and all aboard the *Embolon* were lit by the fiery blaze. Another explosion flashed through the clouds, the monster swallowing another ship.

"That's the way, woman!" Mingan bellowed, leaning above the chart, his face sweaty. He seemed to be following the hurricane's path, where Katka drove it. "Bring them down! Wipe them out, but watch the treasure ships! Careful where they fall!" Katka apparently did not hear him, lost in a trance, bewitched by the roar of the hurricane, the child she had raised—out of the Sun, to warm it up; out of the sea, to wet it; out of the wind, to drive it; out of the Earth, to spin it. Miles away, by the wall, another airship went down in flames. "That's the way, woman! Do it! Sell me the wind!"

They spotted the dirigibles through the clouds. Mingan commanded the car should be retrieved. Branduff was pulled out of it, taking off his gloves, goggles, and helmet as he moved. The machine gunners watched the sky around the *Embolon* tensely, lest somebody jump them. The barrels gleamed in the sun. Katka and Rashelka spotted the airships, too.

"There's the *Santissima Madre*," Mingan declared, watching through his telescope. Perhaps the Spaniards might have seen them, but Mingan did not care anymore. Their escort was scattered and destroyed, the treasure ships were left on their own. Undefended, but not harmless. "And the *San Juan*. The *Algeciras* is... She's damaged. She's down!"

Katka and Rashelka looked through the pane. The ships were resting in a bay like three silvery whales. One was maybe fifty feet above the water, above the coral reef protecting the turquoise lagoon. The other one was above the shallows, close to the shore. And the third one, the *Algeciras*, was lying beached with her nose buried in a narrow white curve of sand separating the sea from the hills which were covered in unspoiled jungle.

"They weathered well," Wayne noticed. "Two can still fly."

"Don't be afraid, they're not going anywhere," Mingan said dismissively, folding his telescope and leaning above the chart. He took another one and spread it out. He studied it for several moments, his eyes skimming across the marked elevations. "Not until they transfer the treasure and men from the *Algeciras*." He called Wayne over to the chart. Without a word, he made a circle across it, going from the lagoon all the way around the island. Wayne looked at the chart; a single glance at the island beneath the clouds was enough for him to understand. He grinned and nodded.

"They don't see us," Rashelka whispered so no pirate could hear her.

"I'm afraid they're not even looking," Katka replied gloomily. She was exhausted, drained, drenched in sweat.

Wayne pushed the helmsman away and took over at the wheel. He steered the *Embolon* starboard, signalling full ahead to the engine room. The bridge shook as the engine sprang to life and the airship, still hidden by the tearing clouds, sped forward, following a wide curve around the island, keeping out of sight of the Spaniards.

"Won't he attack?" Rashelka asked quietly, tension in her voice.

"I think I know what he's up to," Katka murmured. "It's too dangerous to attack from the sea. He'd be headlong against their cannons."

"Gunners to battle stations!" Mingan roared. Just what the crew had been waiting for. The lids slid aside noisily. The coordinated gunners grabbed their *bombardellas*, three at each side, and swivelled their barrels out. They were taking the already prepared charges from storage and starting to load the *bombardellas*. Everybody was working in silence, without the need for further command. In less than a minute, all the gunners pointed their thumbs up. The *Embolon* was ready for battle.

Followed by the tense stares of the pirates, Wayne steered the airship around the island. The Spaniards were behind their tail now. Their airships remained motionless; they were still unaware of the presence of the *Embolon*.

"Altitude three hundred," Mingan ordered, and Wayne swivelled the propellers and vented some gas. The *Embolon* sank, and then she levelled and continued above the sea. At Mingan's signal, Wayne pointed the airship to the island, signalling half ahead at the same time. The airship slowed. It was only then that Rashelka understood Mingan's plan.

The tallest peaks of the island were above the *Embolon*. Rashelka trembled, the jungle-covered hills were approaching. Katka held her hand. On the chart, the island resembled an arm bent at the elbow under a right angle, the forearm pointing west. The bay sheltering the Golden Armada airships was on the shoulder, open to the north.

The *Embolon* flew over the southern outer reef, the huge shadow sweeping across the lagoon and the white beach. They flew over the narrow "forearm" and found themselves above the turquoise lagoon made by the crook of the "arm." And then Wayne turned starboard a little and the ship, more manoeuvrable than she looked, slipped through a valley between two hills. The treetops were speeding right beneath the gondola. Rashelka spotted a flock of green parrots flying from one tree to another, startled by the monster sweeping above them, bringing infernal fire into paradise.

"Hoist the Jolly Roger!" Mingan yelled.

"Aye, aye, Sir!" Wayne replied with joy. He released a lever, and the black skull-and-crossbones pirate flag unfurled to drive fear into the bones of the Spaniards who had barely survived the hurricane and did not suspect an even greater danger loomed ahead.

Wayne followed the contours of the hills skilfully, all the time keeping the *Embolon* hidden behind the forest green. It took great skill to steer clear of the trees, Katka realised. But the *Embolon* was readily obeying Wayne's will and every flick of his hands on the wheel.

Then the hill was no more, falling all the way to the beach, and the lagoon emerged ahead of them. Wayne ordered full speed ahead and the *Embolon* leapt like a cat towards a mouse. They flew over the helpless *Algeciras*. People who'd disembarked onto the beach looked up in confusion, pointing with their hands, scurrying about. Some even waved, thinking help had arrived. Then they saw the flag. Several sailors and passengers ran for the forest, officers yelling after them. Mingan ignored them all. He would deal with them at the end. The *Algeciras* cannons were harmless; he was in their blind angle. The machine gun posts on the *Algeciras* top were unmanned. The Spaniards did not expect this raid.

"Between them!" Mingan barked as he stormed among his gunners. Wayne skilfully manoeuvred the *Embolon* straight between the *Santissima Madre* and *San Juan Nepomuceno*.

"He's mad! He's heading straight in front of their cannons!" Rashelka screamed. She already saw the pirate airship caught between the two Spanish dirigibles, the muzzles of their cannons spewing death, shots to tear them apart in flames —

"No!" Katka grabbed her arm, pulled her back, and pointed. "Look!" And Rashelka understood. Mingan's surprise attack had succeeded fully. He'd jumped the Spaniards unprepared, exhausted by the storm and their attempts to stay together. Without their escort, which had been driven away by the hurricane, they enjoyed some safety by protecting each other with cannons and machine guns. But Mingan tore into them like a wolf into sheep: quickly, suddenly, screaming for blood.

The first luxuriously embellished lids on the silvery Spanish treasure ships rose, the muzzles of the *colubrinas* appearing from behind gilt carvings and painted wooden figures. But the *Embolon* was already between them, spreading even more confusion. Because, Rashelka realised, the Spanish gunners could have easily missed the swift pirate dirigible, and then they would destroy each other. She spotted the gunners taking their positions on the top and mounting their machine guns, hurriedly removing covers from them. Too slow! And the *Embolon* was too low for them. Meanwhile, Mingan's gunners were already taking aim: one side at the *Santissima*, the other at the *San Juan*.

"Give'em Hell!" Mingan roared merrily, and their *bombardellas* fired in unison. Not waiting to see the results, the gunners reloaded and fired again. And again. Deafening thunder made Katka and Rashelka press their hands against their ears. The shots hit their mark. Explosions tore the gondolas into a deadly shower of split decorations and planks, broken glass and splinters. Steam burst out of the *Santissima*'s pierced boiler and ducts, scalding everything in its path. Ballast water spilled, and the *Santissima* started to rise. Somebody fell out of the gondola and plunged in the sea. Several more Spaniards jumped; they had greater chances of surviving the fall into the sea than remaining in the gondola being shredded to pieces by Mingan's *bombardellas*.

And then, a thundering detonation shook the *Embolon*. Katka and Rashelka looked behind them. A chain of explosions was ripping through the *San Juan Nepomuceno*, spreading from one hydrogen cell to the next. Fire was devouring the proud airship, and soon, she was nothing but a burning wooden framework disintegrating in the sea.

Cheers broke among Mingan's crew. Katka felt sick. Her ears covered by her hands, through tearful eyes, Rashelka had witnessed the death of the Golden Armada. A new salvo tore the rear part of the *Santissima*'s gondola away from the hull. It fell into the sea. More men jumped from the airship. Rashelka saw a woman, her skirt flapping around her as she was falling. And another woman. Down in the foaming sea, the survivors tried to swim as far as possible, lest they be buried by the doomed airship.

"Move over!" Mingan yelled, pushing a machine-gunner away. He grabbed the weapon, pointed it down, and turned the crank. The machine gun rattle broke through the cannonade; the barrels turned and spewed a lethal hail on the survivors.

He'll kill them all, Katka realised. *Nobody will survive, he'll kill them all.* It was no battle. It was a slaughter. Cries called towards Heaven, spread arms begged for mercy, but Mingan showered them with bullets, laughing with madness. The sea was coloured with blood, bodies were floating on the surface.

Somebody pushed a piece of white cloth through a window of what was left of the *Santissima's* gondola. Mingan spat and bellowed, "Finish them!" Another volley from his *bombardellas* showered the *Santissima*, and then she too erupted in a conflagration that towered half a mile high. The once glorious treasure ships, the pride of the Golden Armada, were now burning skeletons—like bones of dead leviathans.

"Excellent! Now for the *Algeciras*!"

Wayne turned the *Embolon* towards the last airship. They flew through the smoke of the burning *San Juan*, leaving a grey whirl behind. Several frigate birds flew left of them, agitated by the slaughter above the lagoon. And just like the predatory frigate birds flanking her, the *Embolon* pounced on the *Algeciras*.

There was almost no one left on the beach. Katka saw only several sailors, commanded by a young officer, mounting a machine gun on a tripod while another sailor fetched an ammunition box from the stranded dirigible. And there was a young woman at the edge of the forest, calling. The officer gestured for her to run into the forest, but she would not. *An officer's wife?* Katka wondered. *Why else would she stay?* And then, a machine gun rattle was heard. Katka screamed and threw herself over Rashelka. Glass shattering. Bullets drumming inside the bridge. Wayne cursing and turning the airship. The machine gun was firing from a rear defence machine gun post below the *Algeciras's* top rudder.

The bullets riddled the *Embolon's* gondola. Somebody screamed as they were hit. Mingan barked a command, and the starboard *bombardellas* fired at the *Algeciras*. The next moment, the ship was devoured by explosions and fire, tail to nose. Katka looked up. The burning wooden framework collapsed to the beach and the shallows, burying everyone beneath it. Only the woman remained, screaming at the edge of the forest.

"That's about the end of you!" Mingan spat. He aimed the machine gun at her.

"No!" Katka screamed and leaped, but too late. Mingan turned the crank; the machine gun rattled and mowed the woman down. Katka held back her scream. The woman collapsed to the sand, under the trees, in the shade, and was still.

"There. Done," Mingan muttered through his teeth. He pushed Katka off him, without even looking at her. "Damage?"

"Nothing of importance here," Wayne replied. He called back the helmsman who took the *Embolon* safely away from the wreck of the *Algeciras*.

"Roy was hit," somebody reported from behind.

"Just a scratch, Boss."

Mingan nodded. He was watching the burnt skeletons of the Golden Armada, the bodies floating in the sea and the smoke above the lagoon with satisfaction. "That's the way you do it," he murmured to himself, grinning.

And then he faced his crew. "Now for the treasure, lads!" A triumphant roar bellowed through the *Embolon*. "Get the womanfish!"

Nirveli splashed from the boat into the sea.

She dove deeply into the turquoise blue of the lagoon, carried by exhilaration, her body washed by the sea after days spent in the stagnant water of her glass cage. All Rashelka's efforts in changing the water had made her captivity only a bit more bearable. Still, she felt gratitude to the girl and her mother. They were just like her, prisoners.

And without them, she thought, *I would have lost my mind.*

Nirveli stretched, flicked her tail, rushed playfully down to the sandy bottom. She turned around, stirring the sand with her tail. The *Embolon* and the boat were above her. She escaped their dark shapes and swam along the bottom, flicking her tail and pushing herself through the water with her hands. Then she stopped abruptly and remained still to let a shark pass. The cold eye measured her, the jaws filled with sharp teeth opened and closed menacingly, and then the big fish swam on, attracted by the commotion some hundred feet away where other sharks were going frantic over a body. They twisted around it, biting chunks off and devouring them. Small fish around them darted in for the remains. Nothing is wasted in the sea. There were more sharks around. Nirveli did not fear them. The womenfish were wary only of the biggest ones.

Before her, several spotted eagle rays glided peacefully above the sand, as if flying.

Nirveli looked toward the surface. Mingan's men rowed after her. The *Embolon* was following them. She surfaced, waved to them, inhaled, and dove back. She sped towards the *San Juan*'s frame. It rested on the sandy bottom, collapsed, its polygonal ring-like transverse frames joined by longitudinal girders. Nirveli knew the first severe storm would smash the skeleton completely. Whatever remained would be covered by sand; soon, there would be nothing left to indicate a Golden Armada airship had met its end here.

Nirveli slipped in between the girders amidships. She felt tiny within the collapsed structure. She was swimming above the crushed and dismembered gondola stretching beneath the airship.

This must be the front engine room, she thought. A boiler. A steam engine, cylinders, tubes. A condenser. Transmission chains torn loose. A propeller was resting in the sand, one blade broken.

She looked back. Facing the tail, she saw *colubrina* barrels under the girders, the main battery, which never had the chance to fire a single shot. Mingan had directed her to head for the nose. A flick of her tail and she sped ahead. She saw a burned body pinned beneath a girder. Another one lay a bit further on. The passenger cabins had been torn into pieces; she saw smashed berths, gilt wooden statues of womenfish and tritons holding lamps, broken off and snapped and burnt. A girl's body was suspended among them, swayed by the currents. Nirveli swam through the watery tomb, making her way carefully through the remains of the gondola. Officers' cabins. The captain's cabin. And then she came upon what she was looking for.

Three fire-resistant chests sat under girders, planks, and carvings. Nirveli swam towards them. She looked carefully, checking that everything appeared more or less firm, and then she squeezed herself under the girders. The chests were intact, singed by fire, but Mingan claimed the contents were completely safe. Each was secured with three locks which required codes to release the bolts. Mingan had explained all that carefully to her. No lock could stand against his nitro-glycerine, he had said—whatever nitro-glycerine was...

Nirveli's heart trembled. The Joy-of-Sea was in one of these chests. Her pay for all that death around her. For a moment, she felt dejected. But then Nirveli dismissed the guilt; death was a part of life in the sea. And, after all, what did humans mean to her? And their ships, those on the sea and those in the air—what did they mean to her and her sisters? Nets, dolphin harpoons, clubs, barbs, hooks... Menace, danger, death. That was what humans meant to womenfish. The more they killed each other, the better.

Using such thoughts to drive away the horror of all those bodies, Nirveli wriggled quickly from beneath the girders and swam up. She surfaced right before the boat's bow. She inhaled and yelled to the men in the boat, "Three chests!"

The pirates rejoiced. One even patted her shoulder. Mingan waved to her from the *Embolon* bridge and ordered the ship closer. Nirveli took the steel rope she would tie around the first chest so that Mingan and his men could recover it by a winch.

On the beach, three small simultaneous explosions tore the locks open. Mingan waved away the smoke and raised the heavy lid of the chest. Gold flashed before the pirate's eyes; he was enchanted by the fiery yellow glitter of the coins. His face sweaty, a greedy gleam in his eyes, Mingan took a handful of doubloons. He let them spill through his fingers, enjoying the coolness and tinkling of metal. Then he grabbed a heavy gold chain, raised it for everybody to see and threw it back. He turned over the golden chalices and reliquaries and crucifixes adorned in emeralds, heliodors and fire opals. Finally, he opened a small compartment within the chest and took a cloth purse out of it. Under the tense stares of the pirates, he spilled diamonds into his fist. Nobody uttered a word.

Katka and Rashelka seemed enchanted too, until Katka shook herself, tugged at her daughter's sleeve and they looked at each other. Understanding passed between them; the treasures in the chests were not meant for Rashelka and Katka. There was too much blood and evil on them: evil from when they were stolen from land by slavery, blood from when they were looted from the Golden Armada by slaughter. There was no way that the treasures in the chests, fouled by evil, dipped in blood, could be touched by Katka and Rashelka, for they had lived honestly on the stone, by means of fish traps and nets and hoe; taking their living from poor soil bordered by dry stone walls, scorched by the Sun, whipped by the wind, and salted by the sea. The land that was their home.

A strange silence settled over the beach. All the chests were opened, all the treasures in them laid before Mingan and his pirates. But nobody dared touch them. It looked as if the first one reaching for the doubloons and chains and chalices would cause the rapine, grabbing, and slaughter to begin. Mingan saw the tension among his men. He knew them well, but there was no time to stand there, bewitched. They should run. Mingan opened his mouth to give a command, to have the treasure loaded on *Embolon* and—

"Pay me what's ours, Mingan," a rustling voice said, cutting through the silence. Nirveli was propped on her arms, her tail impatiently foaming the sea washing the beach. "Give us back the Joy-of-Sea!"

Mingan looked at the womanfish. From one of the chests recovered from the *San Juan Nepomuceno* he took out a pearl, as large as a fist and with pink overtones, and he raised it with his left hand for all to see. It was almost painful to watch it in the Sun.

"Is this what you want, womanfish?" Mingan shouted to her.

"Yes!" Nirveli replied. "The Joy-of-Sea! That's what you promised me!"

"Indeed?" Mingan grinned, his brow raised; he smirked at his men, as if it was all a good joke. He lowered his right hand within reach of his revolver and approached Nirveli in a casual manner. "Maybe I did... Maybe I didn't... And maybe I don't care!"

He looked at his pirates. They all burst into laughter. Mingan drew the revolver from his sash.

"No!" Rashelka screamed and leaped after him. She grabbed Mingan by his hand and spun him round. His face contorted in fury; he whipped her with the stare of a beast and swung his gun at her. The barrel cut Rashelka's scalp, blood gushed down her brow. Stunned, the girl collapsed to the sand.

"All three of you forgot," Mingan bellowed, his eyes skimming over Rashelka, Katka, and the womanfish, "that I don't need you anymore!"

"And you forgot," Katka replied in a quiet, icy voice, "we're not on your ship anymore."

Wind coursed through Katka's body and surged into her fingers like a tide. Her anger boosted the wind from a breeze into a *bura*, and she lifted her hands and dropped a strong gust on Mingan. The squall felled the pirate. Katka spun around; the wind was howling around her, roaring, knocking the pirates down. She whirled them like twigs, breaking them like rotten trees.

Mingan cursed. He tried to rise, but Rashelka pounced on him. He kicked her into the water. He leaped forward to strike her, but Nirveli brought him down. Mingan raised his gun. Rashelka pushed his hand up and the revolver fired into nothing. Nirveli grabbed Mingan by his throat, attempting to strangle him. He forced her away with his knee against her chest and kicked her in the head. The womanfish fell back into the waves and disappeared beneath the surface.

Unaware of anything except the *bura* in her hands, Katka scattered the pirates, lifting them in the air. The wind carried them, throwing them everywhere. They screamed and yelled for help, cursed and swore, victims of an unbridled wrath, but she did not hear their cries anymore. After several gusts, the beach had been swept clean of Mingan's gang.

The stutter of machine gun fire came from the *Embolon*. Bullets buzzed around Katka. She raised her hands and cast a gust against the airship. The strength of the wind tore the *Embolon* from her anchor, carried her across the lagoon, and then a new gust whirled her around and ripped the gondola away, steam hissing out of the boiler. Something burst into flames, and the next moment, the triumphant airship was a torch plunging into the lagoon.

A revolver thundered on the beach. An instant later, peace settled over the lagoon. Katka collapsed to the sand. Pain in her chest. Darkness. She shifted her head, found everything was blurred before her eyes. She tried to focus as she felt the power draining out of her hands, slipping through her fingers just like the doubloons from Mingan's fist.

No! she cried inside, trying hard to keep her consciousness and summon her power back.

"Oh yes, woman, you're really something. I knew I wouldn't be bored with you." Mingan stood above Katka, the barrel of the gun pointing at her. He was just a blurred shape to her, a grinning monster, a shadow of imminent death. "Do you think you did me any harm? The *Embolon* was junk anyway. And the crew?" Mingan burst into laughter. "I won't have to share the treasure with anybody now! It's all mine now! Mine alone! Do you hear me, you damned creature?"

Somebody screamed; the cry pierced the darkness that Katka was sinking into. Rashelka! The thought of her daughter left alone with this monster drove Katka to seek out her final shreds of strength. She strained and felt the wind rising anew in her, coursing and getting stronger, drawing out the last breath from her body. She knew that with one more gust of the *bura*, the life would blow out of her too.

"Let's finish it," Mingan growled, lifting his revolver and aiming it at Katka's head. Rashelka screamed and ran out of the waves, bloodied, tears running down her cheeks. She was running at Mingan, swearing and cursing his dog seed.

"Oh, you are a pain!" Mingan muttered as he turned and aimed at Rashelka. Just a little squeeze of the forefinger and—

A shot was fired. A bullet hit Mingan in the head; he flew several feet back onto the sand, leaving behind a trail of bloody drops. Rashelka sank down next to her mother, covering her body with her own. But there was no more shooting.

Who fired? Rashelka wondered. Perhaps it was the Spaniards from the *Algeciras* that had escaped into the forest.

And then an airship descended from above the hill onto the beach. She was flying a yellow-blue-red flag, but Rashelka did not recognise the colours. The unknown ship approached them, and below her, armed men stepped out of the forest. Rashelka counted a dozen of them. They were armed with rifles, *pistolas* and revolvers, and swords and scimitars, with machetes at their belts. Most were dressed in trousers made of coarse, pale fabric and open shirts with sleeves rolled up; their heads were bound in bandannas or covered by broad straw hats. One was wearing a red stocking cap.

They were led by a bearded man with curly hair. He held a repeating rifle, ready to shoot. Rashelka realised these were not regular troops. *Another pirate gang?* she wondered with trepidation. But the men passed by the chests, only a few looking at the gold in them; bandits would not act in such a way. Rashelka looked at the airship once again and decided that perhaps she could have been the very same one seen by Branduff when he first spotted the Golden Armada, the same mysterious airship that had quickly hidden in the clouds.

A tall, strong, dark-skinned youth approached Katka and Rashelka cautiously. He, too, had a rifle and a *pistola* at his belt. He could not have been much older than Rashelka, but all the same, she was a little bit afraid of him. She had heard sailors talk about the black men on the shores of Africa and the New World, but she had never seen one before. As soon as he saw the bloody stain spreading across Katka's dress, he yelled, "Ernesto!"

One of the fighters replied. The youth pointed at the wounded Katka, and Ernesto ran to them. Something in his melancholic gaze touched Rashelka's heart. *That man has known sorrow and misery*, she thought. *He cannot be bad.* She let him examine Katka.

The commander joined them; the youth and Ernesto addressed him as *Comandante*.

"You are her daughter?" the *Comandante* asked. Rashelka nodded. "Come, this is not a job for us." He led her aside. "You need your wound cleaned too. Don't be afraid, *companera*, Ernesto once studied to be a doctor. And if you ask me, I've seen fighters live through worse."

Rashelka was watching the sea and the sky, both burning with sunset. The frigate birds were black shapes with pointed wings against the red sky as they returned to their night roosts. The *Granma*, the airship of the *bolivaristas*, rested above the beach, secured with ropes. Peace had returned to the lagoon; only the remains of the four airships and the crosses on the freshly dug graves testified to the slaughter that took place three days ago.

The *bolivaristas* had erected a camp at the edge of the forest. Campfires illuminated the men as they cleaned their rifles and ate, preparing themselves for rest. In the distance, sentries patrolled the beach; the *Comandante* left nothing to chance. The treasure had already been transferred to the *Granma*, locked away and guarded with machine guns. It had been stolen from the people, and now would be returned to the people, Ernesto had said when they had been loading the last chest. When Rashelka had asked about the escaped Spaniards from the *Algeciras*, the *Comandante* had shrugged and commented that some fishermen would likely pick them up.

"*Hola, companera!*" Rashelka turned. The youth, Camilo, was standing behind her and wore a smile which reached his big eyes. They looked even bigger when his dark face was lit by the flame of the sunset. She was not afraid of him anymore. He had helped Ernesto dress Katka's wound skilfully—the bullet had barely missed her lungs—and they had carried her from the beach into the shadows of the trees. They had made her a place to rest, and Camilo had shown Rashelka how to make a roof out of palm fronds.

"The *Comandante* told me to hand you this," he said as he stepped forward now.

He was carrying a bundle the size of a fist. He unwrapped it to reveal the Joy-of-Sea; the large pearl looked like a glowing hot sphere in the sunset. Rashelka had been afraid the *bolivaristas* would not give the pearl up, but the *Comandante* and Ernesto had felt they owed the womenfish the treasure they had laid their hands on. Besides, as the *Comandante* had pointed out, a pearl like that was not easy to sell.

"*Gracias.*" Rashelka took the Joy-of-Sea. She rolled the pearl between her fingers for a moment, and then she tightened her fist around it and hurled it into the sea with all the force she could. It splashed into the water some fifty feet from the shore. His sadness barely concealed, Camilo watched the waves swallowing up the biggest pearl human eyes have ever seen. And then Nirveli leaped from the waves like a dolphin, holding the pearl and laughing. Her laughter merged with the last calls of the gulls and the murmur of the waves to form a joyous song. She leaped once more and then splashed back into the sea, never to appear again.

"There, we righted that wrong, too," Rashelka murmured. "The Joy-of-Sea belongs to the womenfish. And without Nirveli, the treasure would still be at the bottom of the sea. Come, it will be dark soon." She headed for the camp and her mother who was recovering under Ernesto's watchful eye and receiving careful nursing from one of the girls that had disembarked from the airship. Camilo looked at the waves once again and then followed Rashelka.

Rashelka had learned that when the Andean *reconquista* had crushed the Simón Bolívar rebellion earlier in the century, some of his soldiers had escaped and looked for sanctuary in inaccessible places that were veiled in legends. Enraptured, Camilo had told Rashelka of the hidden city in the mountains where the ancient Incas found shelter before the conquistadors, and of another city, overgrown in the impenetrable jungle. Here, the *bolivaristas* had built their army anew; Bolívar might have been defeated, but his torch of freedom had not been extinguished. The more the whips flogged, the tighter the manacles squeezed, then the brighter it had burned.

But rifles and machine guns and cannons cost. Revolution is not free, as the *Comandante* had commented last night. Ernesto had been sitting next to him at the time. Together they had drafted a manifesto they were to send out to the enslaved and oppressed of the New World. Rashelka had quickly realised Ernesto was more than just a doctor. The *Comandante* might be the commander, but Ernesto was the flame of the revolution.

Camilo had been sitting next to them, absorbing every word they said. But every so often, his gaze would wander to Rashelka. The girl had not missed that, and she had liked it.

Revolution is not free, the *Comandante* had repeated; Mingan's informer had earned his pay twice. Once armed with his information, the *bolivaristas* had set the airship to follow Mingan, knowing how his raid would end and waiting for an opportunity to present itself.

"Will you come with us?" Camilo asked, catching up with Rashelka. The *bolivaristas* had seen Katka's power in action. They had spoken with her, and they knew she had broken the Golden Armada. They wanted her with them. Rashelka knew her mother did not want to kill anymore. But both of them also knew what kind of evil was being nurtured in the New World, in its forests and rivers and mountains. They had witnessed that evil. It gushed out of the earth, burning in the glimmer of gold and silver and precious stones, spilling everywhere, threatening the world. Only the flame of freedom could burn that evil and drive the beasts in human shape away; freedom could heal the wounded land, wash away the spilled blood, and wipe away the tears that had been shed.

"We must take off tomorrow, we're not safe here. Will you come with us? Your mother and... you?"

Rashelka paused; hope was shining in Camilo's eyes. She looked at the camp, then her mother, then Camilo.

"I know how your mother feels... About killing and all. I heard her. But... We need you. The people need you. The revolution needs you..." Camilo looked at Rashelka. And she remembered what her mother had said after the *bolivaristas* had left her to rest. Not every battle needs a monster summoned. It did not take a killer wind to damage moored airships, scatter fleets across the sea, or drench marching soldiers in showers.

They reached the camp to find Ernesto speaking of hope, of a fight, of revolution. Of chains cast off. Of freedom and justice. The rebels listened to his words, exalted; the flame was burning and spreading, unstoppable, across the entire New World.

Rashelka offered Camilo her hand and he took it. The warmth of his hand awoke something new in Rashelka, something she had never felt before.

Perhaps it really is time for the New World, Rashelka thought as they walked along the beach, listening as Ernesto's words were interrupted by applause and cheerful shouts.

Rumiko

Chapter I

In which we meet our heroes

A whistle pierced the sooty autumn evening. Gaslights were being turned on. Although Ilica Street was one of the Zagreb's main streets, the chill kept most people home. Marin let a blue steam omnibus pass him before crossing the street. He stopped in front of a shop. The sign above the entrance read "WATCHMAKER—est. 1873—S. Sigsfeld, prop." Marin removed a lock of dark hair from his forehead, turned the doorknob, and entered the shop.

The doorbell announced him merrily. The young man at the workbench raised his eyes from the pocket watch he was working on.

"You arrived at last," he said, removing a magnifying glass from his eye. Unruly, curly hair gave him an artistic look, but his eyes were curious and calculating at the same time. On occasions, Marin found the look in those eyes cold.

"I was a bit delayed, sorry," Marin apologised and he took a bundle of papers out of his worn out bag. "Here, these are today's lectures. But, really, Jakob, I don't see how you're going to manage—"

"You know I cannot close the shop," Jakob replied, leafing through the notes. Marin noticed he was worried. "Somebody must run it while father is ill. Anyway, this doesn't look much. Digital mechanics, data structures, numerical calculus... When do you need the lectures back?"

"In two or three days. But what are you going to do with the exercises?"

"All right," Jakob shrugged. "I'll attend the exercises. Fortunately, they're not being held every day. Thank you for these."

"Oh, it's—"

At that moment, the doorbell rang again and an unusual pair entered. The gentleman could not have been less than sixty, undoubtedly of oriental origins, with piercing steel-grey eyes, white hair, and a neatly trimmed moustache and beard. He was dressed in a dark suit; the work of a first-rate tailor was immediately obvious. He held a bowler hat in his right hand and a simple but elegant wooden cane in his left.

When his escort followed him into the shop, a lightning bolt pierced Marin's chest. Never in his life had he met such a beautiful girl. Her rich black hair was arranged into a chignon. Her lovely complexion was pale, reminding Marin of snow, and she wore an expensive dress. Their gazes met for an instant. Smiling, the girl looked in another direction, but not before Marin had spotted a mischievous glimmer in her almond eyes.

"*Gutten abend, Herr Watanabe*," Jakob greeted the newcomer in German, putting down Marin's notes. "Your watch is finished. But let me introduce you. This is Marin Stipančić, a fellow student," Jakob added. "Mister Watanabe and his daughter."

"I am Watanabe Shiro," the old man bowed, "and this is Rumiko. We are honoured." His German sounded fluent, although with an accent. Marin bowed in return. He found it difficult to avert his eyes from Rumiko. He hoped he did not look impolite.

"Mister Watanabe was kind enough to entrust me with his watch," Jakob explained as he took a golden pocket watch out of a drawer. Watanabe took it, raised the lid, brought it to his ear and smiled, satisfied.

"Have you been in Zagreb for a long time?" Marin dared to ask.

"Three months now. Expert delegation," Watanabe replied, after pausing a second or two. It was as if he was assessing Marin, weighing how much he could tell him. "You see, our Empire must modernise. So, our delegations visit developed countries worldwide. We gather experiences we can apply in our homeland."

"Oh." Marin nodded. "And what precisely are you interested in, if I'm not being impolite?"

"Railways. As you must have read in newspapers, the Austrian State Railways are hastily laying mountain tracks through Bosnia. And, as you also probably know, mountains dominate Japan, so..."

"Isn't this a Babbage engine?" Rumiko asked suddenly. Marin looked at her. She stood before a showcase in the corner. Among various broken watches, which served merely as decoration, there was a rather small brass box on a wooden pedestal. Its winding key was inserted on the side.

"Precisely, Miss Watanabe," Jakob replied, and he opened the case. "The original IBM portable Babbage engine, weighing a mere fourteen pounds. A bit old, though." Jakob released the locks and raised the engine lid. Rumiko leaned over the frame supporting the complex tangle of axles, cogwheels, and levers that comprised a Babbage computer. Her eyes shone with excitement. "Beautiful, isn't it? Of course, their monopoly expired long ago, but still, nobody makes them as good as Intelligent Babbage Machines Co. It's powered by this spiral spring here, see? It's wound up by the key. Of course, this is a small model. Compared to steam analytical engines..."

"Does it work?" asked Rumiko.

"Unfortunately, no, Miss."

Rumiko turned, visibly dejected. Marin understood why: a running Babbage engine, even when running idle, was a fascinating sight. "The tape reader is broken, and the writer is missing altogether. And some of the bearings are gone, one axle is broken—this is one of the earliest models, after all. Subsequently, they improved upon the durability of the parts. Anyway, I'm afraid I couldn't afford a functional engine myself."

"Such a shame…"

"Maybe, once you finish your studies, you will find the means to repair it," Watanabe commented. "And now, it is time to go. Rumiko-*chan*…"

Once they we're alone, Jakob closed the engine. "Watch your step, my fellow," he said, nudging Marin and winking mischievously.

"I don't know what you're talking about, my friend."

"Come, come, as if I didn't see the way you ogled her. He's got a cute daughter, hasn't he?" Marin said nothing. He could not get Rumiko out his mind; that desire for knowledge as she had leaned above the engine, an unruly lock falling over her forehead, eyes admiring the perfect precision of the Babbagean mechanics which, in Marin's opinion, were the greatest achievement of the modern era of progress. Whenever he tried to describe to a young lady the harmony that was required to carry out complex numerical and logical operations, supervised by algorithmic structures, her stare would wander, her face assuming a dull look of complete disinterest for any technical matter.

"… but one must be careful."

Marin started. "I beg your pardon?"

"They are foreign people, regardless of their familiar clothes. We don't know their customs and traditions."

Foreign or not, Marin mused, *we shall all be finally united by steam, Babbage engine, and telegraph.* These inventions would weave a new world, one with a bright future for young people such as Jakob and Marin. And Rumiko, too. Somehow, Marin felt that the pale girl fully belonged, in some beautiful and unusual way, to that new world.

Chapter II

In which Rumiko and Marin meet again

Marin and Jakob got off the steam omnibus that stopped, whistling, before the entrance to the barracks which were festively adorned with flags. Carried by the cheerful Sunday crowd, they passed the guards and went to the former parade ground. Four moored airships rested around its edge.

The traditional air meeting at the Borongaj field was in full swing. Crowds circulated in all directions. Prominent Zagreb gentry mixed with common folk, students courted ladies, and mothers held their children firmly by their hands, lest they lose them. The sound of a military brass band, playing merry marches from a specially erected stage, contributed to the mood. Several balloons were rising above Borongaj, each carrying two or three passengers in a basket.

Marin and Jakob gave wide berth to the stand belonging to "The Falcon— the Ladies' Lilienthal Club." They both agreed that there were easier ways to break one's neck than throwing oneself off the top of some cliff, hanging under a flimsy biplane flyer and hoping to reach its base in one piece. They also skipped the bingo and the stalls with hot sausages, sweets, and children's balloons. They rushed to the edge of the airfield where the constabulary had a hard time preventing the crowd from spilling in merry disorder across the grassy field.

One airship, painted grey, belonged to the Imperial and Royal Navy. She had flown all the way from Kotor Naval Base to be the crowning glory of the event. Two other ships proudly carried the sign of the Imperial and Royal Air Postal Service on their sides—a pigeon, its wings widespread, carrying a sealed letter in its bill.

There were no Army ships. The relations with the Kingdom of Serbia had grown tense again over the issue of Bosnia, and most of the ships were stationed in Petrovaradin and Sarajevo, from where they took off to patrol the borders. Instead, the Kaiser had sent one of his dark scouting ships from Berlin in a move which, the newspapers claimed, was a sign of support and a warning to the Karađorđevićs.

While Marin and Jakob were making their way through the crowd, a handling party began gathering beneath one of the postal airships. A moustached *Oberleutnant* was issuing orders under the vigilant eye of the aeronaut who was to fly her. The soldiers grabbed the ropes holding the ship and started pulling her in unison toward the centre of the field. It was an experienced crew, and they handled the reasonably large ship as if she was a toy. Soon, she was away

145

from the others, and the aeronaut and the engineer climbed into the car. The time had come to prepare the steam engine that would drive her—something which could take up to half an hour.

During all that elbowing through the crowd, Marin earned a jab in his ribs.

"I'm sorry! Oh, I'm so sorry!" said a lady's voice. He turned and his heart fluttered. He was facing Rumiko. "I'm sorry... Err..." Apparently, it took her a moment to remember. "Marin! Marin Stipančić!"

"Look who's here, Jakob!" Marin happily took Rumiko by the arm and pulled her away from the crowd. She nodded in gratitude.

"Why, Miss Watanabe! Such a small world!" Jakob bowed, and then he looked left and right. "I presume your esteemed father is here somewhere too?"

"My father had to leave on business. So, I was free to come here." She looked at them mischievously. "You won't tell my father, will you? He'd disapprove were he to know I was here unaccompanied."

"Let's say you're not unaccompanied anymore, Miss Watanabe," Marin said, smiling.

Rumiko replied with even more mischief, "My father would approve of student company even less."

At that moment, the music stopped. The Mayor of Zagreb climbed onto the stage, his nose ruddy after some wine. He was followed by the postmaster and the airfield commander. Somebody passed the mayor a megaphone; he cleared his throat and announced above the murmur and shouts from the crowd, "Ladies and gentlemen! Dear visitors! It is time to draw the results of our raffle! I call upon our Lady Luck!"

A young leading lady from the Croatian National Theatre climbed pertly onto the stage to applause and the occasional merry whistle, and bowed, to lots of cheers. Excited, Rumiko took her number from her purse. Marin sincerely wished her luck while the actress on the stage, accompanied by the Mayor's witty comments, drew the winners.

Seemingly everyone who bought a ticket got something; there seemed to be so many lucky winners. But Rumiko's number did not come up. However, she did not seem bothered at all. *Doesn't it matter to her?* Marin was puzzled. *Doesn't she care for prizes?*

At least half an hour must have passed before the Mayor announced the drawing of the three lucky tickets for the main award: a panoramic flight for two in the postal ship that was just being prepared at the field. At that moment, Rumiko grew attentively tense, and Marin deduced that this prize was what she had been hoping for.

The first number drawn was not hers. An elderly gentleman climbed to the stage, leading an eager grandson. Rumiko had no luck in the second draw either; the winners were a fat man of clerkish appearance and his drab little wife, who didn't really look happy about it, as if she put no faith in such novelties. Rumiko slowly prepared herself for disappointment. The actress pulled out a number for the last time. She handed it to the Mayor, who read it aloud. "Thirty two!"

Cheering happily, Rumiko jumped up and raised her ticket high. Then she remembered that it was a prize for two and, not really thinking about it, drew Marin forward by his arm. He looked first at her, then at Jakob, confused.

"C'mon, lucky man, what are you waiting for?" his friend said, laughing and pushing him forward. Marin took Rumiko by the arm, as if they were a couple, and together they made their way through the crowd, which was surprised to see a foreigner from some far away country.

It was some twenty minutes later before the Mayor, the postmaster, and the airfield commander had finished congratulating them. The aeronaut had reassured them that they had nothing to be afraid of, since the ship was perfectly safe. He had given them firm instructions on how to behave during flight. Only then were the lucky winners, followed by fanfares and a march, allowed to climb into the car. Rumiko and Marin settled into wicker chairs right behind the aeronaut. The old man and his grandson sat behind them, while the clerk and his still-not-too-happy wife sat at the very end, next to the engineer.

"All set?" the aeronaut asked, turning to check once again that everybody was settled. Then he gave a sign to the officer on the ground who issued an order, and the soldiers released the ropes. The ship began climbing silently. Marin grew stiff in his seat. He felt uneasy, watching the field and the cheering crowd below become smaller and smaller. Rumiko watched carefully over the aeronaut's shoulder, without the slightest fear or discomfort. Part of her courage passed to Marin, and he looked at the others onboard.

The boy had pressed his nose against the window pane, enraptured. His grandfather appeared calm; it was possible that he had flown on an airship before, or simply that he always appeared unruffled. The clerk's wife was squeezing her husband's arm. "You'll see more if you open your eyes, dear," he said in quiet reproach.

Marin smiled. Unconsciously, his hand reached for Rumiko's. Equally unconsciously, she took it and held it. Marin was filled by an indescribable sweetness. He did not let go of her hand when the aeronaut, having taken a steam pressure reading, started the propellers. He did not let go when the course was set for the northeast. He did not let go throughout the entire flight, as Zagreb spread below them in full splendour.

Their silvery ship glided quietly above the Maksimir park, painted in autumn colours. They startled swans on the lakes, and perplexed rowers with their ladies in boats. Racing an omnibus from Maksimir, they ran west for the centre of the city. They alarmed maids at the stalls surrounding the statue of Viceroy Jelačić, who resembled a toy soldier from so high above. The newly built towers of the Cathedral seemed within touching distance. They greeted buzzards above wooded hills north of Ilica Street and spoiled the lining up of soldiers in the Prince Rudolph's Barracks. They flew across the railroad, and everyone coughed at the smoke from Trešnjevka's heating plant chimneys. They followed the Sava river, and then the aeronaut turned back north, venting the gas at the same time. The Borongaj barracks came closer, marking the end of the flight.

When they finally landed, the handling party grabbed the ropes and moored the ship. The impressed passengers got off, all a bit sad that the flight had to end. Only the clerk's wife was sincerely glad to tread on firm soil again. Rumiko cast one last look at the majestic silver airship, her steps light with joyous excitement as Marin led her back to the crowd where Jakob awaited them.

Chapter III

In which great love blossoms

During the next few days, Rumiko and Marin seemed inseparable. For the first time in two years, Marin neglected lectures he would otherwise have attended regularly and scrupulously. Instead, he guided Rumiko through Zagreb, showing her the sights. From uptown walls, churches and towers, narrow streets and leaning shacks, across the new wide parks and pavilions downtown, all the way to peaceful Maksimir lakes, where Rumiko fed pieces of bread to showy swans.

Marin was amazed at how well Rumiko was faring in the city. She had adopted all the customs—so different from those in her distant homeland—with the ease of someone born in Zagreb, the capital of all Croats. She spoke German as if it was her native tongue.

"For several years now, we have travelled across Europe," Rumiko explained when Marin asked her. "From construction site to construction site. I have almost forgotten the ways of home." Rumiko tossed a piece of bread. The swan stretched its neck and snatched it from in front of the bill of another bird. She tossed a piece to that one too, and there was enough left for the several mallards that had joined them. Finally, when there was no more bread left in the bag, the swans paddled away, wiggling their tails in goodbye.

Later, in the zoo, Rumiko paused before the wolf cage. She contemplated the wolf and his mate as they circled the cage, every so often pausing to sniff the air.

"It's sad," she murmured, "when your entire world is a cage like this. They are almost gone in my homeland," she whispered sadly. Marin said nothing. But he, too, felt compassion for the imprisoned beasts. Then Rumiko walked on and he followed her to the tropical house, where chattering parrots and gaudy finches were sheltered during those chilly days.

They took a steam omnibus back to town. The bell tower clock was chiming nine when Marin finally escorted Rumiko home, a house on Tuškanac hill, rented by her father. The overgrown garden, ringed by cherry trees, maples, and spruces, was entered through a wrought iron gate in a stony wall that was covered in ivy and creeper. A hushed blackbird call greeted them from dense shrubs when they stopped before the gate.

Rumiko turned to bid goodnight to Marin. Then she paused.

"Come, let me show you our home," she said suddenly.

"I'm not sure it's appropriate," Marin objected. Indeed, should anybody see them, it could have the most embarrassing consequences for Rumiko.

149

"Oh, come on, there's no one!" She took his arm and led him through the gate and up the stony stairs. She unlocked the front door and let Marin in. He paused until she turned the lobby gaslights on, and then he followed her into a large reception room.

The house was obviously rented with all the furniture included. Marin saw nothing that reminded him in any way of Japan (and he had studied several books in the last few days, even Racinet, so he believed he had a pretty good idea of an average Japanese home and household customs). Apparently, when in Rome, Mr. Watanabe and his daughter wisely did what the Romans were doing.

Rumiko left Marin in the reception room and disappeared. He waited politely until she entered, having changed into a *yukata*, an indigo-dyed house-coat-like dress, kept closed by a broad sash he knew was called an *obi*. Marin lost his breath. Although simple and convenient, the elegant dress accentuated her sweetness even more. She carried a small tray.

"Won't you sit?" Rumiko asked as she put the tray on the table. Marin sat on a divan while Rumiko settled in an armchair opposite him and offered biscuits and tea. The biscuits were delicious, and Rumiko found some rum to pour in the tea, and the time flew by with pleasant chatter. At one point, Marin became aware that a large clock in the hallway was striking eleven and realised he had remained for an indecently long time. He rose to leave, but then, to his great surprise, Rumiko stood up and took his hands.

"Sometimes, I'm very lonely here," she whispered. Marin felt his mouth drying. He melted in her almond eyes, longed for those sweet lips. As if reading Marin's mind, Rumiko rose to the tips of her toes, embraced him, and kissed him on the mouth. Marin was afraid a single word might break that magic, disperse that intoxicating fragrance enveloping him, destroy that beauty before him, all to be lost in the desert of solitude.

Then Rumiko led him upstairs. She spoke not a word because words were no longer necessary.

What am I doing? Marin asked himself, but the question gave him no strength to resist Rumiko. And why should he resist? What wrong were they doing? Rumiko opened the door to her bedroom and led Marin in. The room was decorated simply but with taste. The bed was enticing with its fragrance of freshly starched sheets and pillowcases.

Rumiko kissed Marin once again. He embraced her, casting away any doubt, and pressed her against him. He caressed her fragile body, surrendering to the whirlwind of her alluring eyes, greedily drinking nectar from her lips. Rumiko moaned through clenched teeth, undid her sash and opened her dress. Marin placed his palm beneath the soft fabric, stroking her pale flesh; he lost his breath upon touching her firm breast. Rumiko unbuttoned his shirt and took it off. He laid her on the bed; it squeaked under their weight. She was opening to him, surrendering in a desire for someone to drive away the solitude of a stranger in a strange land. They looked into each other's eyes, and then she whispered, "Please, don't think badly of me."

"Never, my love! Never," Marin whispered back before finally sinking his entire being into the sweetness that was named Rumiko.

Chapter IV

In which bad news arrives

Marin was awakened by a phone ringing. It came from a study adjacent to Rumiko's bedroom. He opened his eyes and sat up in the bed. It was well after dawn. The phone would not stop, but was persistent, loud; like an intruder, it turned to sourness the sweet taste of last night. Then he heard quiet footsteps and Rumiko lifting the receiver.

He reached for his shirt that had been thrown to the floor. Trousers, where did he lose his trousers last night?

"*Moshi-moshi? Hai?*" Japanese words reached his ears. Perhaps it was her father calling; it would be awkward if so. "*Masaka!*" Rumiko screamed in fear, and Marin realised something had happened. He put on his trousers, listening to her agitated voice. She asked a question. Tense silence followed as she listened to the answer, then another question and silence, a quick reply, and finally the putting down of the receiver. Silence. Steps. Rumiko bursting into the room, her eyes full of dread.

"What was it? What happened?" Marin jumped out of bed and held Rumiko at arm's length. She started, as if she completely had forgotten that she was not alone in the house.

"An accident on the track. Some of the workers are dead."

"Your Father?" Marin shivered.

"They don't know." Rumiko shook her head. "He's gone!"

"What do you mean, he's gone?"

"I don't know. They phoned from the consulate. I should report as soon as possible."

Rumiko stared in all directions, scared, not really knowing what to do. Marin embraced her tightly. The fragrance of her hair, the freshness of her skin, all brought last night back to him, passionate and sweet.

"Don't worry," he whispered into her hair, calming her. "Everything will be all right. I'll go with you."

Rumiko looked at him, shaking her head. "You don't understand! Father—"

"Don't be afraid! You'll see, everything—"

Rumiko tore herself from Marin's arms. "Father had enemies in Japan, perfidious enemies who will stop at nothing! This is their doing, I'm certain of it!"

Rumiko was kept in the Japanese consulate for the whole day. Marin waited for her on a bench under a young plane tree. Dusk was drawing on in Zrinski Square when she finally left the consulate. Marin rose from the bench and went to meet her. Together, they walked through the park to Jelačić Square.

"What did they tell you?"

The first gas lanterns were being lit. Several couples strolled along the paths, their steps rustling the fallen leaves. An elderly lady with a small dog was passing Rumiko and Marin. The white dog stopped suddenly, looked at Rumiko, and started barking.

"Quiet! What's the matter with you?" his mistress reproached him. But the dog would not stop. The woman lifted him off the ground and slapped him gently across his muzzle. "Quiet! You're naughty! You are! Forgive him," the woman said, "he's a bit nervous today."

"It's all right." Marin smiled, and they left the woman and her little dog behind.

"They told me nothing new," Rumiko said, answering Marin's question. "There was an explosion followed by a landslide, and the entire train overturned. It was an engine pulling three wagons and two coaches. Seven people are dead, God only knows how many injured. Father's body wasn't found. He's not among the injured either. The officials said they'll let me know as soon as they learn something new."

"Did you mention your suspicions?"

"It's better that I keep what I know to myself. I'm not sure who's loyal to whom in the consulate."

"I don't understand." Marin did not miss the concern in her voice. Several times, she looked behind her, as if afraid that somebody was following them.

What's going on? he wondered.

"It's not easy to explain to someone who's not completely familiar with our history, but when the Black Ships arrived in our ports in the middle of the century, and when commotions and rebellions began soon after... Well, my father, although a *daimyo*, contributed greatly to bringing down the *bakufu* and forcing the *shogun* to capitulate. Many never forgave him for that. And with time, some of them regained influence and power."

Chapter V

In which dark forces attack

It was already night-time, foggy and dank, when Marin saw Rumiko home. He had done his best to cheer her up. He'd taken her—by a funicular, something she normally enjoyed—to an uptown cellar for supper. In a quiet booth, he tried to convince her everything would be all right. But Rumiko seemed distracted, as if unspeakable horrors swarmed through her head. Finally, Marin took her hands in his.

"You're not alone, Rumiko," he said. "Whatever happens, you're not alone."

Rumiko smiled and—with relief evident in her eyes, as if his words were the first ray of comfort in the uncertain darkness surrounding her—merely whispered, "*Arigato*. Thank you."

And so, following a stroll after supper, they had found themselves before her house once more. As Marin held the gate to let Rumiko pass, he wondered if it would be appropriate to follow her inside. Last night, so sweet, came back to his mind, and shame filled him immediately. No, it was not fair to take advantage of her worry and weakness and...

"Come with me," Rumiko said quietly.

"I thought..."

"I know exactly what you thought," she said, smiling, driving the fog surrounding them away, "and that's kind of you. But you promised I would not be alone."

Rumiko climbed the stairs, Marin following her, and the two of them were swallowed by the darkness of the garden. She unlocked the front door. She was about to step inside when suddenly she turned stiff, tense, as if feeling some danger.

What is it? Marin wanted to ask, but she pressed her fingers against his mouth.

"We're not alone," she whispered into his ear. Marin froze. Without a sound, knowing precisely her whereabouts in the darkness, Rumiko reached for a stand in the lobby and drew a cane out of it, quite similar to the one carried by Mr. Watanabe. She held the cane firmly in her left hand. Marin wanted to go ahead, but she pushed him behind her.

"Let me," she ordered in a quiet but uncompromising tone. She gripped the end of the cane with her right hand and pulled lightly, enough for Marin to see her tender hand drawing a blade.

A sword! he realised with horror. What he had taken to be a cane was actually a weapon.

Suddenly, something whizzed past Marin's ear and lodged itself in the wall behind him. It resembled a sharp-pointed steel star. The resonant clash of steel against steel echoed through the hallway, and another deadly star was deflected by Rumiko's sword. Before Marin could blink, much less realise that she had just saved his life, a dark shape charged at them. A masked burglar, dressed in black, drew his sword and struck, but Rumiko skilfully repulsed his blow, crying out like a demon.

Marin watched in consternation as his fragile belle transformed into a dangerous warrior, excelling in the deadly skills of faraway Japan. Swords clashed, and it was obvious Rumiko would quickly overpower the mysterious fiend. But then her foe reached under his black jacket and scattered some dust across the hallway. Marin screamed as it irritated his eyes. He panicked, thinking he'd lost his sight. Someone rushed past him into the night, pushing him aside. The burglar had escaped.

Marin dropped to his knees, rubbing his tear-filled eyes. The powder stung, bit, and burned all at once. And then Rumiko knelt next to him and deliciously cool water spilled over his eyes, washing the devilish powder away. Marin blinked. Rumiko poured more water on his face from the jar she was holding.

"Do you feel better now?"

Marin nodded. He could see again. "What was that, for God's sake?"

"*Metsubushi*. A blinding powder. Ashes, ground pepper, stinging nettle hairs, and sand, all mixed together."

"Who was that?"

"A ninja. A spy and assassin. Stay here." With these words, she gripped the sword and disappeared. She returned after several minutes which seemed like an eternity to Marin. "Good, he didn't steal anything. And he was alone. Let's go, he's the only lead to my father!"

"But who knows where is he by now!"

"Don't worry." Rumiko led Marin back into the garden. "I'm certain he's up there."

He looked where she pointed and the dark shape of an airship was indeed discernible, like a giant fish swimming through the fog. Was it his imagination, or was there a rope hanging from a car with somebody holding tight to its end?

"We shall never catch them!" he exclaimed. "We should inform the constabulary instead."

"No time! An airship is not fast. We can still catch up with them."

"But how?"

Instead of an answer, Rumiko rushed down the stairs into the street. Puzzled, Marin followed. At that very moment, luck smiled upon them; two eyes glowing in the fog turned out to be a pair of lanterns. A new and shiny topless Stanley Steamer was coming down the street. The driver was a gentleman sporting a pointed moustache, obviously a man of newly acquired riches, and his fair lady sat beside him, both dressed warmly against the damp cold that pierced to the bone.

Rumiko jumped before the steam car, causing the driver to brake and honk the horn angrily, startled.

"Are you insane, Miss? To jump out—"

Rumiko drew her sword and grabbed the man by his fur collar. She pulled him out of the leather seat. His cap flew off his head as he landed on the pavement where, upon seeing a shiny steel blade, he remained, purple with helpless rage. His lady, screaming, clambered off by herself, hiding her face before the insane foreigner. Rumiko climbed behind the steering wheel and looked at Marin. "Coming?"

Somewhat disbelieving his eyes, Marin jumped up next to her. Rumiko knowingly turned the lever under the steering wheel, and the car jerked and rushed down the street at full steam. She held the wheel firmly, cornering, as the owner yelled furiously behind her, completely forgetting himself. "It's not gonna end with this, you'll see! You'll end up in the slammer! In the slammer, I tell you!"

"Was this necessary?" Marin asked, looking over his shoulder.

"It was either this or running to the Head Post Office!"

Chapter VI

In which exciting and terrible things happen

"**R**umiko, I forbid this!"

Immediately adjacent to the Head Post Office building, on a spacious field cleared of cots and fenced for that purpose alone, a small airship was moored. Her steam engine was ready; the ship was to take off soon.

"Those *shurikens* were meant to kill you, Marin! Those people know no mercy. And Father is in their hands."

"I mean, stealing an airship," Marin whispered angrily at her. The aeronauts and the entire ground crew were in the Post, warming themselves with hot tea and rum before departure, recklessly leaving their ship without supervision. Rumiko and Marin were cloaked by the fog as they sneaked along the wrought iron fence with spikes on its top.

"What else are we to do? They went south, they're somewhere above the Sava river by now..."

"But you can't steer!"

Rumiko didn't hear him. She sprang, grabbed the rail, and jumped across it, landing on the other side deftly and as quietly as a cat. Marin was amazed. *What else can this girl do?* He grabbed the rail too and climbed, slipping clumsily, but managed to haul himself over. His coat got caught by a spike and he heard cloth tearing. Cursing through his teeth, he jumped down on the other side. He landed and fell, bruising his palms on the hard soil. A piece of his coat remained hanging on the spike, a trophy of sort. Stooped over, he hurried after Rumiko.

"Cut the ropes loose," she whispered before sitting behind the steering wheel. Marin obeyed, wondering if he was committing a major act of stupidity. The airship, free of her tethers, rose up slowly. Marin ran, jumped, and caught a door frame at the last moment, pulling himself into the cramped car.

At that moment, a clerk exited the Post building, carrying a tied bag. He saw the ship climbing and called out in surprise. At his shout, the crew rushed out, cursing and yelling and running after the ropes hanging from the ship. Marin spotted the three mail bags. He threw the first one out, followed by the remaining two.

"What are you doing now?" Rumiko demanded.

"Stealing an airship is one thing. Stealing Imperial and Royal mail is something else entirely, believe me! And we also lose ballast this way." As if hearing him, the ship rushed up even more briskly, and none of the hands reaching for the ropes caught one. Several tense moments later, they were some hundred feet above the building spires.

"What now?" Marin closed the door and settled behind Rumiko.

"Did you forget the air meeting? I was watching how to fly this thing!"

"You were watching how to fly it? Oh, God!" Of course he remembered the aerial sightseeing of Zagreb. That ship had been of a different mark, considerably bigger and with a more spacious car. But her levers and dials had not differed much from these. Even so, it all seemed very complex to Marin, yet Rumiko's entire aeronautical training consisted of simply having watched how it worked!

What was I thinking? Marin thought, stewing, angry at himself for not restraining this crazy girl from rushing mindlessly into peril.

To Marin's surprise, Rumiko pulled the lever knowingly, releasing steam into the cylinders. The engine came to life and the propellers behind the car turned, pushing the ship forwards. Watching the compass, she turned the steering wheel and gave it more steam. Almost without a sound, the ship rushed south above the city, leaving a whitish trail behind. The fog below them was like a grey sea, out of which roofs and spires broke here and there. They flew over the railroad then, in the distance, Marin saw the rooftop of his faculty building. From then on, they saw only fog and treetops. Then, after some ten minutes, two lines of poplars and willows. It was the Sava river, its course outlined by the trees, Marin knew, despite the river being covered by the fog.

"I can't see them," Marin muttered. "What if they're following the river to Sisak and on, into Bosnia?"

Rumiko said nothing. She merely released some ballast. The ship bolted up, rising and rising until she stabilised again at about half a mile altitude.

"Is there a flare gun here?" Rumiko asked. Marin looked around and found a pistol with flares right behind his seat. "Fire three flares downwards, in different directions."

He obeyed, puzzled. He opened the pistol, inserted a flare, and closed it again. Then he pushed the barrel through a round opening in a window—seemingly meant for just this purpose—and fired. Then he understood. A screeching rocket flew towards the ground, merrily burning above a landscape veiled by fog. Marin fired the second flare through an opening on the other side, and then the third one. The bright flares illuminated the fog, which now resembled an opaque white glass pane. Against such reflected light, Marin spotted the black silhouette of an airship, some two hundred feet above the Sava course and some two miles away.

"Down there!" He pointed. Rumiko nodded, turned after the second airship, and accelerated.

"What if they saw us too?"

"Maybe they haven't yet," Rumiko replied. "Although now they know somebody's chasing them." The flares fizzled, and they lost their prey again. But they knew she could not get far. After several minutes, Rumiko ordered, "Fire another."

Now they spotted the pursued ship above groves growing on some fertile flooded soil south of Sava. She had not gained any altitude, but she looked closer. They flew above a village, leaving behind the bell tower and Lombardy poplars sticking out of the fog. And then there was forest below them, seemingly spreading into infinity. "You think your father is onboard that ship?"

Rumiko shook her head uncertainly. "I don't know." She pulled a lever and valved some gas. The ship descended. "Another flare!"

"But—"

"Unless they're blind, they know we're at their heels! Another flare!" Marin obeyed, and the flare shone upon the forest shrouded in fog. "Oh, bloody Hell!"

The enemy ship was straight before them, presenting her side, several hundred feet away, like an ambushing pirate. Only then did Marin realise she was painted black. That was why they had not seen her climbing into the night. And now she obstructed their path.

"What...?"

A flame flickered from the black airship's car.

"Down!" Rumiko screamed, throwing herself from the chair, grabbing Marin and covering him on the car floor. A blink of the eye later, the car windows were shattered by a hail of bullets from a Gatling gun. Loud staccato bursts were lost amid the noise of slugs ripping the wooden boarding, tearing the wicker seats, breaking the levers, and severing the control chains. Another burst tore the rudder off, and again slugs rained down on the car. Glass shards cut Marin; he felt blood flowing down his forehead. Steam hissed behind them. Fortunately, a bullet pierced the pipe outside and steam whistled into the night instead, otherwise the heat would have scalded them like pigs.

A new burst hit the ship. Bullets pierced the envelope and the gas, hissing, rushed through countless holes.

"Burners out!" Rumiko yelled, and Marin cut the fuel to the firebox burners at the last moment. The ship was swiftly losing altitude as the envelope lost gas. The fog-shrouded ground grew closer and closer. "Hold tight!"

Marin squeezed Rumiko in a tight embrace, trying to protect her. Then came a jolt, a breaking, the cracking of branches, the tearing and ripping of the envelope, and the hissing of gas. They fell through a treetop and hit the moist soil beneath hard. The impact shook their bones so badly that Marin thought his spine would break.

"Out!" Rumiko pushed him away, grabbed her sword, and kicked the door open. They both scrambled out of the smashed car and splashed into mud. Marin rose to his feet and stumbled through the quagmire, following Rumiko. Behind them, a detonation deafened them and a hot blaze burst up, devouring what was left of their airship.

Veiled by fog, surrounded by centuries-old oaks, Marin and Rumiko paused. Somewhere behind, in the forest, the fire began to die down.

"Did we lose them?" Marin whispered. His face was bloodied, his clothes completely muddy. Rumiko was no cleaner, but from her bearing, he deduced with relief that she was not injured. He could not believe what they had passed through. Even the most experienced officer, even the toughest soldier, would be shaken after a night like this, yet here a fragile girl stood next to him, brave and unflinching in her quest to rescue her kidnapped father. *What would the spoilt Zagreb young ladies say to that?* Marin wondered. He wanted to praise Rumiko for her courage.

She put a finger to her lips and he stayed silent. She listened to the night tensely. The distant hooting of an owl. A rustle somewhere behind them. Marin turned, uneasy. Beasts foraged here, and it would be no good should they stumble upon a wild boar. Rumiko pulled his hand and he ran after her. To where, he did not know. They would not be able to find their way before morning when the fog would have cleared. Suddenly, Marin thought he heard the quiet thrum of a steam engine, transmission, and propellers. He strained to hear. Yes, he was right! He cursed. The black ship must be quite close. He looked up, but the fog hid her.

"They're at our heels," he whispered into Rumiko's ear. She merely nodded. She gripped her sword, ready to draw it. *Are we already surrounded?* Marin despaired. *Is it possible that they could be as quiet as apparitions?* He looked around and saw a branch lying on the ground. He seized it with both hands; it felt like a good, solid club. Rumiko looked at him, an expression of pity on her face.

Suddenly, a figure stepped out from behind an oak some twenty feet away and stood facing them. They were in a small clearing. Marin turned when he felt—by the instinct of an animal being pursued—that somebody was behind them. Two men had cut off their retreat, and figures were approaching them from left and right. Apart from the first man, they were all wearing black, with hoods on their heads, masks on their faces, and swords in their sashes. *Ninjas,* Marin recalled. And the one before them, dressed in an expensive-looking *kimono,* must have been their leader. He wore no mask. He appeared almost as old as Watanabe, but stronger, with a black moustache and an arrogant bearing. He was wearing both a long and a short sword in his sash.

"Watanabe-*ke no gosokujo?*" he growled.

Rumiko replied in Japanese, then she asked a question. The man replied contemptuously in several sentences. At that, Rumiko shuddered and staggered. Marin realised the worst must have happened. But then she clenched her teeth, drew her sword and gripped it with both hands above her head, challenging all five of them to try their skills. Their leader lifted his hand and spoke in not quite fluent German.

"I think the esteemed gentleman, since he was foolish enough to find himself here, deserves an explanation as to why he will die."

"Indeed, I do. Only it is custom here for gentlemen to introduce themselves first."

"You are right, I apologise. I am Seki," the man replied, and he bowed.

"Marin Stipančić." Marin tried to keep a tremor out of his voice. There was no doubt that blood would be spilled here. He only hoped it would not belong to Rumiko or him. But hope alone would not be sufficient to save them.

"You met Watanabe-*san*, I believe. And I noticed that you understand he's dead. We caused the accident and kidnapped him in the subsequent commotion."

"So, you are the followers of the deposed *shogun*," Marin interrupted. Seki laughed.

"I see Rumiko-*san* hinted at our recent history. True, Watanabe-*san* and I were on opposite sides. But my side grew interested in his subsequent work, work that became his obsession. We approached him discreetly, not revealing who we really were, and we offered him significant funds. He—well, let me put it this way—used them against our agreement."

"So that's why you killed the man?" Marin said through clenched teeth.

"After several years, Watanabe-*san* realised with whom he had entered into partnership and to what cause he had aligned himself," Seki continued, ignoring Marin's interruption. "After that, his work became completely inaccessible to us. We needed to find out how far he had gotten with his research. It took a long time for a good opportunity to present itself. When it did, we failed. He bit his tongue off instead of telling us." Marin shivered. Seki had just admitted in cold blood that they tortured the old man to death, as if this was something common. "It was an act demanding great strength of will."

"And then you sent a ninja to break into our house," Rumiko said, cutting across him.

"And you came home at an ill time. But at the same time, you revealed yourself." Seki smiled. "As soon as my man told me what happened, I realised

Watanabe-*san* had indeed made great advances with his work. I realised he had succeeded beyond all our expectations, he—"

"Enough!" Rumiko yelled, and she charged at Seki. He shouted something in Japanese and the four ninjas rushed at her. Weighted chains and a rope with a hook at its end flew at her from four sides. But with incredible agility she evaded the attacks supposed to restrain her.

Marin realised they wanted her alive. He charged at the nearest ninja, hoping to jump him from behind. But the man in black must have sensed his intention with some uncanny instinct because he could not possibly have seen him, and the weight on the end of the chain struck Marin's temple. His vision blurred, he staggered and fell; he rose quickly, still clenching the branch, but found himself feeble on his feet.

The rope with the hook coiled around Rumiko's waist. The ninja pulled her strongly towards him. But Rumiko skilfully switched her sword from one hand to another and stabbed the ninja between his ribs. He whined silently as she withdrew her blade from his body. She cut the rope with the next strike and it fell away from her. Seeing blood spurting from the ninja's deep wound made Marin realise just how lethal the Japanese swords were.

"Your father taught you well, Rumiko-*san*," Seki murmured. The other ninjas now approached her with much more respect.

"Did you think *kaginawa* and *kusari-fundo* will restrain me, you swine? You'd better grip your swords, lest I cut you all down barehanded!"

Seki nodded. "So be it. If that is what you wish." The remaining three warriors drew their swords. "After all, if your father did his work well, we can afford to cause a little damage to you."

Marin was afraid Rumiko's threat might have been a bit premature. The three men surrounded her. They had completely forgotten Marin, as if he was not an opponent worthy of their attention but merely a stranger to be dispatched after finishing the serious business at hand. With his pride a little bit hurt, Marin gripped his club and set to charge at the nearest ninja.

"Stay out of this!" Rumiko commanded him. "You stand no chance against them." Screaming like a beast, Rumiko attacked the first ninja. Steel rang against steel, blade screeched against blade. The next moment, without Marin even seeing what happened, a man fell down. With a victorious cry, Rumiko threw herself at the remaining two. Swords sliced through the air; one ninja repelled the attack while the other charged. Rumiko struck back, the three of them exchanging savage blows. It was a fight with no mercy, to the death. Seki merely watched from the side, his right hand resting on his sword, pleased with what he saw. And then a scream, and one ninja was stumbling back a few feet, blood spurting from his neck. A moment later, the last ninja collapsed in the mud. With horror, Marin realised the man's belly was cut open. Finally, Rumiko was alone, surrounded by four corpses.

"This is all you planned to send against me?" she said, facing Seki with contempt. "I know a good ninja is hard to find these days, but these…"

"I assure you they were among the best." Seki smiled. "Your father did great work, Rumiko-*san*. And he taught you better than I could have imagined. But then, his skills were legendary. Even at his age, I doubt we'd have overpowered him if we hadn't stunned him with explosives first. Nevertheless, I don't believe you're better than me." Seki drew his sword. The time had come for the two of them to face off.

Marin looked at them helplessly. Seki raised his sword in a slow, threatening movement. Rumiko did not even flinch. They measured each other for several moments, and then charged. Their swords struck as they passed each other, yelling, before both stopping dead, frozen in the mud.

What's happened? Marin was surprised, having expected a protracted fight. Then he noticed a bloody blotch spreading across Seki's *kimono*. When? How had Rumiko's sword found its target? What was that deadly skill that can cut a man in an eye-blink, in a movement seeming to stem from a demoniac dance? Marin did not understand. He had witnessed some swordsmanship exhibitions, but this was an entirely new world, entirely different skills. And his Rumiko possessed them.

Seki opened his mouth to say something. Blood gushed out. The sword fell from his hand. He dropped into the mud, dead.

"It's over! You cut them down, Rumiko!" Marin rushed to her. Suddenly, without a word, Rumiko collapsed to her knees. Marin's heart froze. He caught her before she fell to the ground, and she hung with all her weight against his arms, almost pulling him down with her.

"No," he muttered, "God, no!" He had seen how deadly those swords were, and he instantly realised that, in the same invisible manner that Rumiko cut Seki down, he had mown her down too. Her gaze was empty. Marin felt her dress getting wet under his palm. Suddenly, something felt out of place. He looked at his palm and gaped in surprise. He could smell it. Along with all the mud and blood, his palm was soaked in machine oil.

Chapter VII

In which Jakob has a lot of work to do

An impatient ringing of the doorbell broke the night-time silence in Samuel Sigsfeld's shop. *Is it some drunken fool?* Jakob asked himself. *Or perhaps the constabulary? But why?*

"All right, all right," he muttered. He opened the door a crack, only meaning to take a peek, but as soon as he unlocked it, an untidy, staggering apparition burst into the shop. It was surrounded by the stinking fog that blanketed the city, and it was carrying something in its arms, something wrapped up that had the shape and size of a body.

"For God's sake!" Jakob exclaimed. Marin stood before him, his face dirty, his coat filthy and torn, his hair encrusted in blood, his stare half-mad.

"Where can I put her?"

"Put who, man?"

"Where can I put her? And lock the door!"

Jakob obeyed and indicated the workbench. Marin placed whatever he was carrying atop the work surface with care and stepped back. He wiped blood and mud from his forehead. He wiped his hands on his trousers and then unwrapped the bundle he'd been carrying. Jakob barely suppressed a scream when he recognised Rumiko bundled in coarse cloth.

"Is she dead?"

"No. I need—"

"Why did you bring her to me, man?" Jakob screamed. "You're wasting time here with me, instead of taking her to a doctor!"

"I can't, you'll see—"

"What happened? Tell me!"

"Actually, I don't understand myself. Old Watanabe is dead. So Rumiko cut a host of ninjas down with a sword... I know it sounds crazy, you should have been there and seen for yourself! And then she fell, too!" Marin was shaking as he tried to explain what had really happened.

"But why not take her to the doctor?"

"Because of this!" Marin hissed, and he uncovered Rumiko fully. Jakob stared at her stained dress. He touched the stain, smelled his fingers; his eyes widened. Words failed him. Then he took a deep breath.

Not impossible, he decided after thinking it over, *not impossible...* His brain started running like clockwork.

"This is what we are going to do now." He looked at Marin with a firm stare. His voice became calm. "Whatever damage has been done, it's done. This isn't an urgent case and we have time. Go upstairs to my room, tidy yourself as much as you can. Try not to wake my father up. And wash your hands well. I'll need your help, and if this is what I think it is, then we need clean hands."

It was in the small hours of the night when the two of them, after a meagre supper and several cups of strong coffee, returned to the shop. Rumiko was laying there, her eyes staring dully at the ceiling. First, they took off her clothes. They both paused when confronted by her perfect figure, an almost snow-white complexion without a slightest blemish, perfect down to her seducing intimate curls and what lay beneath them.

"Did you know her?" Jakob asked.

"In the Biblical sense, you mean?" Marin asked. After a brief silence, he nodded.

The fatal cut, the only one to mark her perfect skin, was deep, slanting across her belly. Jakob teased apart the cut skin which was greasy with oil. Marin cast some light on the wound, and a steel spiral spring flashed inside. It was obvious something was wrong with it.

"Navel," Jakob murmured. "The winding key probably goes here. Do you have it?"

Marin shook his head. "Maybe at her home. We left in a hurry."

"Never mind, it's easy to make a new one. Let's turn her over on her belly."

Her skin was sewn in neat and firm stitches, from somewhere beneath her hair, down her nape and all the way down her back. "You didn't see this?" Jakob asked. If he had not noticed Marin's worried look, he might have winked.

"It was dark and she was wearing a *yukata* and—"

Jakob dismissed the rest with a wave of his hand. He realised there was no time to waste, after all.

"Listen, you must go back to their house. It will soon be swarming with constabulary. Go, right now, while it's still dark, and make sure that you're not seen." Jakob realised that he would also have to think of some story. The investigators could easily visit his shop as well. He would have to hide the body.

"What am I looking for?" Jakob's calculating coolness calmed Marin. He had done a good thing, bringing Rumiko here. If anybody in this town could fix her, it was Jakob.

"Blueprints. I don't believe Watanabe was taking her around without any blueprints. Maybe they're on paper, maybe on transparencies."

"All right, I understand," Marin said with a nod before grabbing his coat. He unlocked the door, peeked out as if checking for an ambush, and then disappeared into the fog. Jakob locked the door behind him and cast a thoughtful look at the body. Although he had not yet checked the full extent of the damage, he had already guessed what might be the matter and was calculating the possible expenses.

Chapter VIII

In which all ends well

The doorbell rang merrily as Marin entered the shop in a Christmas mood. He took off his cap and shook the snow off it, unbuttoned his coat, and removed his scarf. "It's cold outside," he said as he rubbed his palms.

"Well, it's wintertime, isn't it?" Jakob replied and locked the door behind him. He looked at Marin. "It's finished!"

"Really?" Marin asked, rejoicing. He took his friend's shoulders. "I don't know how to thank—"

"It cost me quite a lot," Jakob said gravely.

"Look, I'll make it up to you one day—"

Jakob interrupted him. "There are interesting things in those blueprints. Things that one could make a patent or two out of."

Marin had spent enough time with Jakob above the opened Rumiko to know how revolutionary she was. Instead of human bones, Rumiko had bamboo sticks. Lightweight, yet firm. Her vertebrae were made of jointed shorter pieces of bamboo. Only her skull was a two-piece steel case. And inside it was the most perfect and complex Babbage engine Jakob and Marin had ever seen. Every part was a miniature masterpiece, and the complexity of the entire machine far surpassed even the large steam-driven IBM 11-30 that college exercises were held on. And instead of punched tape, which had replaced the original looped Jacquard cards in modern Babbage engines, Rumiko's memory consisted of round plates, like disks lined on a single axle. Both students immediately realised the novelty that old Watanabe had dreamed up. While data on tape could be accessed only sequentially, one bit after another, the memory installed in Rumiko could access data directly, the moment it was needed. They both realised that this increased the speed of the Babbage engine inside her, and they also knew well enough just how much capital an interested party would invest in something like that.

The greatest expense had been replacing the spiral winding spring. Jakob had been forced to order it from Switzerland. The spring was driving all of Rumiko, just like an alarm clock.

"I heard once that the Japanese make mechanical dolls," Jakob had said to Marin one night as he was leaning over Rumiko, studying the camera obscuras she had for eyes. "I think they're called *karakuri ningyo*. Some use clockwork mechanisms, others sand or quicksilver. Some of them are even steam-powered. Not to mention de Vaucanson's and Jaquet-Droz's automatons. But something like this..."

They had spent hours and hours studying blueprints. They passed night after night above Rumiko's exposed insides until they understood all the fine points of that brilliant and deliciously beautiful machine. Jakob was right; Marin had found the blueprints quickly, neatly wrapped in wooden cylinders. But he also discovered their copies, reduced onto celluloid. He'd handed Jakob just the containers. He'd also kept silent about some gold that he had found in a drawer of Watanabe's writing desk. He felt he was going to need it, once his friend finally repaired Rumiko. It was rather unfair not to cover his friend's expenses, but the gleam in Jakob's eyes as he was studying the blueprints suggested that he would manage to make his efforts profitable somehow.

Marin had kept another secret from Jakob: the sketches and notes he had found among the blueprints. Of course, he could not read them, but the drawings were sufficient for him to finally understand the allusions made by that cursed Seki. Watanabe's task had been to build an invincible mechanical soldier. And when one had been created, soon whole regiments would spring up. Then Seki's comrades could re-establish the overthrown regime. Marin could only guess what drove Watanabe to make Rumiko instead of a soldier; the old man took that secret to his grave.

A swineherd had discovered the destroyed airship and dead bodies the next day. Carrying Rumiko, Marin had used the fog to make good his escape long before that. The black airship had also disappeared, driven away by the dawn; whoever was inside had given up the chase. Of course, the investigators made enquiries about Watanabe. They interrogated Marin, too, but they did not suspect for a moment that he knew more than he told them. They did not discover that Watanabe had taken his watch to Jakob for repairs. Finally, no doubt due to instructions from above, they concluded their investigation, explaining it all with some old political dissensions.

Marin was well aware that Rumiko was not safe in Zagreb. On the other hand, she would be like a fish in a shoal in Japan. And there were quite a few foreigners in Japan; their expertise was needed there. While waiting for the spring to be delivered, Marin made up his mind.

"Coming?" Jakob startled him from his musings. With Jakob holding a lantern, they descended the steep cellar stairs and stopped before a heavy locked door. Jakob took a key out of his pocket and unlocked the door. Marin followed him, holding his breath.

When Jakob turned the light on, Marin saw Rumiko. She was lying on the table, just like all the nights before, covered with a white sheet. All the tools around her had been set to one side. Marin approached the table and looked at Jakob who nodded. Marin uncovered the lifeless body. The wound was tightly closed and neatly stitched.

"The stitches will remain, I'm afraid."

Marin caressed Rumiko's cheek. "Key?"

"Here." Jakob passed him the tool. Marin took the large key. He used his fingers to gently pry open a hole at the place where a navel would be in an ordinary girl, and inserted the key. He began turning it and heard clicking from inside as the spring wound tighter. With every turn, the resistance grew stronger, and then, finally, the key would turn no more. Nevertheless, Rumiko did not move.

Marin looked at Jakob.

"I don't know," Jakob replied with apology in his eyes. "I didn't try it before now. I don't know what happens when the machine is restarted after a rest."

Maybe the machine should not have stopped in the first place? Marin thought wretchedly. Maybe Rumiko was dead the moment the broken spring ceased powering the mechanism. What if all the repairs were in vain and it would all be just a strange memory Marin could reveal to no one? Because who would ever believe he had loved a machine, a doll? Or that the doll had responded with love, with more care and tenderness than any girl he had known before?

Marin sighed with resignation, leaned above Rumiko, and placed a tender kiss on her lips.

There was complete silence in the cellar. Marin straightened, ready to turn away. He was about to leave that Hoffmannian fantasy behind, because it was all just a foolish dream, when all of a sudden Rumiko opened her eyes wide. She leaped up like a furious wildcat and grabbed a screwdriver from the table next to a wall.

"Rumiko!" Marin yelled, facing a sharp tip pointing at his belly. "Rumiko, it's over! It's over, you killed them! You cut them all down!"

It was only then that she became aware of who stood before her. Her eyes darted from Marin to Jakob and back to Marin.

"You cut them all down, Rumiko. It's over, they're no more."

Rumiko paused, keeping her eyes on Marin. Her face crinkled up in concentration, as if the Babbage engine in her head was searching through all the memories, trying to remember details after she had been shut down for months. And then, with joyous cry, she dropped the screwdriver and flew into Marin's arms, nude as she was. Jakob wanted to object; her clothes were neatly stacked on a chair in a corner. But then, taken by some unusual peace and warmth in his heart, coming to the realisation that a good deed was done, he silently crept out of the cellar, as befits a true gentleman, and left the enamoured ones in a tender and passionate embrace.

Epilogue

Jakob Sigsfeld tapped his cigar. Ash fell onto the stony slabs paving the terrace of his new villa. Before him spread the vista of the promenade and shoreline. Pines rose above the shore and downy oaks arched over the path. Beyond them, a dead calm sea. There were several boats on it and a passenger steamer's smoke was visible in the distance. On the rocks, gulls squabbled nosily over a morsel. There were scaffolds on a new hotel; the construction was nearing its end. It was a warm, hazy, autumn morning in Opatija, and Jakob reached for the newspapers on a table next to him.

The IBM stocks had risen again. Jakob smiled in satisfaction. They were not happy when he had demanded partnership in the company instead of a fixed fee for his patent of a random-access memory. They were by no means happy; they could count the money just like he. But they had no choice; they could not allow anyone to overtake them in the market. And Jakob had invested his dividends cleverly. Shares in a steam-shipping company. The hotel that was being built before his very eyes. Yes, and that fellow Schwartz whose patent for the *Metallballon*—a rigid aluminium-clad airship—looked promising.

A servant stepped onto the terrace, carrying a smallish parcel. Jakob raised his eyes from newspapers. "Mail for you, sir."

"Thank you." Jakob took the parcel and dismissed the servant. He looked at the address; the package had gone first to his Zagreb apartment before being forwarded here. Then he saw the Japanese postage stamps and read the sender's address. He frowned as his heart started beating faster. *Marin!*

The last time he had seen Marin was three years ago, the night he came to pick up Rumiko. He took her into the winter night and he had not called or written since. Until now...

Jakob tore the wrapping, taking care not to damage the chrysanthemum stamps. For a moment, his newly discovered passion urged him to fetch a magnifying glass and take a closer look at them, but then he saw what was in the package, carefully wrapped in fabric. A framed photograph. Marin and Rumiko, both in *kimonos*. And a boy with Japanese features, black hair, in a dark student's uniform. Jakob frowned; he did not understand it. Rumiko was a perfect, but still, childbirth was impossible. And then it dawned upon him. The blueprints! Watanabe must have had an additional copy of them which Marin had held back.

For a moment, Jakob was upset, but then he thought it over. *Marin won't try to cash the blueprints,* he realised. His secrecy about them would repay his debt to Jakob.

Jakob looked at the photograph longingly. Who knew how many of them would soon walk this Earth, machines like Rumiko or the boy.

Machines? Or our successors on this Earth? he wondered, staring at the happy family. The boy held a white puppy in his arms.

The puppy seemed alive, made of flesh and bones.

As the Distant Bells Toll

Winter night embraces me like a skilful lover. It wraps around me, seducing me into its game. It knows exactly where to touch with icy fingers, where to blow with chilly breath, where to lick with cold tongue. Cursing the winter, I raise the collar of my thin jacket. Won't help me one bit though since I have but a T-shirt beneath and nothing more.

If I'd known, I would have put on something warmer before I died.

A blizzard whirls across the broad street, cutting through my jeans. A chill licks across my skin, ice clings to my wet hair. Snow enters my sneakers and melts, wetting my socks. I can barely feel my feet. I rub my palms against each other and blow warm breath on my wooden fingers, trying to bring some life back into them. In vain. Damn, it is cold!

I try flapping my wings; maybe that would warm me up. I try, with all my strength. Nope. I try harder. Nothing; they won't even spread. They're a useless decoration, as pointless as if I didn't have them at all. Then I realise that this power has not yet been given to me. I still haven't passed the Exam.

A car passes me by, lights penetrating the blizzard. The driver drives slowly, carefully, afraid to accelerate along the snow-covered street. He has no chains; the snowstorm must have surprised him like so many others. I measure the car up as it leaves me behind. An Opel, one of the better models. Oh, if only the driver would stop! If only he'd give me at least a bit of warmth... I would be very grateful to him, I would be glad to make him warm in return. Oh, I would make him warm all right; the night is just right to make each other warm and...

But he does not stop, he does not see me. He does not want to see me, he does not care. There is a celebration going on around me, and nobody cares about the freezing apprentice in the street.

I am back in the snowstorm, alone. Soon, it will be midnight. People in the distant apartment buildings celebrate His birth, looking forward to the feast. Gunshots and petards echo across the suburbs, mixing with shouts and drunken songs. The chill stabs me and penetrates deep inside, filling me completely, binding me with icy shackles. I wonder if all this is just the Teacher's twisted sense of humour.

Because if I do not pass tonight, I'm afraid I could soon become very, very warm.

And I would sell my soul to the Devil himself...

Enough! I cut myself off. *Stop! Quiet! Don't even think about it!* They are everywhere, just waiting. I know, I have convinced myself based on many examples. The Teacher was very descriptive. They are waiting; all they need is for you to make a small slip, and then they catch you in their net and you are cursed, cursed for all eternity, without salvation, without escape. The more you resist, the more you are theirs.

And I don't want to become *that* warm.

The wind slaps me back into the night, snowflakes dance in beams of yellow light above the street. I should pass tonight. I do not dare think what would happen if I don't. Patience is almost exhausted. The Teacher let me know clearly that the time had finally come to correct the administrative error, one way or another.

I know very well that the wings on my back are an error. The Teacher reminded me of it more than once. They let the issue hang above my head, like a sword on a thin thread, ready to judge me at any moment. And opportunities to do so were plenty: I was stubborn, foul-mouthed, spiteful, a girl from the street. And the Teacher wasn't exactly around when patience was being distributed either.

If all had turned out the way it should have, I would be hot now. Very hot, Hell-hot. But the day I died in a screech of brakes—my body swept over the hood, thrown aside like a rag doll, hitting the tarmac—that day, Death was everywhere. Wars, killings, disasters—she was reaping mercilessly left and right, without question, innocents and sinners alike, children and old men. An avalanche of souls buried the Reception in cries and screams, and in all that confusion, one condemned soul ended up on the wrong list.

Sometimes, at night, when I am alone and it's quiet around me, I dream of the confused apprentice. He barely finds his bearings in all that mess; shouts, crying, howling all over the place. Our eyes meet for an instant, and he puts me on the list for Heaven, not even thinking about it. The notion that I was cursed does not even occur to him; his hand writes down my name by itself. And angels in white come for me and take me, and I dream of finding him and thanking him, the way only I know how... But these are the dreams of a lonely girl during long nights. I never met him again; they never let me search for him. Maybe once I pass the Exam.

Of course, those down there saw the error sooner than those up there. So, the phoning started, frothy and impudent enough for the Reception to get obstinate. But, at the same time, they had a problem: according to the Laws, my place *was* down there, and they all knew it. And then somebody at the Reception, perhaps Peter himself, came up with a brilliant idea. Without even asking me, they enrolled me in the School, claiming I was chosen *before* they were warned of the error. Once earmarked for the School, I couldn't have been returned. And that was that.

When I think about it carefully, I was lucky. Because I offered pleasure in my life. Or, if I'm being honest, I sold it, several minutes of ephemeral joy, a hundred euros in a dark doorway. A girl has to make a living. And sometimes, I was bold enough to enjoy it myself.

And someone, somewhere, a long time ago, had hypocritically decided it was a sin.

A hospital, almost on the edge of Zagreb, a new, big, green concrete block looking like it had been thrown onto the meadow opposite the forest. An ambulance is approaching from afar, blue lights and a siren howl. I cross the broad street. The blizzard does not abate, it still isn't tired, a long night is before it. Warm, it must be warm in the hospital.

I cross the parking lot. It is almost empty, only a few cars. The snow merges vehicles into whiteness, covering bodies, erasing shapes. I pass the concrete jardinières. Snow-covered conifers and cotoneasters (gardening is the Teacher's passion. In his words: "Eden was a garden." And he always needs some help, whether I want to help him or not) are white fingers, reaching out to stop me from getting closer. But I hurry on, barely feeling my feet, fingers, or nose. Warm, it must be warm inside.

I hurry through the snow to the entrance. The ambulance is here now; it stops and the siren dies. The building breaks the wind; snowflakes dance, illuminated by the flashing blue. The doctor and the paramedic are already out of the vehicle, red windbreakers in the white of the blizzard. Two medics from the hospital open the rear doors of the vehicle and pull the stretcher out. Somebody drank too much by the look of it. They rush through the entrance, nobody paying attention to me. Warm...

I use the commotion to follow the stretcher through the entrance doors, past the night watchman in his booth. He does not ask anything, probably thinking I accompanied the sick man in the ambulance. The doctor on duty arrives while I retreat behind a pillar and slip through the doors into the nearest corridor. I hurry, not looking back. Nobody shouts after me as I disappear in a labyrinth of waiting rooms, leaving the chill behind me.

I relish the warmth with all my senses. I begin shaking, my legs barely holding me so that I almost collapse to the floor. A radiator! I snuggle next to it, soaking up heat. Warmth creeps through my fingers, thaws my hands, crawls up my arms and into my body. Life pours back into me, driving away the freezing night which is howling beyond the thick walls.

I do not know how much time passes before I come to my senses again. Finally, I rise and sit on a plastic chair next to the radiator, looking around.

I'm in a long waiting room, plastic chairs against both walls. There are regularly spaced doors, numbers, nameplates. A fire hose, a glass-covered announcement board. More announcements stuck on the doors.

I probe with my senses. Tremors of the daily rush still vibrate in the waiting room, echoing, throbbing through my mind. Nervousness, tension, disease. Disease is all around me; people brought it with them, people bring it in every day, like sin, like punishment. It wants to enter and overwhelm me, strangle me and drown me in a flash flood of pain. Cascades of suffering pour from upper floors. The rooms are up there. Patients are up there, alone on this night when His birth is celebrated; alone with their diseases; alone with their pains; alone, without anybody.

I long to shut myself off from the tide of disease that washes through me. I know I shouldn't; I'm not here by accident. This is my chance to do something good, to pass the Exam. But I must shut myself down at least a little. I've never felt anything like this before, never has pain possessed me this way, completely and thoroughly.

And for the first time, I realise how hard it is to be an angel.

Then it cuts me, suddenly, without a slightest warning. Something else breaks through the pain and suffering and solitude, something I've felt only a few times before, always just for a moment, during my lessons, under Teacher's strict supervision. Something cold, mean, truly evil, capable of destroying me in an eye-blink. I know I should run away while there is still time. I should run out of here before it feels me, run back into the winter, through the snow, as far as possible, before it discovers me and lurches at me.

A demon has arrived at the hospital. Searching...

One thing I'm certain of: the demon did not come for me.

I climb the stairs silently, sensing him all the time. I am closer to him with every step, and I know he is searching. He is looking, probing, hunting. He wants something special, something hard to get. I wonder if he feels me too, or if I evade him, cloaked in whirls of pain all around me. Maybe I have avoided his notice. I hide myself as well as I can, the way the Teacher taught me. It is possible that he really did not detect me, that he's so certain of his power, convinced nobody can touch him.

I stop at the next floor where glass doors lead into a corridor. He is here somewhere. Black letters on the glass: paediatric ward. I enter the corridor.

177

Suddenly, as if a furnace door blew open, the hot gust of his trail almost slams me against the opposite wall. A moment of unspeakable horror, but the demon is much further ahead; it is only his trail that emanates from the door in front of me.

Hesitating, I walk to the door, waiting, listening, trying to find him. Silence, silence everywhere. I grab the door handle; his fingers held it a mere ten minutes ago. I feel his power in my palm, dark, merciless, cold in all its heat. I open the door. It's a closet, filled with brooms, brushes, rags and pails, sponges, rubber gloves, detergents, and disinfectants, their sharp smells assaulting my nose. And through them all, I catch the unmistakable whiff of sulphur. A pentagram the height of a man burnt on the wall; I can still feel its heat. The gate through which he came here, uninvited, into this night. The gate of Hell, which he opened himself.

Hunting...

I follow the demon through the corridor. I clearly see his trail in the darkness, visible just to me. It leads me from room to room; the demon was quietly opening door after door, entering, searching but not finding, continuing on.

The corridor turns left. I stop; he must be here somewhere. I feel him. I feel him so clearly, and I am afraid he feels me too. It is impossible that he does not know I'm on his trail, but he is not in the corridor. He must be in one of the rooms. I continue, following hot prints on the door handles and then, suddenly, I stop, holding my breath. The next door handle is not marked by his hand, he didn't get that far. This means he is here, in the room right before me.

I see his print on the handle and fingerprints on the door where he pushed the door silently to enter. I stand there, hesitant. The horror in me grows, rises, and spills over. I should turn back and run away before he jumps on me, before he grabs me, but my legs will not listen, and I wonder what is he waiting for. Why doesn't he strike? Is he playing games with me, now that I'm caught in the net from which there's no way out?

"Come in, little one, it's unlocked." A mocking voice echoes in my head, filled with arrogant superiority and disdain for everything below him.

"Come in, don't be afraid. You don't interest me tonight."

I close the door quietly behind me and look around a single-bed room, the kind just for the rare ones who can afford it. A bathroom is adjacent to the room, the light from it illuminating a tiny child's body on a bed, connected to life support. The little girl lies in a coma, almost consumed by disease. Her life is hanging on with the help of plastic tubes and needles stuck under her tender pale skin and fastened by a strip of surgical tape.

Her father sits on a chair next to her. He does not see the demon and me, his head in his hands. He has been crying, and now he is just sitting as time slowly drips away, drop by drop, like the solution in the plastic bag hanging by the bed.

I pass him by. His life unfolds before me, and I learn all about him, as if reading an open book, one written in blood. He is rich, powerful, influential; many people in the town fear him. If only they could see him now. His soul is already cursed, condemned; he has judged himself by his deeds. And his hands, which have grabbed mercilessly throughout his entire life, are now clasped helplessly.

The demon stands next to the bed, looking at the girl. His dark grey business suit fits him like a glove, clothes appropriate for a client. Dark hair. Deep, piercing eyes under dense eyebrows, there is nothing they will miss. Lips, just for a moment drawn in a cynical smile. And horns, massive, strong, spiralling, like a crown on his head. He is old, regardless of his appearance as a man in his late thirties. And experienced—oh, how experienced; he could eliminate me in a moment.

As I watch him, I find something in him. Something unexplainable, deep, beyond the moulds in which the Teacher stubbornly insists everybody is cast, demons included. Is it only me or is there a trace of sadness in his pupils, sadness within eyes that have seen everything? I feel myself drawn to him, like opposites attract each other. Who knows—if he was someone else, and if I wasn't who I was, and if we were someplace far away from here, alone, without the girl and her father...

"What do you want?" I whisper.

"What do you think?" Cold, disdainful, the sadness is gone. Perhaps it was never there at all, perhaps it was all just an illusion, a trick, a game.

"Him?" I incline my head towards the father. But if that's the case, I don't really understand—he is already theirs. As soon as his time runs out, they will come for him; he's eternally cursed, even if he does not know that yet. None of them know until it is too late.

The demon grins. He walks over to stand before me, the fire in his eyes piercing me.

"Listen and learn, little one. They don't teach you things like this up there. And they'll come in handy, should you ever pass."

The father does not see us or hear us, alone in his pain. He rises, his eyes red from tears. He passes us by and disappears in the bathroom. There is the murmur of water as he washes his face.

179

The demon straightens himself up and winks at me as he adjusts his tie, looking like a magician about to show me the masterly, unstoppable sleight of hand in a game he has played with mortals for time immemorial.

Water keeps on running in the bathroom. The demon heads that way, leaving me alone with the girl. I want to follow him, but his look stops me cold.

"Listen," he commands.

The demon pulls the door closed behind him, but he does not shut it completely. I approach the girl on the bed; her lifeless body is covered by a sheet, her head resting on a pillow. She is six. Her pale face is emaciated by disease. I can feel it mercilessly eating her body from inside, gnawing, tearing, devouring, certain of another victory. I push a lock of blonde hair away from her forehead. The girl does not feel me, she cannot feel me. Her body surrendered a long time ago. She will not live to see the morning.

A muted cry of surprise from the bathroom. Through the crack in the door, I see the father lurch back from the sink, water dripping from his face. Several moments of silence stretch out as human and demon measure each other up. The father does not see the horns and hooves, but I can see questions multiply in his head frantically. "Who are you?" The father tries to sound confident, but in vain; he cannot hide the anxiety after many nights keeping vigil. "How the devil did you get in here?"

"We don't have much time." The demon's voice is quiet now, calming, bewitching, like a snake hypnotising a mouse. "She'll die by the morning, won't she?"

"What do you want of me?"

"She'll die by the morning." The bare statement pushes all questions aside; they become so unimportant, disappearing before its finality. The father measures up the stranger before him, a slight dash of hope awakens in him. Oh, yes, the Teacher warned me of this game, the demon works strictly by the book. Hope is one of the most dangerous weapons to be found in desperation; like a fire, it bursts and blurs reason. It just has to be started and fed skilfully.

"Tell me, just tell me – what do you want?"

The demon remains silent for several moments, letting the hope grow, blaze up, grow comfortably warm; it is the first trace of light after months of darkness and despair, pain and relentlessness. "I have an offer for you," he replies finally. Silence again, flames flaring even higher, obscuring everything. "Your daughter will survive. She will recover completely. Not immediately, but she will recover in a week. And she will live a long and happy life. Rich... And healthy... That's what I'm offering you."

The fire burns in the father. The girl is everything he has ever really loved; she is the only thing he ever had, no matter how much he had amassed and stolen.

"In return..."

"What do you want? Name it, say the price, money is no issue!" Desperately, the father still does not understand completely. The stranger before him may be a miracle worker. A miracle is the only thing that can still save his little girl. And the demon just grins, knowing that the bait is taken and that the catch is almost certain.

"I want a soul."

The father stops dead, speechless. It is only now that he realises who stands before him. This is the most critical moment in any bargaining. Fear and disbelief wash over the hope like a torrent, almost extinguishing the fire. This is the last chance to refuse, but the demon is experienced, he is already possessing the father, calming him down and convincing him without words. His lies become the father's thoughts; the offer becomes so attractive, irresistible, the last straw he can still hold on to.

"Mine?" he asks in a low, shaky voice. He would give it. Even the way he is, he would give it. He loves her so much, his precious...

"You pitiful fool. We already have yours." The demon looks him in the eyes, his voice becoming quiet, almost inaudible. "Hers."

And it is only now that I understand. Stupid, stupid, stupid! Why didn't I get this from the start? The father's soul was condemned a long time ago; not even a demon apprentice would bother about it. But the girl in bed before me is still pure, unblemished by the crimes of her father. Down there, in the heat, a soul like hers is a true jewel, the best gift to the Lord of Darkness this night. Oh, yes, it takes someone old and experienced to play a hand like this.

The father remains silent, not answering as the demon takes the contract out. Something is breaking in him; he knows what he is condemning his precious child to if he signs. But, on the other hand, her entire life... That is a lot of time, maybe enough to get around the contract. And a new hope stirs, a new flame. The demon kindles it himself. You can get around every contract, including the one with the Devil. Enough prayers and paid masses, perhaps even an endowment, anything it takes. Money is no issue, God must see that and have mercy on her soul, even if it is already too late for his.

The demon grins as he stirs false hopes. His master is a prince of lies; a lie is omnipotent; a lie conquers everything. In his claws, a lie is a reverse of hope. The demon takes a golden fountain pen out of his pocket while the father looks up slowly, agreement in his eyes. The demon passes the pen to the father, showing with his finger where to sign.

I stand above the girl, helpless to help her as her father prepares to sign the eternal damnation on her behalf. I know there will be no forgiveness, no matter what she or her father do, because a signature is a signature, and when the time comes, when the demon has fulfilled his part of the bargain, he will come to take her into the deepest heat of Hell.

The father stops suddenly, wondering if he should, if he has the right to sign in her name. The demon, grinning, drives the clouds of doubt away. It's all right, he persuades, the girl would sign herself if she could. The father remains uncertain; he knows what it is that he signs, he knows what it is that he condemns his precious to. But the lies fan the flames anew, the fire burns with all its might and makes him warm. Every sin can be redeemed, and every contract can be cancelled, even the one with the Devil...

And I can do nothing. A few more seconds and her destiny will be sealed. If only I could heal her, but I cannot, not in time, not before the father signs. The disease is deep in her, in her marrow; it has overwhelmed her body completely.

The shaking hand brings the pen towards the parchment while my brain works feverishly, running in circles, caught in the trap of my own helplessness. The tip of the pen touches the parchment, the first stroke, slow, uncertain, as if in trance, condemning his own daughter.

And then I realise the answer in a flash. I do not even have time to feel the full horror of what I have to do, the only thing still left to do. There is no time for horror as the pen signs the verdict for the innocent.

I grab the pillow under the girl's head and cover her face with it, holding it with both hands and pressing down with all my weight. Her body resists feebly, arching in bed, thrashing about, but I don't let go, I won't let go. I do not know how long it lasts; I lose all sense of time as I suffocate the little girl. Behind the door, the demon triumphs in his victory. It is done, an innocent soul is his, has just being signed over to him. He admires his own genius, so certain of himself. He had it all worked out; he roars with laughter, completely forgetting about me. The pen writes down the verdict, etching a little bit more of her name, shakily, just a few more strokes, while the body beneath me gives up. I feel the last spasm of feeble muscles passing through my arms, like the spasm of a clothes moth that I once squeezed between my fingers, a long time ago, when I was still alive. It shakes me from within, filling me with cold and terror. And I know when it is over. Her soul becomes free and rises up, high up, as the pen makes the final stroke too late. The body is dead, the soul is free, the demon cannot fulfil his part of the bargain any more, and the contract is void.

Numb, I lift the pillow. The eyes, wide open from the spasm of dying muscles, stare at me as I return the pillow to under the small head. I close the eyelids with my fingers, covering the dead eyes so they won't see me. I do not want them to see me; I'm afraid of them as I silently remove the locks of blonde hair from her cold forehead.

I feel nothing as I cast a last glance at the empty shell in the bed, and I feel nothing, complete emptiness, as I exit into the corridor. I am empty as I leave the ward. I hear the demon entering the room and stopping, shocked. It takes him time to understand what has happened, to realise that the signed contract in his hand is just a worthless piece of parchment. And I feel the father as he enters and stares at the dead body in disbelief. He rushes to the bed, takes the body in his hands and falls down to his knees, in grief, and I am empty, completely empty, as I hear his broken moan. The demon simply walks away, before the father raises an accusing stare in his direction. No explanation, no words, just anger. The father's nightmare, fuzzy, buried in grief, is all that will remain in that room.

I run down the stairs and on, down the corridor, through the waiting rooms and into the lobby, passing the watchman, his face coloured blue by a small TV in the booth. He does not see me as I pass the heavy glass doors, out, into the blizzard, into the cold, into the Christmas night.

The hospital remains behind me, lost in the whirls of pain and solitude. Lights are on in the distant apartment buildings. The midnight hour is long past, His birth is celebrated, drunkenly, in the warm, at tables filled with food.

Around me there is just cold. The blizzard rages, wind licks my cheeks. The winter night is like a skilful lover, but I do not feel anything. The night's chill is nothing against the ice that I carry deep within me.

Suddenly something grabs my shoulder, a hand like a claw, and turns me savagely to face it. I stagger in the snow, barely staying on my feet. The demon stands before me, fire in his eyes, he wants to fry me. There is not a trace of charm in him anymore, not a bit of sadness; it was all just a deceit. Only hatred is raging in his eyes.

The demon lifts his clenched fist and opens it. Ashes are carried by the wind, whirled around, thrown into the snowflakes. The contract: worthless, a fistful of ashes was all that remained of it.

"Well played, little one," he hisses through clenched teeth. "Well played indeed."

The demon turns and walks into the night without a further word, leaving me alone; the blizzard covers the hoofprints he leaves in the snow.

I remain standing under the yellow floodlight. The game is over, and it is only now that fear surges through me. I struggle to inhale the freezing air. The demon's hatred burns in me, but I am still here, he did not destroy me. And he wanted to, oh, how he wanted to. But he could not; he was not permitted to, and I know why.

I try my wings. I spread them in all their magnificence. I flap them, then a second time, once more, and again, harder, stronger. I rise from the ground. My white wings take me up, high, above the buildings in which His birth is celebrated drunkenly, and higher up, above the blizzard, and above the highest clouds and upwards... Bells reach me through the night. Only I hear them; they toll just for me. They toll grudgingly, they never fully accepted me and they never will, but they toll, they must toll, announcing my arrival to the place where I belong after all, now that I have passed the Exam.

And when I get there, I will look for the girl. I will be hers, and she will be mine, and I know that she will need me. Because Heaven can be a cold place.

ALEKSANDAR ŽILJAK

Afterword

I cannot recall the precise moment and situation in Summer of 2007 in which Deniver Vukelić—an editor of *Grifon*, a magazine then published in Zagreb, Croatia, and devoted to fantasy and medieval culture—invited me to write a text for the magazine. The new issue had two themes: knights and sea monsters.

I don't really see myself sweating under a chain-mail and helmet, and wielding a sword, but I was dabbling in cryptozoology, a science of mysterious animals, that include various sea monsters. So I wrote an article on the most famous on them, sea-serpent and kraken and mermaids and megalodon. But I also offered a story, which Mr. Vukelić agreed to read. The result was "The Law of the Sea", one of the stories included in this book. As a matter of fact, three more stories gathered in this collection were first published in the *Grifon* magazine.

When I write fantasy, I attempt to steer clear from post-Tolkien practice. Incessant imitating of *Hobbit* and *Lord of the Rings* in literature and media inevitably restricts us to a limited set of ideas, themes, characters and props. I believe that, if fantasy is to live and develop as a genre literature, it must reach for new environments, traditions and heroes.

It will be quite obvious to a reader of this book that I relied on history, but with a "what if?" touch, stemming from science fiction. In this case, what if various mythical and fantastic beings, present in folk tradition and fables, actually existed in certain periods of human history? How do they influence everyday life of people? Will there be a conflict or co-existence? Will the dragons, unicorns and sea-serpents be our friends? Or menace? Both? This is also a bit of a science-fictionalish approach. Because, when not being metaphors for Nature and her forces, the mythical *others*—unicorns, dragons, sea-serpents, divine she-wolves (as well as elves, orcs, goblins, dwarves, I guess)—may serve the same purpose as the SF others: extraterrestrials, aliens, robots, artificial humans. In both instances, they are metaphors for *them*. *Them* as in humans that are not *us*.

The reader of this book will also notice that I don't care much for kings and princesses, knights in shiny armour or muscular sword-wielding heroes, ages-old sorcerers and forgotten deities. When I have them in my stories—and I do, from time to time—they are most often the antagonists, threat, menace, exponents of unchecked power—magical or by virtue of social position—that, seemingly infinite, corrupts infinitely.

186

I am more interested in ordinary human beings, peasants, serfs, craftsmen (and women), students, servants... People snatched out of their daily struggle to survive and forced to face evil that humans do, or the wrath of unbridled nature, or frightening and beautiful beings of pasts forgotten. Vulnerable people, I guess, even when they are trained in ancient martial arts or have mastered the arcane magical skills. And yes, more often than not, my main characters are female.

"A Unicorn and a Warrior Girl" is my attempt at a story set in ancient China. The idea about a virgin forced to lure a unicorn was gestating in my mind for quite a long time, but then I decided to move it into space and time of Qin Shi Huang, the man who united China, the man belonging equally to history and myth. And yes, I was inspired to no small extent by Hong Kong and more recent Chinese martial arts films, that very often slipped into a specific form of fantasy. (I still remember the days—I was a young teenager then— when my classmates went to see *Enter the Dragon* dozens of times. I began to appreciate that movie considerably later, together with the rest of Shaw Brothers and Golden Harvest production. More recently, I was also fascinated by the films of Tsui Hark and Zhang Yimou, when they were at their directorial peak.)

"The Divine She-Wolf" is based on the folklore of the vicinity of Varaždin, a Croatian town north of Zagreb. While small, Varaždin was a capital of Croatia, until the great fire in 1776 razed the town, and administrative institutions were moved to Zagreb. Local tradition contains several fables about wolves, wolf-shepherds, and the divine she-wolf. To these, I added the dog-heads. They were much older bogeymen, but when the Mongols started raiding Croatia in the 13th century, the name passed to them, probably because of their squinting eyes, and fur caps and beast skins that they wore. As for wolves: once universally feared, hated, and persecuted almost to extinction, the wolves in Croatia are now protected and despite all the challenges of wolf-management, their numbers increased to an estimated 150-200 animals, concentrated in the central, sparsely-populated regions of the country.

"The Nekomata" was written for an anthology of vampire stories, published in Serbia. But since I considered vampires a bit boring (After playing with them in "The Eyes of Opal", a novelette about a lesbian gun-slinger vampire in a Wild West world ruled by dinosaurs. NOTE: when pulling something like that, you don't bother with explaining. Instead, you *immerse* your reader into such a world, no matter how crazy it is.), I decided to go for another angle. So I used the Japanese tale about a shape-shifting blood-drinking giant cat with two tails. In order to add some motivation, I introduced a clan of female ninjas, and political ambitions of Iyeasu Tokugawa, the famed warlord who unified the country, put all the warring barons under check, and introduced a long era of peace, that lasted until mid-19th century.

"Elsbeth and the Book of Dragons" is dedicated to women artists who illustrated 18th and 19th century natural history monographs. Perhaps the best known of them was Elisabeth Gould (1804-1841), who illustrated her husband John Gould's monographs on European, Asian and Australian birds, as well as the monographs on toucans and trogons. She produced plates for Charles Darwin too. Of course, she also fulfilled all the expectations from a Victorian woman and wife, giving birth to eight children. And she died quite young, after returning from a two-years' journey to Australia. Maybe some of you keep Gould's finches. They are named after her.

The shipwreck described in "The Law of the Sea" actually happened in 1724 off Hispaniola. Two Spanish galleons were sunk in a hurricane. The majority of survivors from the first one managed to reach the land. The second galleon sunk in shallow water, with most hands and passengers killed. The few survivors spent more than a month on the maintop, unable to swim to the shore because of the sharks below. Both wrecks were found and explored in second half of the last century, giving insight into trade and economy of early 18th century Spanish possessions in Latin America. These two galleons also carried mercury, necessary for getting gold and silver. There has been speculations that the loss of that particular cargo perhaps marked the beginning of the end of Spanish rule in the Central and South America.

"The Aelomancer" was directly inspired by an entry in *Dictionary of Mythology* by Bergen Evans, a book dating from 1970. Under "Aeolus", one reads: "Until very recently it was widely believed among sailors that one could buy a favourable wind. Certain old women sold winds for sixpence in the Orkneys and the Hebrides as late as 1903." Since I was writing a steampunk story, I added airships. I *love* airships. They are majestic. I saw one over Zagreb some fifteen years ago, silvery (with a BMW logo), sailing over the city almost without a sound. And yes, some of the first airships were steam-driven. And yes, there were large airships (German World War 1 Schütte-Lanz series) with wooden structure. And there is a Tower of Winds in Athens. And there are winds with strange names in the Americas: so says the Webster dictionary. And there are womenfish: Croatian Adriatic version of the sirens, most likely inspired by now almost-extinct monk seals.

"Rumiko" is another steampunk story, written for an anthology that combined steampunk and space opera. I brought the Japanese in the somewhat shifted late 19th century Zagreb. I also introduced the mechanical computers, having assumed that Charles Babbage mechanical computer, a.k.a. the analytical engine, did work after all. And yes, I introduced the *other*.

"As the Distant Bells Toll" is the oldest story in this collection, dating back to 1998. This is one of the several urban fantasy demon stories that I wrote. It takes place in the Dubrava hospital, on the eastern edge of Zagreb. If you are wondering about shooting at Christmas Eve: in Croatia, Christmas and New Year eves sound like war zones. Not just the firecrackers, petards and fireworks. But pistols and an occasional AK-47, particularly in the late 1990s, when quite a few of them remained in private hands after the war.

Most of my stories, in this book and otherwise, deal with relations between humans and nature. I believe that these relations can be particularly well-studied in fantasy, because I see this genre as a reaction to the modern (post)industrial urban environment, physical, but also economical, social and emotional, that was created by the capitalist expansion within the last two hundred years. Fantasy and its growing popularity in the last five or six decades are certainly the expression of resistance to that process, unfortunately still insufficiently articulated to move visibly from personal escapism towards the efficient social action.

This, when all is said and done, is mostly a book about humans and animals. One may wonder what is the purpose of all those unpredictable, perhaps harmful, perhaps dangerous, sometimes messy creatures? Practical reasons aside: we still go hunting, just like our ancestors did ten thousand years ago, only now we go to the butcher's—somebody else is doing the unpleasant work for us. Something else is more important. If the animals disappear, if we exterminate the birds, whales, elephants, pandas, rhinos, tigers, we are left without any standards—biological, ethical, moral, cultural—to measure our existence against. We lose diversity created through hundreds of millions of years of unpredictable processes. Instead, we get the fascist nudity of steel, concrete and glass, geometrically regular landscapes through which rivers flow by straight channels (to use an image from an old Soviet SF story) into dead seas. The unfathomable beauty, comparable to and even surpassing all our achievements in art, is replaced by the grey monotony and absurdity of boring consumer existence.

Only when we remember again who we are actually—and folktales across the world remind us of that—we can build better and safer future for us and all the other living beings. However, we should not haze our vision, as is often done in fantasy, by tearful idealising of the times long past. The dilemma nature vs. science & technology is false. The true answer is *both* nature *and* science & technology, with (and there lies the problem) significantly different social relations, freed from economic, thus any other, exploitation. One of the starting points of that journey is the change of our present-day destructive attitude towards animals and nature, towards the environment in which we all live.

So, love the animals. One is facing you every time you look at the mirror.

Finally, what is the purpose of fantasy today? Is it just an escape from unbearable reality of our lives? That may tend towards glorification of feudal patriarchal system, racial and ethnic supremacy, and sexism? You may wonder what am I talking about? But I have seen history reduced to synopses of bad fantasy novels in order to mobilise crowds for the 1990s wars in Yugoslavia, and I have seen fantasy images, including the wielding of real swords, used to celebrate the darkest Nazi puppet regime of the World War 2. The danger is clear and present.

Or, on the other hand, is fantasy literature a tool to consider and discuss a new and better world, with new relations between races, nations, genders, human beings? (Remember what the fantasy others actually stand for!) And new relations towards the environment that surrounds us and still supports us.

If fantasy is taken as a tool—and literature is a tool—it all depends on the way it is used. I believe that the times in which we live demand pushing away the escapist purpose of the genre, and accepting the activist one. I believe it is time that fantasy, as the closely related science fiction has been doing for quite a long time now, needs to become a test tube to study something new and better through thought experiments, to propose new social and environmental relations, to look at the magic as—the way Arthur C. Clarke said—far advanced science. I find this very important, because if we fail in sketching, designing, and finally building this brave new world, I am afraid there is no hope for mankind in the long term. And time is running out.

Finally, acknowledgments are in order. First, to Cheryl Morgan for entering an adventure of publishing a book by an author little-known outside of his country and language. I hope this will be a successful endeavour. To Paul Mason and Keiko Kito for pointing out errors in my Japanese-subject stories. Despite my best efforts, some things can be known only by those who live in Japan. And last, but not least, to Charlotte Bond for proof-reading/editing the manuscript. Her painstaking efforts made the stories infinitely better. Thank you all!

Aleksandar Žiljak
Zagreb, August 20th, 2020.

ALEKSANDAR ŽILJAK

Publication Histories

NOTE: All the stories were originally written in Croatian, and later translated into English by the author. All the subsequent translations into other languages (save one) were made from the English versions.

A Unicorn and a Warrior Girl

• Originally published as "Jednorog i ratnica" in *Grifon* #12, Zagreb: Red Srebrnog zmaja, August 2009.
• Published in *Božja vučica*, Zagreb: Mentor, 2010.
• Published in Romanian as "Inorogul şi râzboinica", Societatea Română de Science-Fiction şi Fantasy (SRSFF) (http://www.srsff.ro/4008/inorogul-si-razboinica/), November 24th, 2010. Translated by Antuza Genescu.

NOTE: Red Srebrnog zmaja (The Order of the Silver Dragon) was a Zagreb history re-enactment society. *Grifon* was their magazine devoted to fantasy and medieval themes, reaching issue #13. *Božja vučica* (*The Divine She-Wolf*) was my second story-collection book.

The Divine She-Wolf

• Originally published as "Božja vučica", *Grifon* #11, Zagreb: Red Srebrnog zmaja, January 2009.
• Published in *Božja vučica*, Zagreb: Mentor, 2010.
• Published in Bosnia-Herzegovina on *bh fantasy* / http://bhfantasy.wordpress.com/2011/07/08/aleksandar-ziljak-bozja-vucica, July 8th, 2011.
• Published in the magazine *Omaja* #5, Velika Plana, Serbia: Udruženje umetnika *Zavet*, 2013.
• Published in Romanian as "Lupoaica divina", Societatea Română de Science-Fiction şi Fantasy (SRSFF) (http://www.srsff.ro/proza/lupoaica-divina-aleksandar-ziljak/), February 12th, 2013. Translated by Antuza Genescu.
• Published in English in POD anthology *Wolf Craft*, edited by Ron Koppelberger, Static Movement, June 2013.
• Published in *Sarajevske sveske* #47/48, Sarajevo, Bosnia-Herzegovina: Mediacentar Sarajevo, 2015.

NOTE: *bh fantasy* is a blog/page by Ante Zirdum, Bosnian fan and SF and fantasy editor. *Omaja* (named after a Serbian mithological creature) is a magazine dedicated to fantasy and folk beliefs, published by Udruženje umetnika *Zavet*

(Artist Society *Oath*). *Sarajevske sveske* (*Sarajevo Volumes*) is a literary magazine from Sarajevo.

The Nekomata

• Originally published as "Nekomata" in the anthology *U znaku vampira - muške priče o krvopijama*, edited by Goran Skrobonja, Belgrade, Serbia: Paladin, 2012.

• Published in *Knjiga beštija*, Bizovac, Croatia: Ogranak Matice hrvatske Bizovac, 2013.

NOTE: *U znaku vampira - muške priče o krvopijama* (*Under the Sign of Vampire - Male Tales of Bloodsuckers*) was the male authors' part of the two-part anthology of vampire tales, edited by Goran Skrobonja, the renowned Serbian horror writer and translator. *Knjiga beštija* (*The Book of Beasts*) was my third story collection. Matica hrvatska (*Matrix Croatica*) is the Croatian cultural non-profit institution with numerous branches throughout Croatia, this branch (ogranak) being in Bizovac, in Eastern Slavonia.

Elsbet and The Book of Dragons

• Originally published as "Elsbet i Knjiga zmajeva" in *Grifon* #10, Zagreb: Red Srebrnog zmaja, May 2008.

• Published in Bulgarian as "Elsbet i knigata na drakonite", *Irin Pirin* #1-2, 2009, Sandanski, Bulgaria: Mednik, 2009. Translated from Croatian by Ivan Topalski.

• Published in *Božja vučica*, Zagreb: Mentor, 2010.

• Published in Romanian as "Elsbet şi Cartea Dragonilor", Societatea Română de Science-Fiction şi Fantasy (SRSFF) (http://www.srsff.ro/surfer/aleksandar-ziljak-croatia-elsbet-si-cartea-dragonilor/), February 10th, 2012. Translated by Antuza Genescu.

NOTE: *Irin Pirin* is the Bulgarian literary magazine.

The Law of the Sea

• Originally published as "Zakon mora", *Grifon* #8/9, Zagreb: Red Srebrnog zmaja, October 2007.

• Published in *Knjiga beštija*, Bizovac, Croatia: Ogranak Matice hrvatske Bizovac, 2013.

The Aeolomancer

• Originally published as "Eolomant" in *Knjiga beštija*, Bizovac, Croatia: Ogranak Matice hrvatske Bizovac, 2013.

- Published as "Eolomancer" in e- and POD anthology *Gears and Levers 3*, edited by Phyllis Irene Radford, Clinton, MT, USA: Sky Warrior Publishing LLC, June 2013.

Rumiko

- Originally published as "Rumiko" in *Parasvemir*, edited by Tatjana Jambrišak and Darko Vrban, Zagreb: Mentor and SFera, 2010.
- Published as "Rumiko" in e- and POD anthology *Gears and Levers*, edited by Phyllis Irene Radford, Clinton, MT, USA: Sky Warrior Publishing LLC, April 2012.
- Published in *Knjiga beštija*, Bizovac, Croatia: Ogranak Matice hrvatske Bizovac, 2013.

NOTES: *Parasvemir* (*Steamspace*) was an anthology of steampunk and space opera stories. It is one of the annual anthologies published by the Zagreb SF society SFera (with or without publishing partners) since 1995.

As the Distant Bells Toll

- Originally published as "U daljini se čuju zvona" in *Kvantni portali imaginacije*, edited by Davorin Horak, Zagreb: SFera and Nova stvarnost, 1997.
- Published in English on my blog *Napredna inteligencija* (www.naprednainteligencija.blogspot.com), December 27th, 2011.
- Published as "As the Distant Bells Toll" in POD- and e-anthology *You'd Better Watch Out!*, edited by Kevin G. Bufton, UK: Cruentus Libri Press, 2012.
- Expanded into a theatre play *Salvata*, written and directed by Rebecca Agić, and performed during 2017 by Teatar Gaudeamus from Zagreb.

NOTE: *Kvantni portali imaginacije* (*Quantum Portals of Imagination*) was an anthology of SF stories. It was one of the annual anthologies published by the Zagreb SF society SFera (with or without publishing partners) since 1995. *Napredna inteligencija* (*Progressive Intelligentsia*) is my currently neglected blog, with more stories and texts in Croatian and English.

ALEKSANDAR ŽILJAK

About the Author

Aleksandar Žiljak was born in Zagreb, Croatia, in 1963. He graduated on the Faculty of Electrical Engineering in Zagreb, and got Master of Computer Sciences degree on the same Faculty in 1990. After working as a professor in several high and trade schools, he became a freelance illustrating artist, specialising in wildlife art.

He published his first short stories in 1991, writing relatively sporadically throughout the 1990s. His first book was a story collection *The Blind Birds* (*Slijepe ptice*, 2003), but his SF and fantasy output increased considerably in the following two decades, currently amounting to six story collections, a book about cryptozoology under a pen-name Karl S. McEwan, and four novels: *Irbis* (2012), *The Poseidonia* (2014), *Mystery of the Dragon Islands* (*Zagonetka Zmajskih otoka*, 2015), and *The Ndanabo Children* (*Ndanabova djeca*, 2018). Žiljak translates his prose into English himself. His stories have been published in numerous European countries, USA, India and China. *Irbis* and *The Poseidonia* have been published in Serbia, while *The Poseidonia* has also been published in the Czech Republic. A collection of his SF stories has been published in Germany, in both German and English edition (*Welche Farbe hat der Wind?* / *What Colour is the Wind?*, 2017). He also published a collection of SF movie lectures titled *Stars in the Night* (*Zvijezde u noći*, 2019).

196

ALEKSANDAR ŽILJAK

Beside being a writer, Aleksandar Žiljak is also an editor. Together with Tomislav Šakić, he co-edited *Ad Astra* (2006), an anthology of the Croatian SF stories 1976-2005. He also edited several story collections by prominent Croatian SF writers. Currently Šakić and Žiljak edit *UBIQ*, a Croatian SF and fantasy magazine, that was voted the best European SF magazine on Eurocon in Stockholm in 2011. Aleksandar Žiljak is also known as a translator, and is famous for his lectures on numerous Croatian SF conventions.

Aleksandar Žiljak won numerous SFera Awards for his SF art, stories, editorial work on *Ad Astra*, the novel *Irbis*, and *Stars in the Night*.

Lightning Source UK Ltd.
Milton Keynes UK
UKHW021842201120
373785UK00003B/42/J